N

To every reader who has taken this journey with me
since the release of Breathe

SIMON PULSE
An imprint of Simon & Schuster Children's Publishing Division
1230 Avenue of the Americas, New York, NY 10020
This Simon Pulse edition November 2015
Text copyright © 2014 by Abbi Glines
Cover photograph copyright © 2015 by Michael Frost
All rights reserved, including the right of reproduction in whole or in part in any form.
SIMON PULSE and colophon are registered trademarks of Simon & Schuster, Inc.
For information about special discounts for bulk purchases, please contact Simon & Schuster Special Sales at 1-866-506-1949 or business@simonandschuster.com.
The Simon & Schuster Speakers Bureau can bring authors to your live event. For more information or to book an event contact the Simon & Schuster Speakers Bureau at 1-866-248-3049 or visit our website at www.simonspeakers.com.
Cover designed by Jessica Handelman
Interior designed by Mike Rosamilia
The text of this book was set in Adobe Caslon Pro.
Manufactured in the United States of America
2 4 6 8 10 9 7 5 3 1
Library of Congress Control Number 2014038505
ISBN 978-1-4814-3621-2 (hc)
ISBN 978-1-4814-3620-5 (pbk)
ISBN 978-1-4814-3619-9 (eBook)

ACKNOWLEDGMENTS

I need to start by thanking my agent, Jane Dystel, who is beyond brilliant. Signing with her was one of the smartest things I've ever done. Thank you, Jane, for helping me navigate the waters of the publishing world. You are truly a badass.

My editor, Sara Sargent. Working with you has been awesome. I look forward to many more books! Mara Anastas, Jodie Hockensmith, Carolyn Swerdloff, and the rest of the Simon Pulse team, for all their hard work in getting my books out there.

The friends who listen to me and understand me the way no one else in my life can: Colleen Hoover and Jamie McGuire. Knowing I can call them and they'll listen anytime is priceless. They always have my back. Love them both very hard.

I need to give a big shout-out to Abbi's Army, led by Danielle

Lagasse. She has pulled together an amazing bunch of readers who promote my books and make me feel incredibly special. I love every one of you, and I am humbled that you would spend your time sharing my books with others.

Natasha Tomic, for always reading my books the moment I type "The End," even when she has to stay up all night to do it. She always knows which scenes need that extra something to make them a quality "peanut-butter sandwich scene."

Autumn Hull, for always listening to me rant and worry, and for still beta-reading my books for me. I can't figure out how she puts up with my moodiness. I'm just glad she does.

Last but certainly not least: my family. Without their support I wouldn't be here. My husband, Keith, makes sure I have my coffee and the kids are all taken care of when I need to lock myself away and meet a deadline. My three kids are so understanding, although once I walk out of that writing cave, they expect my full attention, and they get it. My parents, who have supported me all along. Even when I decided to write steamier stuff. My friends, who don't hate me because I stay lost in my stories most of the time. They are my ultimate support group, and I love them dearly.

My readers. I never expected to have so many of you. Thank you for reading my books. For loving them and telling others about them. Without you I wouldn't be here. It's that simple.

Chapter One

Present day . . .

ROCK

"Daddy, watch this!" Daisy May exclaimed excitedly. As if she didn't already have my complete attention.

"I'm watching," I assured her.

She ran and began doing cartwheels across the backyard before flipping backward into what I now knew was called a back handspring. My baby girl was a little gymnast, and with that came a lot of practices. But every time she beamed at me and said, "Daddy, watch this!" I couldn't think of anything else I'd rather watch.

The past two and a half years of being my little girl's daddy had been some of the best years of my life. Only one other smile moved me as much as Daisy May's.

Trisha stepped out the back door, smiling at me, with two

glasses of lemonade in her hands. *That* smile was the other one that owned me. Daisy May had become my little girl a few years ago, but Trisha had been my girl for much longer. I had been entranced by the teenager who wouldn't give me the time of day, and completely captivated by the woman she had become.

She was the best mother in the world if you asked Daisy May, Brent, or Jimmy. She was the most incredible woman in the world if you asked me. And she knew damn well we all adored her.

"You nailed that, Daisy, baby," Trisha cheered, and Daisy May instantly lit up. Our little girl had lived the first seven years of her life without the love of a mother. The woman who had given life to our children hadn't been able to love anyone. She'd been angry and bitter and had neglected not only the children we now claimed as our own but her oldest son too—one of my best friends, Preston Drake. He'd been the only love these kids had known until their mother overdosed, leaving them in need of a home. Preston had been ready to take his younger siblings in, but Trisha and I had fallen in love with all of them. When we'd asked him to let us adopt the kids, he had agreed. He'd wanted them to have a home life with parents who loved them. Something he had never experienced.

They all worshipped the ground Preston walked on. He was still their older brother, and he watched them every Thursday night and any other time Trisha and I needed a night out alone. It was a family unit that worked.

I was one lucky son of a bitch.

"Momma, do you think I'll make the team next week?" Daisy May asked as Trisha handed her a glass of lemonade.

"I think you've worked hard and you have as good a chance as anyone. But no matter what happens, you are number one to us."

Like always, Trisha knew the right answer to everything, and Daisy May beamed at her.

"Preston said he would be there," Daisy May said, plopping down on the grass beside me.

"Then he will be. You know he wouldn't miss your try-outs for anything," I replied, taking the glass Trisha held out for me—then pulling her down onto my lap. I liked having my woman in my lap. Always had.

"I'm nervous," Daisy May added, then took a sip.

Trisha reached over and pulled Daisy toward us and tucked her under her arm. "We will be right there cheering you on. You've worked hard, and no matter what happens, you will be our star. We will be so proud of what you've accomplished. Most of those girls have been taking gymnastics since they were very young. You've managed to get a chance at the team in only two years! That right there is a reason to be proud."

I loved this woman. She could make anyone feel better. I was sitting out here, getting nervous thinking about Daisy May trying out to make the competitive team, and Trisha wasn't making just Daisy feel better—my nerves were easing too.

Truth was, I didn't like the idea of anyone telling my baby girl no. But Trisha kept reminding me I couldn't fight all their battles in life. It was so damn hard, though. They'd suffered enough in their earlier years.

"Next week I get to be a flower girl again," Daisy said, grinning up at us. She didn't stay focused on one thing too long. She was already thinking about Preston and Amanda's wedding.

"You have several weddings coming up. But I imagine next week's is the one you're most excited about," Trisha said, ruffling Daisy May's brown curls.

"Yep! I can't wait. Amanda said me and Brent and Jimmy get to all stand up there with them when they say their . . . uh . . . them things they say. I forgot what it's called."

Trisha leaned back against me as I chuckled. "While they say their vows," I said, and Daisy May nodded.

"That's it. We get to stand up there. And Jimmy gets to hand Preston the ring. The one he puts on Amanda's finger. And I get to give Amanda the surprise . . ." Daisy's eyes got big and she shut her mouth.

"What?" Trisha asked before I could.

Daisy May shook her head and grinned, then twisted an

imaginary lock on her lips and tossed away an equally imaginary key.

Apparently, Preston had some kind of secret only Daisy May knew about.

"Well, now I'm even more anxious for the wedding," Trisha said as she sank farther into me. My arms were wrapped around her waist, and I was beginning to think about where I'd like to move my hands. My wife was smoking hot. She always had been. It never got old seeing her in a pair of tiny shorts and a tank top. This body could stop traffic.

Our fifth wedding anniversary was coming up in four months. I had already prepared Preston that I'd need his help. I intended to take her somewhere special. We'd never had a real wedding. We couldn't afford one. But I had been desperate to make her mine. Back then I kept thinking she'd figure out she could do better and leave me. When I had convinced her to go to the courthouse and become mine forever, I hadn't thought about the fairy-tale wedding she deserved. I had just wanted Trisha.

It was time my woman had the fairy-tale wedding she deserved right before we went on the honeymoon we'd never gotten.

The first time I'd seen her, she had taken my breath away. Getting her attention had been one hell of a ride. She'd been so determined to stay away from me. Or any man. Then I'd found out why . . . and I'd sworn to myself she'd never have to live in fear again.

Falling in love with Trisha had changed my life. My friends and family had said I was an idiot. I was throwing away my future. Butch Taylor, my father, had never been a big part of my life until I had become a high school football star. For once I had a parent who gave a shit about me. It had been something I'd craved since I was a kid. Making him proud and proving I was worth loving had been what drove me to work harder. My dream was within my reach. I had my father cheering me on, and I would make it to college and then—I knew—I'd play pro ball.

Until my dream changed the day a pair of the prettiest blue eyes I'd ever seen stared at me across the parking lot one morning before school started. That was the first day of my sophomore year, and it would be another twelve months before I would be able to get Trisha Corbin to even speak to me.

With one look, that girl had changed my dreams.

Chapter Two

TRISHA

Most kids agonized over going back to school. I sat on the bus, listening to others talk about their summers on the beach, sleeping late, going to parties, and how much they dreaded school. It was like they were speaking a different language. A foreign world I knew nothing about.

I glanced over at the seat across from me, at my younger brother, Krit, and his best friend, Green. Krit was as relieved as I was to be going to school. We had looked forward to this day all summer. Having an excuse to escape the life we lived at home was a blessed relief. Green was excited because they were eighth graders now. Two years ago Sea Breeze had moved the eighth grade to a section of the high school building because the middle school had gotten too full. They were still separated from the high school students for the most part, but they would use the high school's cafeteria and gym.

My brother had grown at least six inches this summer. He reminded me of a weed. Overnight he'd gone from scrawny kid to tall and slightly intimidating. Didn't mean his mind had caught up to his almost six-foot-tall frame, though. He was still a kid. A scared kid. One who needed me to protect him. Even if I did have to tilt my head back to talk to him now. He had passed my five feet eight inches sometime around June.

I crossed my legs and tugged at my shorts. Not that it helped. There had been no money for me to go buy any school clothes this year. I had to wear last year's things. Krit had grown way more than I had, and he'd required an entirely new wardrobe. Every dime I'd made lifeguarding at the pool went toward buying him decent clothing at the consignment shop.

The problem with me wearing last year's things was that, although I hadn't grown in height, my breasts and butt had gotten bigger. So although I was still five eight, same as last year, my shorts were shorter. I wasn't sure how my legs had gotten longer, but they had—or my butt was just taking up the extra room.

My hips seemed wider too. That probably wasn't helping either. Krit turned his head to see me tugging on my shorts, and I stopped. The frown that wrinkled his forehead told me he wasn't happy. We had argued about me spending all my money on his clothes. He'd said he needed two pairs of jeans and two shirts. He could wash them every day. I refused to let him go to school in only two outfits that fit him. I had plenty. I would just need to go on a diet and make them fit me right again.

I wasn't sure how I had managed to gain weight, but that was all that made sense. This was my fault. Not his. I smiled at him reassuringly and acted like the short length of my shorts was no big deal. Picking up my book bag, I placed it in my lap as the bus pulled to a stop in front of the high school.

"We're here," I said, standing up.

"They're too short. I told you to buy new ones," was Krit's response. He wasn't going to let that go.

"My butt and hips got big. I just ate too much over the summer. I'll lose weight and it'll be fine," I told him. "Now, forget it and focus on school."

"We don't get to eat enough for you to have gained weight," he snarled.

"Please, for the love of God, don't lose weight. It would break my heart," Green said with a flirty grin.

Krit shoved him back down in his seat and scowled at him. "Don't. Seriously, dude. Don't."

I was used to Green's flirting. He'd been at it since last year when he discovered he loved girls. It was only getting worse. I knew he was harmless, and I remembered when he was scared of the dark and wore Superman underwear. He was like my other little brother.

"I don't like you in those shorts. Shows too much," Krit said in an angry whisper as we stepped off the bus.

"I'm fine. No one is looking," I told him.

He lifted his eyebrows at me. "Really? You're gonna tell me shit like that and expect me to believe it?"

I started to tell him to shut it, when my heart rate picked up and my breathing hitched. He was here. I hadn't seen him yet, but I knew he was here and he was close by. My body always reacted that way when Rock Taylor was around. It had been like that since I'd stepped off the bus the first day of school last year and made eye contact with the most beautiful boy I'd ever seen.

For almost three hours I had waited anxiously for another glimpse of him. Then finally at lunchtime I saw him again. He had a girl on each arm, and one even sat on his lap while he ate. His friends were all the same. Girls acted ridiculous to get their attention and threw themselves at the guys, who seemed to think it was their due. Like they were supposed to get to pick and choose females. When Rock had gotten up to leave the cafeteria, he had looked back at me and winked. Right before another girl grabbed his arm and he walked out the door with her. By the end of the day I knew more than I wanted to know about Rock Taylor.

"Is that Rock Taylor?" Krit asked in awe. As if Rock were a celebrity. The guy was a high school football star. So what? He was gorgeous and talented, I would give him that much. But he wasn't anyone I wanted my little brother idolizing. Rock Taylor used girls. I'd seen it firsthand. Over and over again.

But no matter how many girls I'd seen in the bathroom in tears on a Monday morning when Rock had ignored them after sleeping with them on Friday night, my body still reacted to him. Like it was on high alert. I understood why girls always went willingly into his arms, even while knowing it would end badly.

The difference was, I had real issues to deal with. Survival being the number one issue. For me and my brother.

Ignoring Krit's comment, I changed the subject. "Do you have your schedule? And remember, give yourself at least five full minutes to get from the upstairs classrooms to the downstairs classrooms. Don't be late for lunch or you won't have enough time to get your tray and eat. And eat it all. Okay?"

Krit gave me a crooked grin. "I got this, Sis. Seriously, chill."

He was going to be a hit here. He had been in middle school. Krit had always been a beautiful child. Girls were noticing that more and more. I was proud of him, but I also hated for him to define himself by his looks. He had so much more inside him.

"I know you do. It's just a big day and I want it to go well for you," I replied.

"That's them. See 'em?" Green said, pointing back toward where I knew, without even looking, Rock stood. "They own this school. See the girls all over them? Day-um, that's awesome. We're so gonna be them in two years."

Krit turned to look back, but I fought the urge. I knew what I would see. Dewayne Falco, Preston Drake, Marcus Hardy, and Rock Taylor looking like the kings of the world while the females did everything in their power to get their attention. They personified every cliché in the book. Dewayne was the bad-boy rebel, Preston was the playboy with the smile that dropped panties everywhere, Marcus was the wealthy privileged kid, and Rock was the football star. All of them had bodies and faces that sent girls into a frenzy.

"Y'all get to your side of the building. It takes longer to get over there than you think. Be good. I'll see you out here at three. Don't be late or we'll miss the bus."

They both rolled their eyes, then headed right, toward the eighth-grade side of the school, while I turned left toward the high school section.

Chapter Three

ROCK

It had been almost three months since I'd seen her. I had tried everything to get that girl out of my head, but damn if she still didn't take my breath away. Last year she had been new. She was a transfer student from a nearby city. Her name was Trisha Corbin, and she starred in every fantasy I had. That was all I knew about her. Not from my lack of trying. She just wouldn't give me the time of day.

Admitting that I'd been looking forward to school starting again just so I could see her was pathetic. But damn if it wasn't the truth. Even if she ignored me, I got to watch her. Every gorgeous inch of her.

Today she had stepped off the bus with a guy walking close to her like he was warning anyone who looked her way. Didn't know who the fuck he was, but he was young. I could see that in his face. His body hadn't grown into his height. He was lanky.

"Looks like her brother. That hair color. He has to be related," Dewayne said beside me. He'd been watching me watch her. Shit.

"Doesn't matter," I said, jerking my gaze off her and back to the swarm of females trying to get some attention.

"Fuck, whatever," Dewayne muttered.

Hiding anything from my friends was impossible. We'd been close since second grade. They knew me well. My fascination with Trisha Corbin was something they had all picked up on last year.

But after she'd shot me down not once but *twice*, I had backed off. Being turned down wasn't something I was used to. Ever.

"I heard you and Gina broke up," a blond cheerleader—Kimmy something or other—said, running her nails up my arm.

"Never dated Gina," I replied, annoyed. Kimmy was cheap. I wasn't interested in that. Not when I had just seen Trisha Corbin looking like a dream.

"Oh, well, she sure is telling people you fucked her good up against the wall, on the car, and over the table," she said, then giggled, batting her eyelashes at me.

"I fuck. I don't date," I replied, then threw her arm off me and stepped around the girls. I was a glutton for punishment—I was going to see if I could find Trisha and get her to talk to me.

"I like it hard," Kimmy said as I walked past her.

"I can help you with that," Preston drawled, and I knew pretty boy would get her off my back. She'd found just the guy to scratch her itch.

The guys with Trisha turned toward the eighth-grade wing. Dewayne was probably right. The blond was more than likely her brother. I hadn't paid enough attention to the guy to notice.

Trisha stood looking at the schedule in her hands. The way she pressed her lips together when she was thinking was fucking cute. She had the best facial expressions. You could almost read all her thoughts just by watching her face.

"Ain't fair that you get prettier every time I see you," I said as I came up beside her and stopped. It was lame, but the girl made me nervous. I said stupid shit whenever I was around her.

Trisha tensed up just like she always did when I got near her. I hated that. Not once had I done anything to make her dislike me. I'd been knocking myself out to get her to notice me for more than a year now.

"You gonna talk to me this year, or do I continue to get the silent treatment?" I asked.

Her frown deepened, but I waited. I wasn't going to let her lock me out. She could at least speak to me. Why she was the one girl at this school who didn't want to talk to me, I didn't know. Hell, even the girls I'd pissed off thawed easier than she did when I wanted them to.

"I'm not giving you the silent treatment. I just don't want to encourage you. I've tried to be nice about it."

Ouch. Damn, the girl was mean. Problem was, I didn't believe her. I had seen her watching me when she didn't think I was paying attention. And there had been interest in her eyes. Something else was making her put up a wall.

"I'm real nice. Wish you'd at least give me a break and be my friend." Had I really just asked to be put in the friend zone with this girl? Dammit, I was slipping. I didn't want her to be my friend.

She finally turned her head and tilted it back to look up at me. She was tall for a girl, but I was taller. The confused expression on her face almost made me laugh out loud. She was thinking I had lost my mind too.

"You don't have girls who are friends. You have your little gang, and none of you are friends with girls."

She had me there. But she was different.

"I'm thinking I want to test the waters. Besides, if the only way I can get you to talk to me is to offer friendship, I will."

She raised her eyebrows in disbelief, and then she laughed. I had never seen or heard her laugh before, and goddamn, it was something else. I wanted to record it and play it over and over again, soaking in the fact that I had made her laugh. Memorizing the way her eyes danced with amusement. I forgot where we were and everything else around me.

"You think that's funny?" I asked, unable to keep from grinning like a fool.

She let out one more soft chuckle, then shook her head. "No, I think that's hilarious. You wouldn't last a day without flirting with me." As she said those words she snapped out of her moment of amusement. The tense, frustrated girl was back. "I need to get to first period. Excuse me," she said, and started to walk off. But I wasn't caving in now. This was the most she'd talked to me, and I didn't want it to end. I needed reassurance she'd talk to me again.

"Give it a chance. Be my friend." I was begging. The boys were going to tease my ass for weeks over this.

She let out a sigh and turned back to look at me. "Sure. Whatever. Now I need to go to class, *friend*."

At that, I flashed her a grin that had most girls wrapping themselves around me, and I let her go. "See you later, buddy," I called out as she hurried down the hall without looking back.

I watched as guys did double takes at her retreating form as she passed them. She was oblivious. The urge to shove them all into their lockers so they never glanced at her sweet ass again was hard to resist. But that wouldn't stop them, and I would end up suspended.

I settled for giving warning glares as I walked toward my locker. They all needed to know she was mine. Friend or not, Trisha Corbin was off-limits. Every one of their horny asses needed to understand that.

Chapter Four

TRISHA

Friends? Was I crazy?

After three classes this morning I was still replaying my conversation with Rock Taylor over and over again in my head. It was like watching a train wreck on repeat. I couldn't be Rock's friend. He didn't want me as a friend. He wanted in my pants. Or panties, to be specific.

Ignoring him was so difficult. He was huge. Bigger than life. Those arms of his looked like they could protect anyone. Guys in high school shouldn't look like him. He was built like a wall. The men our stepmother brought home didn't have anything on Rock. He could take care of them.

No. Shaking my head, I cleared that thought right out. Rock had no clue what baggage came with me. He wanted to add me to his list of girls he'd nailed. He didn't want to protect me from the men who enjoyed slapping me around when I didn't let them touch me.

Focus, Trisha. Focus. Keeping Krit safe was my only goal in life. Well, that and getting us the hell out of her house. The only thing I could find any solace in was that there was a line with Krit she would never cross. Fandora Daily didn't let the men she screwed around with hurt her stepson too much. She preferred they hit me. Her unwanted stepdaughter who she also liked to hit. My mother had taken off when I was eight, and I'd been left with my father and his current wife, Fandora. When he took off, he'd left Krit and me behind. The only thing that kept Fandora from tossing me out with the trash was that I took care of Krit. She could go out on dates and live her life knowing she had a built-in babysitter.

So I was given a home. By the time I was ten years old, both my mother and father had deserted me. All I had left was my little brother. And I made it my goal to keep him safe and to keep us together.

Krit was the only person on earth who loved me. I would sell my soul for him. He was what kept me from just giving up and letting Fandora's men beat me to death. I fought to live for my brother's sake.

Touching my side, I inhaled sharply. I was afraid this time my rib was broken. I didn't know what to do about that. I'd taken medical wrap and wound it around my ribs tightly. That was all I knew to do. Going to the hospital could land both Krit and me in foster homes, and I couldn't risk being split from him. He needed me.

Yeah . . . Rock Taylor didn't have a clue. Next time he hit on me, I should show him the black-and-blue bruises under my shirt. Or maybe the ugly green tint of the bruise healing on my ass. Or the scar that marred the skin on the left side of my hip where I'd been whipped with a belt so hard it sliced me open. I'd definitely needed stitches for that, but I'd never gotten them. Fandora was smart. She didn't want me to be harmed where people could see.

She was also completely selfish and bitter. And yet she loved Krit—well, to a degree. She was proud of the handsome man he was turning into, and I think she assumed he'd take care of her one day. So she kept him. And because he loved me, she kept me.

But she made sure I understood that I was a burden on her and always had been.

The end-of-class bell rang and I grabbed my books before standing up. Riley Owens stepped in front of me and grinned. Her dark brown hair was cut into a cute chunky style this year, and she was wearing more makeup than she had last year. I had always thought she was pretty, but she was really attractive now.

"You were in a zone, chick. I tried all class to get your

attention. I haven't seen or heard from you all summer. What gives?" Riley asked, bumping my shoulder with hers as we began walking toward the door and into the hallway.

Riley was one of the two good friends I had here. There were others who were friendly, but coming into this close-knit crowd last year was hard. They didn't accept new faces that easily.

"Sorry. I was working mostly. How was your summer?" I replied.

She sighed in a dramatic fashion that made me smile. "Well, I had to go visit my dad and his new wife up in Pennsylvania. And, girl, let me tell you, they have rednecks up there too. Some people would give folks around here a run for their money. He lives out in the country, and his wife went barefoot to the grocery store! Seriously! Who does that?"

That was another thing about Riley: She always made me smile. "Sounds traumatic," I replied.

She almost nodded in agreement, then squinted at me. "You're being a smartass, aren't you?"

I bit back a grin and started to say something when her dark green eyes went wide as she looked up at something behind me. I started to turn and stopped. I could smell him. Peppermint and leather. Why did that smell so good?

Riley's eyes went from amazed to flirty real fast. She was preparing to grab my new friend's attention. With her new look,

I had no doubt she could. She would be an easy target. I needed to save her.

"Hello, Rock," I said, turning to face him. He was completely focused on me, missing Riley's fluttering eyelashes and come-hither smile.

His lips did a sexy smirk. "What lunch period did you get?" he asked me, keeping those determined eyes directed at me.

"Second," I said, wishing my voice didn't sound affected by him. But he was so close and he smelled so nice. I liked peppermint and leather. It worked. Totally worked.

"Me too," he replied, his smirk turning into a pleased smile. "Let me walk you."

Walk me. Rock wanted to walk me to lunch. *Deep breaths, Trisha. Deep breaths.* "Oh, I was going to walk with Riley to lunch." It was the only excuse I could think of.

Finally Rock shifted his gaze from me to Riley, and I am pretty sure she made a swoony sigh. "Care if I join y'all, Riley?" Rock asked her.

"No. Not at all. I mean, you can walk us both. I don't mind. Or if Trisha doesn't want to, you can walk me. Anywhere at any time." She was babbling like an idiot.

I shot her an annoyed frown. She had just told him he could walk her anywhere at any time. Really? Dear God. No wonder the guy thought all women should fall at his feet. Apparently they all did.

He chuckled. "I'd really like to take Trisha. She's my new friend, and I'm working hard to get her to keep me." His gaze was back on me.

Riley nudged me hard in my battered ribs, and I fell into Rock's chest as I let out a small cry. Pain shot through me, making my vision blur and my eyes water. I was going to be sick. If only I could breathe, I would have run to the restroom.

Two strong arms wrapped around me and held me steady as I focused on not throwing up. "You okay?"

I couldn't answer him. The pain was still shooting through me, and I was struggling to breathe.

"Shit, how hard did you hit her?" he asked angrily. His arms were gentle but held on to me firmly. I didn't fight him. The pain was ebbing, and I could hear Riley apologizing as the pounding in my head eased. I needed to tell her it was fine, that this wasn't her fault. But I was still fighting back the nausea.

"You okay? You need me to walk you down to the nurse? Have her take a look?" He was concerned. If he hadn't held on to me, I would be on the floor in the fetal position.

Pushing past the lingering pain, I managed to nod and take a deep breath. Straightening my shoulders, I stepped back, trying to move out of his arms. At first I didn't think he was going to let me go, but he dropped his arms slowly, reluctant to let me move away.

"I'm so sorry," Riley whispered. "I didn't mean to hit you

hard. I was just trying to get you to go with him. I mean, it's Rock Taylor, for crying out loud. He's . . ." Riley paused.

"It's fine. I think you just hit the wrong spot and, uh . . . hit my, uh . . . funny bone." That didn't even sound believable.

Riley scrunched her nose up and frowned. "I thought I hit your side. . . ."

I glanced back at Rock. He was going to think I was crazy. But maybe then he'd give up on trying to get me to like him. "I'm not going to lunch. I need . . . to go get a book from the library," I said in a hurry, then turned and walked as fast as I could down the hallway. No footsteps followed me, and I took that as a good thing.

With me gone, Rock would probably turn the charm on Riley and she'd let him sweet-talk his way into her panties. The idea of that made me ill. I didn't want Rock hooking up with Riley.

Shoving that thought away, I passed by the library and headed toward my next class. Lunch was one of my favorite things about school: I got a hot meal. I was hungry, and I doubted I would get much, if anything, to eat tonight. Fandora was in a bad mood. Her latest boyfriend had left her.

I had gone longer than this without food. I could make it until tomorrow at lunch if needed. What I wasn't ready to do was face Rock after that fiasco in the hall. I doubted he'd try to speak to me again. He and Riley probably thought I was insane.

Chapter Five

ROCK

I didn't like Trisha's friend. First she hurt her, then she didn't run after her. Instead the brunette had started flirting with me. Which pissed me off.

After grabbing the burger off my tray in the cafeteria, I headed for the library to find Trisha. Eating would have been impossible while worrying about her. Something had been off about that whole scene. Riley had only elbowed her in the ribs. I'd seen it and I hadn't liked it, but I didn't think it was hard enough for the reaction it caused. Hell, if I hadn't gotten a look at how pale Trisha's face had gone and the pain in her eyes, I would have thought she was acting just to get my attention.

Her body had been trembling as I held her. She'd really been in some serious fucking agony. The more I thought about it, the more it bothered me. The only reason someone would react like that was if they were hurt already. And if she was hurt there already, why not just tell us instead of making up some library bullshit and running off?

Preston had lipstick smeared on his face and messy hair, plus a blonde on his arm whose name I couldn't remember, when I stepped back into the hallway from the cafeteria.

"You leaving already?" he asked, frowning at me.

"Got somewhere to be," I replied, and headed past him before he could ask me any more questions.

"Need me to go with you?" he called out after me.

"No!"

Preston was always ready for a fight. He assumed that was the only thing that would pull me out of the cafeteria. He had his future riding on his baseball career just as much as I had my future riding on my football career. Pisser didn't think about that, though. He'd jump into a fight without thinking about it if he thought we needed him.

I would too. But I'd worry. I would be careful. I was too close now. I didn't just have a college career waiting on me. I had a dad for the first time in my life. He was proud of me. Someone cared, and that meant something. I hated that I needed my dad's attention like a damn kid. But he'd never been around before.

If I could keep us out of a fight, I did. For me and for Preston. Dewayne and Marcus had parents. Good parents who would make sure they went to college. They had parents who loved them. Preston and I had to work a little harder. Hell, we had to work a lot harder.

Shoving open the library doors, I stepped into the quiet room stacked full of books. I only came in here if I absolutely had to. The place gave me the creeps. Too many damn books and no one was supposed to talk. Then there was the librarian. She was older than a human should be and mean as hell.

Her sharp eyes squinted at me and I froze like a naughty child. She was all of five feet tall and hunched over slightly. The little bit of white hair she had left was on top of her head in a tight bun. Seriously, I think she might have been sipping some everlasting life concoction.

I scanned the room, but none of the tables had the pretty blond head I was looking for. She had lied. This wasn't where she had been headed. Deep down I'd known she was lying. But I'd still hoped I would find her here.

Turning, I stepped back out of the library and began my search of the empty classrooms. I didn't know what her schedule was or this would have been easier.

"Rock! Come on! Coach just called an early meeting in the field house. We're supposed to go directly there," Marcus called out as he, Preston, and Dewayne came walking down the hallway.

"We have fifteen more minutes left of lunch," I pointed out, annoyed.

"Coach is fired up about the game Friday night," Marcus said with a smirk.

Shit. After lunch I went to the field house to work out that period, then came back for Algebra II before heading out to practice. Coach was messing it all up. I wanted to find Trisha and make sure she was okay.

"Heard we're leaving after a half day on Friday to get on the buses and head to Rock Creek. Coach told Simmons he wants us rested and ready to go by game time. So he's getting us there three hours early."

Glancing back into the hallway, I looked for the white-blond hair that fascinated me, but I saw nothing. I'd have to find her later.

Chapter Six

TRISHA

Krit and Green were already waiting at the bus stop in front of school when I got there. Both of them had big smiles on their faces and were talking animatedly about their days. I didn't have to ask how they liked eighth grade. Just watching them talk answered that for me.

My problems vanished as I watched my little brother grinning like he owned the world. He hadn't been given many things in life to smile about. Knowing he'd had a good day was a relief. My ribs had throbbed the rest of the day, but I had managed to dodge any questions from Riley because we didn't have any other classes together.

"Hey, babe," Green called out when he saw me.

I shot him a warning glare and he started laughing. Krit

rolled his eyes, not amused by his friend's constant flirting with me.

"Don't call me 'babe' again if you want to live," I informed him.

Green waggled his eyebrows at me, and Krit shoved him and said, "Dude, stop it. Seriously."

Green's tall, lanky body hadn't had time to adjust to his overnight height either. He stumbled back, then laughed. "Jeesh. You two are uptight."

"Was your day good?" I asked Krit, ignoring Green.

Getting Krit through a school day without him losing his temper or having some kind of emotional snap was an accomplishment. He was severely ADHD, and I was beginning to think he also suffered from some sort of personality disorder that we didn't know about. Fandora wouldn't take him to have him checked out. She hated giving him meds at all. It took time out of her day to get them.

When one of her boyfriends had slapped me and Krit threw a brick at his head, she had gone and gotten his meds. But we were getting low again. Krit tended to get addicted to things. He was like a live wire, unable to stay still. Ready for the next adventure. And if you stood in his way, he lost it.

Keeping him calm was my job.

"I was an angel today," he informed me, then gave me his crooked grin. My heart squeezed. I loved my brother. So many times I felt like he was mine. I wasn't old enough to be his mother, but the way I felt about him was what I believed a real mother's love would feel like. There was nothing I wouldn't do for Krit. Nothing. When he was happy, it made me happy.

"Don't lie to her. You got sent to the office once," Green added.

"What?" I asked, my heart sinking.

Krit shrugged, then glared at Green. "Nothing big. I told the teacher I'd get to the assignment in a minute. I was finishing up something. She got all pissy."

That was typical Krit. He didn't like being bossed around. Not by anyone but me. I could get away with it. In his eyes, everyone else needed to step back. Even his mother.

Krit started to say something else but stopped as his eyes lit up at something behind me. Frustrated with his erratic attention span, I turned to see who had his interest.

Rock Taylor was walking up from the football field dressed in pads and that tight uniform they wore. His helmet was in his hand, hanging forgotten by his side. As impressive as all that perfection was, the breathtaking part was that his eyes were locked on me. *Me.*

"He's headed this way, I think," Green whispered.

I wasn't ready to deal with him again. What if he asked about my side in front of Krit? Crap. I had to get out of here.

I reached for Krit's arm. "Let's go. Bus is almost here. We

don't want those back seats with the thugs. Let's be sure to get in line."

"But I think Rock Taylor is coming this way. Like, to us. Or . . . you," Krit said, watching Rock carefully now. He wasn't so mesmerized anymore. He seemed to be thinking this through.

"He's not coming for us. Let's go," I said, pushing them both toward the bus line.

"Trisha." Rock's voice stopped me. Green's jaw dropped, and Krit's eyes no longer held fascination. He was studying Rock hard now. A tight frown came over his face, and I watched my little brother turn into a man as he stood up straighter and stepped in front of me.

"What do you want with my sister? She don't seem real excited about seeing you," Krit said in a hard, cold tone.

Rock was a wall of muscle, and Krit had to tilt his head back to make eye contact with him. But Rock didn't seem to care or back down. Krit was determined to protect me. He was doing that a lot now. I was so worried he was going to get hurt. It was my job to protect Krit. Not the other way around.

Rock's jaw twitched, and it looked like he was trying not to smile. "Trisha and I decided to be friends today. Didn't we, Trisha?" he said, looking over my brother's shoulder to me.

I had to calm my little brother down. I nodded and stepped around Krit. "Yes, we did," I confirmed.

"Then why were you trying to get us on the bus before he could get to you?" Krit asked, not buying this at all.

"Yes, why were you doing that, Trisha? Hurts my feelings," Rock added. This time he was smiling. Dang him. He was amused by all this.

I stepped in front of Krit and lifted my eyes to meet Rock's. "I just didn't want to be left with the seats in the back of the bus. I don't like those."

Rock's grin grew even bigger. "I got a truck. Lucky for you, I like giving my friends a ride."

Oh, no. I wasn't letting him see where we lived. Not today. Not ever. "Uh, no, that's okay. The bus works just fine." And as if on cue, the bus rolled up and Mr. Freds called out over his megaphone for the riders of A138 to board.

I grabbed Krit's arm. "That's us. I'll see you tomorrow," I told Rock quickly, and pulled my brother to the bus line. I didn't look back, and I was almost afraid Rock would get in line with us. Even though he was supposed to be at football practice.

Getting this guy to back off wasn't going to be easy. Getting my heart to stop going into a frenzy whenever he spoke to me was also not going to be easy. He was every daydream I had allowed myself to have since I was a little girl. A big, beautiful, strong man who could keep me safe. Someone who would love me and ride in on his horse and wrap me up in his arms so that no one could hurt me again.

Rock Taylor did not want to save me and my brother. He was a teenager with a football career ahead of him. Everyone knew the college scouts were watching him. He was going to be big one day. I would be a waste of his time.

"Rock Taylor has the hots for your sister," Green announced to Krit as we sat down. I ignored his comment.

"Yeah, I saw that," Krit replied, sounding pissed.

I turned to look at my brother. I would have thought he would love any excuse to get to talk to Rock Taylor. "He doesn't have the hots for me."

Krit scowled. "Yes, Sis, he does. I saw it. He's not what you need, though. He ain't got time to deal with our shit. He won't stick around, and you'll get hurt. Then I'll have to kill him."

Green let out an amused, hard laugh. "You can't kill Rock Taylor. He can step on you and squish you like a bug."

"You have no clue what I can do," Krit said, staring straight ahead with a determined gleam in his eyes.

I had to deal with Krit. But not here on this bus where people could hear us.

Rock needed to understand I didn't have time to be his friend or anything else. I wouldn't fit into his world. I had my world to survive.

Chapter Seven

ROCK

"You good tonight?" I asked Preston as we walked from the field house out to Marcus's truck. This was a daily thing. Preston's home life was shit. If it weren't for his younger brothers and baby sister, he wouldn't ever go home. His mother was a user. In a very bad way.

"Yeah. It's all good. I'm anxious to hear about Jimmy's first day of school," Preston said with his easy smile that the world believed. But I knew better. Behind his pretty-boy looks and carefree smile was a guy who had seen bad shit. He was basically a father at seventeen. He was the only love and protection his siblings got.

"Jimmy start kindergarten?" I asked.

Preston nodded, then sighed. "He was scared as hell this

mornin' too. It was hard not going with him. I wanted to sit in his class with him all day. You know?" He chuckled and shook his head. "I can't imagine doing this with Daisy May."

Daisy May was the baby. She was only one. Preston had been taking care of her since she was born. His mother had come home from the hospital and then left for a week. Preston had lost his job that summer because he couldn't leave the trailer they lived in. Jimmy was only five then and Brent was about two, I think.

"We'll all go sit with Daisy May on her first day of school. Threaten anyone who looks at her. She'll be the most protected first grader there is," I assured him.

Preston laughed, and then his smile turned into something real. I was reminding him that he wasn't alone. That all he had to do was let us know when he needed us. We were his family too. Sometimes he needed reminding. He was bad about figuring shit out alone.

"Saw you talking to Trisha Corbin today," Preston said with a smirk. "Two days in a row."

Trisha had been hard to track down today. It was like she was avoiding me. I found her anyway. Chasing a girl like this wasn't something I excelled at. But damn, she smelled good. And that smile of hers. . . . If I could get her to smile, then it made everything worth it.

"She's not gonna be easy," Preston warned.

He had no idea. "Yeah. I got that. I wasn't looking for easy. It ain't about fucking."

Preston tossed his bag into the bed of Marcus's truck and frowned. "Then what the hell is it about? Have you seen her tits and ass? Day-um."

I would have snapped if it was anyone else who had said that. But it was Preston, and he graded all girls on their tits and ass. He was a player in a very bad way. He didn't have a good opinion of females, thanks to his mom. Daisy May was the only female he put on a pedestal. Well, Amanda Hardy, Marcus's little sister, too. But she was so off-limits it wasn't fucking funny. Like any of us, Preston would beat anyone's ass who touched her. But he wouldn't talk about her body or go near it.

"It's more. Something about her . . ." I wasn't getting into this with him. He'd make fun of me for weeks. Months. Hell, all fucking year.

"Y'all ready to go?" Marcus called out as he slapped Rachel Mann's ass and left her staring after him longingly. Rachel had been after Marcus all last year.

"You finally decide to dive into the Mann girl pussy?" Preston asked, amused.

He'd messed around with Rose Mann, who was Rachel's cousin. Both girls had rocking bodies and heads full of brown curls. They were hot. But I wasn't going there. They paled in comparison to Trisha.

Marcus rolled his eyes and tossed his bag into the back of his truck. "Stop being an ass."

"She's clingy. Don't say I didn't warn you," Preston said as he put his hands on the sides of the truck, then jumped up and slung his legs over into the bed. It was his turn to take the back. "Where's D?" he called out, looking around for Dewayne.

"He was preoccupied with two of the cheerleaders. Can't remember their names, though. They're new ones," Marcus answered him.

"Shit. Does this mean he won't be home so we can't go swing by and get some of Mrs. T's cookies?" Preston whined.

"We can still go get some cookies. Mrs. T doesn't care if Dewayne is with us or not," Marcus assured him.

Sometimes Preston reminded me of a kid. But it was part of his charm, I guess. Girls loved it. Until he brushed them off once he got some. Then they didn't love it so much.

Marcus closed his door and looked over at me. "Do you think he'll always be this way?"

Chuckling, I shook my head. No. I knew he wouldn't. He had three kids to raise. When he was with us, he was free to do what he wanted, so he lived wild. When he went home, he became a dad.

"He needs this. When he isn't home, he needs to live," I replied.

Marcus frowned. He had the easiest life of us all. Although

Dewayne's was pretty sweet. Marcus had the happy family and the money. The life Preston had was something Marcus didn't completely understand. He'd been trying to take care of Preston since we were kids, when Preston would come to school without a lunch. But he didn't know just how bad shit was. Preston didn't talk about it much.

I only knew because my life wasn't roses either and Preston felt like he could talk about it with me.

"Yeah, I guess you're right," Marcus finally said.

I leaned forward and turned up the radio as Marcus pulled out onto the road.

I had to wait until tomorrow to see Trisha. Damn.

Chapter Eight

TRISHA

"Just go," Krit snapped at me. He was scared. I could see it in his eyes. He knew his stepmother wouldn't hit him too hard. But she had no limits with me. I didn't care, though—I wasn't letting her hurt him.

"No," I replied, standing up from the table where Krit and I had been having an after-school snack. We weren't supposed to eat the cereal without permission. It was for breakfast only. But we had both been hungry and thought we had time before she got home. If she wasn't lying on the sofa watching trashy talk shows with a beer in her hand when we got here, it meant she was out and wouldn't be home until later.

"What the FUCK?" she screeched as Krit shot up out of his chair to stand in front of me. Granted, he was taller than me now, but he was still younger. I was supposed to protect him. Not the other way around.

I tried to shove him aside, but he wasn't budging. "Stay behind me," he warned with a much more commanding voice than I was used to hearing my little brother use.

That made her cackle—a hard, sadistic laugh. "What, boy, you think you're gonna protect that mooching sorry-ass slut from me just because you're bigger than me?"

She took a step toward Krit, and his entire body tensed. "You. Won't. Hurt. Me," she said in a soft voice that gave me chills. "I'm your momma. You won't touch me."

"We wanted a snack. We've been at school all day and we were hungry. Lunch didn't fill us up," Krit explained. I heard the little boy come out of him. The scared one who always tried to reason with his crazy-ass stepmother. I wasn't going to let him touch her to protect me. He'd never forgive himself.

I moved fast and jumped in front of him. "Get out of here, Krit," I yelled at him, and barely had time to prepare myself for the slap across my face.

"SHIT! Mom, stop it!" Krit demanded, and I felt his hands clasp around my arms.

"Stupid, stupid, ugly slut." She hurled words at me that she thought hurt me. Coming from someone I cared about, maybe they would. But she'd been calling me names all my life. I didn't care what she said about me.

She pulled back at first, and Krit tried to move me out of the way. But instead her swing hit my hurt ribs. The scream that erupted out of me sounded like it was coming from somewhere else as black spots formed in my vision and I crumpled to the ground, trying to breathe.

I heard Krit yelling, but I couldn't move. The pain was paralyzing, and I hadn't been able to draw a breath yet. The black spots all bonded together until there was just darkness.

"Dammit, Trish, wake up." Krit's desperate voice worried me.

I fought to open my eyes. The pain had started to subside. I was breathing again. Looking around, I tried to sit up in case the crazy woman we called Mother was getting ready to strike again.

"Be still. She's gone," Krit said, pressing a hand to my shoulder to keep me from getting up. "She probably won't be back tonight."

"You sure?" I asked, then winced because I had tried to shift. The pain was there, but if I didn't move I was okay.

Krit looked angry as he nodded. "Yeah. I hit her. I've never hit her. I was scared because you weren't moving, and so damn mad that you had to deal with her shit. I just lost it." He sighed and hung his head. "She said she was calling the cops."

Krit had hit his mother. Exactly what I'd been trying to protect him from. He'd feel guilty about it later. And he'd question himself.

"If the cops come here and see me like this, she'll get locked up. She isn't calling the cops. She was trying to scare you," I assured him.

He nodded and straightened his shoulders like he was trying to be brave. "You need to see a doctor. Your ribs look bad, Trisha."

If I went to the hospital, they'd take us away from her and we'd be split up in foster homes or group homes. I wasn't letting that happen. I couldn't protect him there. He needed me.

"Not chancing that. Just help me stand up, and then I'll need help wrapping it tight," I told him.

He stared down at me with a frustrated frown. Then growled angrily. "I'm not a little kid anymore. When are you gonna see I can take care of myself, Trisha? Stop getting hurt for me! I can protect us both. And I want you to see a doctor."

"They will split us up," I reminded him.

He looked defeated. "Maybe. But at least you won't be beat on."

"There is no promise of that if we escaped from here. At least here I know what to expect, and I have you."

Krit leaned down and kissed the top of my head. "One day we won't live like this. We will have a real life. We will be free."

Tears burned my eyes. When had my little brother become the one who comforted me?

Chapter Nine

ROCK

Trisha wasn't at school today. I'd watched her brother and his friend get off the bus, but she hadn't been with them. The kid studied me as he walked by where I was standing. As if he was trying decide something. His blue eyes were so much like his sister's. And there was a haunted look in them that I remembered seeing in Preston's when we were younger.

Something was wrong.

That feeling stayed with me all day. When the last bell rang, I didn't head to the field house. I made my way to the eighth-grade hall. I was finding her brother.

Krit was walking toward the door leading outside when I got to his side of the building.

"Krit," I called out. There was a crowd of kids between

us, and I knew if he got out that door, the[...]
the rush.

He turned and his eyes found me immediately. Whic[...]
ably had to do with the fact that I was more than a head tallei
than most of these kids.

After telling his friend something, he pushed through the
crowd and made his way back toward me. Thankfully, his friend
continued on outside. Krit pulled his book bag up higher on his
shoulder and stood up straighter, making his tall, lanky frame
seem even taller. "What do you want with her? She's not some
chick you can just screw and move on from. She'd never sleep
with you. She's a good girl. She's also got shit to deal with, and a
player like you wouldn't understand. So back off her if you're just
after her as one to add to your many."

I was impressed. Not once did he falter in his demand. He
was standing up for his sister, and he wasn't afraid of the fact
that I could snap him in two. I liked this kid.

"Not after her to sleep with her. I like her. A lot," I assured
him. "Where was she today?"

Krit frowned like he wasn't sure he believed me. But I could
see there was hope in his eyes. He wanted me to like her. "She's
hurt," he replied slowly, and I could tell he was holding something back.

"How is she hurt?" I asked, wishing I'd not waited all damn
day to figure out why she wasn't in school.

He looked away from me and his jaw clenched. After a few too many beats of silence, I was beginning to think he wasn't going to tell me. Finally he turned his gaze back to me, and the pain in his eyes didn't make me feel better.

"Mom hit her. She already had messed-up ribs. And she punched her there again. I tried to help her." He stopped, and his eyes watered as a hardness came over his face.

Shit.

"She at home with your mom?" I asked, trying not to let the horror pounding inside my chest show on my face. The kid needed me to be strong. He was about to break down, and he was fighting it.

"I . . . I, uh, hit Mom. When Trisha crumpled to the ground, I lost it and I just . . ." He looked down and I saw him swallow hard.

"Did your mom leave?" I asked him.

He nodded.

Motherfucker. Why did her mother hit her? Sick fucks didn't need to reproduce. God should have made that a rule.

"Yeah. She was angry, but she was bleeding. She left and wasn't back this morning. Trisha was in a lot of pain, and I convinced her to stay in bed. She needs to get better."

"I'm taking you home," I told him, and grabbed his arm and headed for the exit doors. I wouldn't get any fucking sleep tonight if I didn't see Trisha with my own eyes.

Krit tried to jerk his arm free. "Dude, let go. I've already missed my bus. I need the ride. You don't have to break my arm."

I wasn't aware my grip was so tight. I let go of him.

"Sorry," I muttered.

He shook his arm as if to get feeling back in it, but he continued to walk beside me.

"Don't you have football practice?" he asked, glancing back at the field I had been due at twenty minutes ago.

"Yeah," I replied, jerking open the door to my dad's beat-up truck. I only got to drive it when he was working nights and sleeping all day. That was this week. I just had to fill it with gas and wash it.

"You gonna get to play Friday night if you miss? I heard that you had scouts watching you all season."

If my dad found out I'd missed a practice, he'd be furious. The only reason he hadn't kicked me out was because I could play football. He liked knowing his boy was going to be something.

When I was younger, he had left me with my mom and had barely come to visit me. Then one day in middle school I had begged him to let me play football and he'd been excited about it. When the coaches praised me and I became the star of the team, Dad had taken me away from my mother more and more.

The day I had come home from school to find all my things packed up in the back of his truck, my mother had been standing on the porch with the man she was dating. She explained that she needed a life and it was my dad's turn to take care of me. Plus, she couldn't afford it anymore.

The next month she moved to another state, and I hadn't heard from her since.

So Dad was all I had. A man who only loved what I could do. Not me.

"If you don't get to play, everyone's gonna be pissed. We can't beat the Dolphins without you."

I would get to play. Coach would be mad, and he'd make me pay for it with longer practices. But he'd let me play.

"I'll play. Tell me how to get to your house."

Krit pointed to the left. "Take the main street until you're almost out of town. Then turn right onto Forts Road. Fifth trailer on the left."

Forts Road was in the bad area of Sea Breeze. I'd been on that road once before with my mother when I was a kid. She'd been buying pot from someone there. We didn't live in a great part of town, but it wasn't this bad. And Dad had an apartment that wasn't so bad. It was better than the house I'd lived in with Mom.

But Forts Road . . . Shit. Trisha shouldn't be there by herself.

"It ain't all that bad. Stop looking so damn horrified," Krit grumbled.

I started to argue with him, but I let it go. No need to make him feel bad.

Chapter Ten

TRISHA

From my bed, where I had lain all day, I could hear the school bus pull up by the road. Mommie Dearest came home sometime after noon. She stumbled down the hall, and I heard her door slam. Then nothing else. She was hungover or still high and sleeping it off. The door to my room was closed, so she never thought to look inside.

I waited for the front door to open and Krit to come in, but I never heard it. Once the bus was gone and he still hadn't come inside, I knew I had to get up. Something was wrong. If he missed the bus, he'd need me. I held my breath and tried not to groan as I sat up and slowly moved my legs off the bed. Once I had them both on the carpet, I stood up and took short breaths.

Today I had babied my side. Tomorrow I couldn't do that.

For starters, the wicked witch was now home. Then, of course, if I missed more school, they'd start calling here. That would be bad. Very bad.

Just as I took a step toward the door, I heard someone pull up outside. I froze and waited. Krit's voice drifted through the window. I let out a sigh of relief. He'd gotten a ride. I continued to walk to the door, but then I heard another voice.

Once again . . . I froze.

Rock Taylor was here. Oh no. What had Krit done?

"That's Mom's car. She's home," I heard Krit tell Rock *freaking* Taylor! What was he doing?

Forgetting the pain, I opened my door and made my way down the hall and into the living room just as the front door opened up and in walked my brother, followed by Rock. Holy crap.

He was so big. Stepping into our trailer, he looked so out of place.

"Krit," I croaked out, while my eyes were locked on Rock.

His gaze dropped to my ribs, and I remembered what I had on. Wrapping my arms around my waist, I tried to hide the tape we had used on my ribs. I hadn't wanted my clothes to touch my injured ribs, so I was wearing a sports bra and a pair of cutoff sweatpants.

"I missed the bus. He gave me a ride," Krit started to explain.

That didn't make sense. "Why did you miss the bus?" I asked, still trying to figure out why Rock was here. In our trailer.

"He asked about you. When you didn't show up at school. I told him . . ."

I snapped my gaze off Rock and glared at my brother. Surely he hadn't told Rock what had happened. "You told him what?"

Krit shuffled his feet nervously. He had told him about Mom. Why would he do that? Rock Taylor wasn't going to run in and save the day. He was interested in me. Now that he'd seen me like this, I hoped his fascination with getting in my pants would go away. My hair wasn't washed and I looked awful.

"Thanks for bringing him home," I bit out, trying to sound like I meant it. But I had a feeling it was Rock's fault Krit had missed his bus. "But we got this. You can leave now."

Krit's eyes went wide. "Trisha! Seriously, why are you being like this? He isn't—"

"He's seen enough, Krit. Mom will wake up any minute, and he needs to be gone."

"He said—"

"It doesn't matter what he said. I am telling you that if you care about me at all, you'll go back to your room and start your homework quietly. I don't want her waking up, and you don't either. She'll be angry we woke her. I'm not up for another round just yet."

Krit hung his head, then nodded and started walking toward his room. He stopped and gave Rock a nod. "Thanks, man."

"Anytime," Rock replied.

Krit glanced at me, and I could see the frustration on his face. I knew he thought Rock was here to save us. That little boy inside his big body still held on to the hope of a hero. Finally he went on down the hallway.

I waited until his bedroom door clicked closed before looking back at Rock.

"Don't talk to him again. He doesn't need you using him to get to me," I said in the coldest tone I could muster.

Rock didn't move. He held my gaze, then looked down at my ribs again.

"You need to see a doctor," was his reply.

I let out a hard laugh. "Really? Aren't you brilliant. News flash: If I see a doctor, DHR steps in and I lose my brother. Not gonna happen. Back off, Rock. I'm not up for grabs. I'm so off-limits to all men it's not even funny. You are wasting your time and playing with my brother's head. He thinks you can do something to help us. Stop it. Just. Go. Away."

"She hit you a lot?"

Really? Did he not hear anything I just said?

"I said to go away," I hissed.

"Let me help you. I know a doctor who can see you. It won't get back to DHR. I swear."

"GO. AWAY." I bit my tongue and closed my eyes. I had yelled. Shit. He was making me so mad. I needed to keep my voice down.

"Can you stay in bed tomorrow? Will she make you go to school?"

Either he was deaf or he thought he was above listening to what others told him. "Rock, I need you to leave. I need you to forget all of this. Go play football and be the star this town loves to talk about. They want you. I don't."

He stood there and watched me for a few more seconds. Then, just when I thought he wasn't going to listen yet again and I started to feel a small twinge of hope that maybe he wanted more than to get in my pants, he turned and walked outside.

His perfect, beautiful body walked down the small steps and back toward his truck. He didn't look at me when he climbed inside and pulled away. He left. Just like I thought. He wanted something I wasn't going to give him.

Guess he got the message.

If I admitted it to myself, it hurt. But I wouldn't admit that. Or think about it. I didn't have the luxury of fantasizing about anyone. Especially a guy who would be leaving for a college of his choice in two years.

Chapter Eleven

ROCK

Friday was finally here. The first game of the season. I was playing tonight, but I wasn't starting. Coach was benching me for the first five minutes. It was part of my punishment for coming to practice late on Wednesday. He had kept me running the bleachers for three hours. I'd been so damn exhausted that after throwing up twice, I had barely made it to the truck. Dad had been pissed because he had needed his truck back.

All that shit for nothing. Trisha Corbin had made it very clear she didn't want me near her.

Didn't stop me from asking Krit about her yesterday when she didn't show up again. He said his mom had a new boyfriend and had stayed out with him last night so Trisha had taken one more day to heal.

Unable not to watch for her damn bus this morning, I had waited to see if she stepped off it. When she did, her gaze had gone right through me as if I wasn't there. She walked by me without a glance or a word. I was fucking invisible to her.

That shit hurt. I hadn't done anything to deserve this from her. I just wanted to help. I wanted to be near her. But she obviously hated me.

So tonight I was going to play like a fucking pro and then go out and celebrate when we won. If I had to drink Trisha Corbin from my head, I would. Letting her consume me like this was ridiculous. Yes, her life was shit, but did that mean she had to hate me?

Dewayne sat down beside me in biology and tossed a Snickers bar on my desk with a grin. "Mom stuck two in my bag this morning. Looked like you needed something to smile about."

Dewayne had the best mom in the fucking world. We all loved Tabby Falco. I picked up the candy bar and tore the wrapper open with my teeth. "Thanks," I said before taking a bite.

"Tonight's the night. Thought you'd be all smiles," Dewayne pointed out.

Normally, I was. But Trisha Corbin had fucked with my mood. "I'm just staying focused."

Dewayne chuckled. "Bullshit. I've seen you staring at the Corbin girl like you want a taste. She not interested?"

He'd better be glad he'd just given me a damn candy bar.

I shot him a warning glare. "Moving on from that" was my only reply.

"There's always Ellie Nova. That piece of ass is the best around here. But I'm working on getting a bite of that."

Ellie Nova was the high school princess. Not my type. She knew she was gorgeous and she worked it. I didn't tell Dewayne I had actually already had a taste. She'd come onto me at a party at the end of last year. I'd kissed her, but it didn't do anything for me.

"She's all yours," I assured him, then took another bite of my candy bar.

Dewayne nodded and leaned back, crossing his arms over his chest. "Guess if Trisha Corbin worked it, she'd be just as fucking hot. She hides away from everyone and doesn't say much. Her group of friends is small. But yeah, I can see the attraction. The girl has a body. And her face . . ." He let out a low whistle.

I didn't realize my hands had curled tightly into fists until Dewayne's gaze dropped down to them. He smirked. "Yeah, I can see you've moved on from that."

Books dropped onto the desk on the other side of me. "Damn, D. What'd you do to piss him off? And where'd you get the candy?" Preston asked as he slipped into the desk.

"He's pissy over Trisha Corbin," Dewayne said, smiling smugly.

Damn asshole.

Long, tanned legs caught my attention and I let my gaze travel up to see a short little navy skirt that so didn't meet the dress code. But damn, was it nice. The small waist and perky tits weren't bad either.

Noah Miller, a senior with dark red hair and big brown eyes, smiled at me just before taking the seat in front of me. "Hey, Rock," she said in a soft voice as she leaned over and batted her long eyelashes at me.

Sure, she was wearing a lot of makeup, but not everyone could look like Trisha without makeup. Noah's face wasn't hard to look at. Never had been.

"Hello, Noah," I replied.

"You ready for tonight?" she asked. The top three buttons on her white shirt were unbuttoned, showing me her cleavage. Not a bad view.

"Yeah. You coming?" I asked.

She gave me a small shrug, then grinned. "I guess I would if I knew I had plans afterward."

This was an invitation. Did I want to go there with her? Shit, why not? Trisha wasn't interested. Hell, Trisha hated me.

"Party at the beach tonight. Bonfire win or lose. But we're gonna win," I added.

She bit her bottom lip, then pressed her arms against the sides of her tits to squeeze them together. It was a move I knew and appreciated. "I don't want to go alone."

Dewayne cleared his throat to keep from laughing. This was what I was used to. What I knew. Maybe that was the way it was supposed to be. I didn't need to go after girls who weren't interested. The ones who wanted me were where I needed to stay.

I leaned forward on the desk and dropped my gaze to her tits she wanted me to look at so badly. "I think I can fix that for you," I told her boobs. "After the game meet me at the field house."

She shivered and I was back in territory I knew. "Okay. We can take my new car," she said. "It's a Charger and completely badass. I'll let you drive it."

I wouldn't have the truck tonight. Fixed that problem.

Lifting my gaze to meet her brown eyes flashing with attraction and excitement, I grinned. "Sounds good, baby."

"And he's back on the horse," Dewayne drawled.

I ignored him. Instead I reached over and tucked a lock of Noah's hair behind her ear and winked. She melted just like I knew she would.

This was much easier.

So why didn't it fucking feel good?

Chapter Twelve

TRISHA

Riley opened the door to the cafeteria before I could get to it. "Let's eat!" she said in her bright, cheery tone.

I was starving. This morning Fandora's new boyfriend had come out of her bedroom while we were getting ready to go. His eyes had scanned my body, and then he'd gotten that creepy grin I'd seen before on her boyfriends. "Fandora didn't tell me her daughter was so fucking hot" had been his oh-so-intelligent words.

"She's also too young. Jail bait," I had replied in a warning tone. Then I'd hurried out the door with Krit. Luckily, he had gotten to eat his bowl of Frosted Flakes. Me, not so much. I was still moving slow, and getting ready took me longer than it normally did.

"You coming to the game tonight?" Riley asked me.

That was all anyone talked about today. The football game. I was so sick of hearing about it. Rock's name was always attached to the conversations. He wasn't getting to play the first five minutes, and everyone was panicking.

I felt guilty about that but didn't know why. It wasn't like I had asked him to miss his practice and come to my house. But he had. And he had also been sure not to approach me today.

I was certain he was going to try to speak to me when I got off the bus this morning, but he hadn't. My words had sunk in. Hadn't taken much for him to figure out I wasn't worth it.

"Doubt it," I replied, standing in line for food. Fandora had made sure to apply for free lunch for Krit. She hadn't bothered for me. However, the school system had added me too since they could see we came from the same home. I never let her know. I was afraid she'd take it out on me.

"You can ride with me," Riley said hopefully.

And leave Krit at home? No way. Not with a new guy hanging around the trailer.

"Can't tonight," I replied, wishing she'd drop it.

She sighed. "Fine. Might as well give up my hopes of you and Rock Taylor anyway. I was going to live vicariously through you, but it looks like Noah's got his attention now." She snorted. "Not surprising. Look at her hanging all over him."

Why I turned my head to look, I do not know. Maybe to

prove that I had been right about Rock Taylor. For whatever reason, I turned to see Rock sitting at the end of his table like the king of the world, with Noah Miller leaning on him and laughing at whatever he was saying. The other football players also filled that table, with girls much like Noah sitting in their laps or beside them. This was what I expected of Rock Taylor.

He was smiling like he didn't have a care in the world. He had Noah's breasts against his arm and her long legs wrapped around his like she was trying to hold on to a moving target. When he lowered his head to whisper something in her ear, his gaze met mine.

For a brief moment he paused. Something flashed in his eyes, but he blinked it away quickly, then moved his eyes back to Noah and continued to make her giggle.

Yuck. Just yuck.

"That's his speed. He likes them fast and cheap," I told Riley, trying not to sound jealous.

Riley didn't reply at first. I was thankful because I needed a moment to figure out why my chest hurt. Rock had never been mine. It made no sense that I cared he was with Noah.

"Yeah . . . I was just hoping for a moment that he wasn't like the others," Riley finally said.

"Me too," I whispered before I could stop myself.

Riley gently squeezed my arm. "You're so much prettier than her. And you have class. He missed out."

My eyes burned and I hated that. But Riley was a good friend, and she was trying to make me feel better. It was sad that any devotion or encouragement I got from someone made me emotional. But it was rare. So when it came at me, I always felt weepy.

"You're coming tonight," Davey Marks said as he broke in line to wrap his arm around Riley's shoulders and grinned at me. "Both of you. I'm not going to this testosterone-filled barbarian thing by myself."

Davey was one of the only other real friends I had at school. He was short. I'd guess he was five nine, maybe. He wore thick glasses and had freckles all over his body and face. But he was always smiling and happy. He was also brilliant. He'd be the valedictorian our senior year. I had no doubt. The guy was a genius.

"I thought you'd be in the library solving world hunger," Riley teased him.

He rarely came to the cafeteria for lunch. He really did spend it in the library or doing extra-credit work for one of his advanced classes. Last year we saw each other more, but this past week Davey had been scarce.

"I did that during break. I'm good to go for lunch today. Mrs. Barnaby said I needed to attend more school functions, like football games, and socialize with other students more. I need to be more well rounded."

Mrs. Barnaby was the counselor. She had to bring Davey off the ledge of being the ultimate overachiever every year . . . several times.

"Trisha can't go," Riley said in a pouty voice.

Davey's eyes went wide. "What? You gotta be kidding me! It's what this town worships. It is our god, Trisha. Do you not know this? Rock Taylor is a demigod. We should all bow to him in worship."

This time I laughed. He was joking. When Davey got carried away poking fun at the world around him, it was hilarious.

"Sorry. I hate to not come worship at his altar, but I have to hang out with Krit tonight."

Davey waved his hands wide like this was no big deal. "The Kritmeister! Bring him too! And that friend of his. Turquoise, is it?"

"His name is Green," I replied with a laugh.

"Yes, young Mr. Green with the weirdest name in the world except for Krit's. Bring them both! We will watch the demigod trash the other team and yell like we all give a shit."

Taking Krit out might be good. Fandora would be thrilled we were out of her hair. She'd probably be happy with me for taking Krit somewhere. Might get me on her good side long enough for my ribs to heal up.

"They'd like that. If you're sure. We would need a ride," I told him.

"YES!" Davey punched the air. "My dad is letting me take the minivan. So we will party like rock stars. Might even get some burgers afterward."

This would be good for Krit and me. Even if it was Rock I'd have to be watching on the field all night. I could deal with it.

That little whatever it was had ended. I could go back to being invisible to Rock Taylor.

Chapter Thirteen

ROCK

She didn't look at me again. *Fuck!*

I'd had her attention and I'd blown it off. Whispering to Noah had screwed that shit up. Trisha didn't glance my way one more time. Not even a peek. She had taken a seat with her friends. Instead she kept laughing and talking to Riley and the nerdy guy who had shown up in line and made her smile. I hated him. Didn't know him, but I hated that she smiled so easily for him.

Noah kept slipping her hand up my thigh, and I had to grab her hand and squeeze to get her to stop trying to cup me right here in the damn lunchroom.

"Why are you stopping me?" she whispered in my ear.

Because I wanted to watch Trisha and see if she looked at me again. I wasn't fucking it up this time. Playing games with someone like her was stupid. I knew better than that. I'd just been so pissed about her blowing me off and pushing me away.

"Not here," I replied, watching Trisha cover her ribs and laugh. The laughing was hurting her. Dammit. Her eyes danced as she looked at the nerdy guy. Did she like him?

"Let's go somewhere, then," she said, trying to wiggle her hand free of my hold.

"Not now."

Damn, she was getting on my nerves already.

Trisha distracted me by standing up. Several guys turned to look at her. She was oblivious, though. She continued talking to Riley, and then walked with her over to the trash cans. I moved Noah off me and headed over to her. I wasn't sure what the hell I was going to say, but I had to get her to look at me again.

Riley stopped talking midsentence when she saw me over Trisha's shoulder.

I had to say something to Trisha or she'd leave. "Trisha."

Her body tensed and I hated that. I didn't want to be the one who she tensed up around. I wanted to be the one to make her smile.

Slowly she turned around to look up at me. Those bright blue eyes I dreamed about looked guarded. "Yes?"

What now? It wouldn't make sense for me to apologize about Noah. I had nothing to apologize for. Not really.

Hell.

"I'm going to go," Riley said, and Trisha glanced at her.

"Wait on me." The pleading in her voice wasn't hard to miss.

Riley nodded and dropped her gaze to the floor.

"How are you?" I asked, needing to say something.

"Fine, thank you" was the only response I got.

I needed to get her to talk to me. But how?

"You coming to the game tonight?" Shit. Had I seriously just asked her that? As if she didn't have bigger issues than coming to the football game.

She glanced over at Riley. "Yeah, Krit and I are going with some friends."

So she was coming. Okay. I had to change my plans.

"Rock, you ready to go find a closet to finish what we started?" Noah wrapped her arms around mine and whispered loud enough for everyone to hear her.

And just like that, Trisha's eyes went wide and she forced a smile that wasn't real. This was not going well at all. Why couldn't I stop being a guy for a fucking minute and not screw shit up?

"You better, uh . . . get back to that," Trisha said, then turned and hurried off. Riley glared back at me, then rolled her eyes before closing in fast behind Trisha.

"Why were you talking to her? Who is she, even? Those clothes sure have seen better days. Someone needs to tell her they don't fit anymore." Noah's catty tone didn't win her any points with me.

The nerdy guy stopped in front of us, his disgusted gaze on Noah. "She's class. Something you couldn't possibly comprehend," he said. Then he looked at me. "And something you're not good enough for."

Then he walked off.

Noah let out a high laugh. "Seriously? That dork just said that to us? About her? Puh-lease. She wishes."

No, I wished. Fucking hard.

Shaking Noah loose, I stepped away from her. "I've changed my mind, Noah. Tonight's not good for me," I told her, then left her standing there. She'd recover soon enough. I just didn't have time to care.

Dewayne walked up beside me and slapped me on the back. "And he's off the horse again, folks. Trisha Corbin has got him all kinds of fucked up."

I didn't respond to him. Dewayne was typically a smartass. He liked to say shit to fire you up. And unlike Preston and Marcus, he could take me on. I glared at him and headed for my next class.

"For what it's worth, she didn't take it well when she first saw you with Noah. Girl's face went pale, and I think it hurt her. So maybe you're onto something. Just don't try to make her jealous. That's not her style."

I hated it when Dewayne was right.

Chapter Fourteen

TRISHA

The crowd was already loud, and the game hadn't even started. There were big paper banners that the cheerleaders had made lining the fence. The stupidest one I saw was ROCK WILL ROCK YOU! I mean, seriously? It takes the whole team. I've watched football before. Rock couldn't win the entire game for them.

Krit and Green had taken off with some other friends once we got here. I told him to check in with me every thirty minutes. He'd rolled his eyes and muttered, "Whatever."

Going to a football game wasn't something he had ever gotten to do. I knew it was a big deal to come and hang out with friends. It was a normal thing that most kids did, but we were limited. Seeing as our mother was crazy.

I searched the crowd until I saw his blond head in a group of guys I'd never seen before. They seemed older. "Who are they?" I asked Riley, concerned.

"Calm down, mama bear. They're in his grade. That tallest one with the oddly impressive gun show for a thirteen-year-old is Dewayne Falco's little brother, Dustin. He's the big shit in his grade. Apparently, when Krit picks friends, he goes big."

I wasn't sure I liked the idea of Krit hanging out with Dewayne Falco's brother. "Maybe I should go get him," I said, chewing on my bottom lip.

"And make him hate you? I don't suggest it. And Dustin Falco never gets in trouble. The Falcos are good people. Their dad owns Falco Construction. I've met his mom. Really sweet. She came in the office last year to drop off some pain medicine for Dewayne when I was working in there third period."

Okay, fine. Just because Rock and Preston slept with every woman on earth didn't mean Dewayne did. I was being judgmental again. Ugh. I wish I didn't do that.

"Okay. You're right. I can see him, anyway. He's fine."

A pretty redhead walked up to them, and Dustin Falco slipped his arm around her shoulders and pulled her against him. Not sure I liked that, either. That seemed way too familiar for eighth graders.

"You sure he's Krit's age?" I asked as he kissed the girl's head.

"Yeah, I'm sure. That's Sienna Roy. She's Dustin's best friend," Riley explained.

How did she know this? And they so didn't look like friends. "How do you know all these people?"

She shrugged. "Small town. I've gone to church with Sienna Roy most of my life."

Davey walked up the steps toward us, drawing my attention off my brother. Davey had gone to get "rations," he had said. I had to hold my side because I couldn't not laugh. He was carrying three nachos and cheese, three hot dogs, three bags of cotton candy, and what looked like an assortment of candy piled on top. There were bottles of soda sticking out of both his front pockets. I assumed he had one more in a back pocket.

"You buy out the refreshments?" Riley asked, standing up and taking things from his hands.

"Not exactly. But I tried," he replied.

I took the items she handed me, and we managed to fit them around us. There was no way we were going to eat all this, but I knew Krit and Green probably would. I was going to save Krit a nachos and cheese and a cotton candy. He'd be up to check in soon enough.

"Whatever we don't eat we can give to the bottomless pits Trisha brought with her," Davey explained.

"Thank you, Davey. You didn't have to buy us all this food," I told him. I knew his parents were generous with him and gave him spending money so that he didn't have to work a job and could focus on getting into Yale. Still didn't mean I expected him to do something like this.

He winked at me. "I got two hot dates tonight. I must feed them well so they'll come back with me again."

Smiling, I reached for a hot dog and took a bite. It had been a long time since lunch and I was hungry. I wasn't going to turn this down.

Before I could finish the hot dog, people jumped to their feet and cheered. I heard hoots and hollers. Different players' names were shouted from the stands. I watched in fascination as they shook little pom-poms on sticks. Riley reached down and pulled me up.

"They're running out onto the field. Show some school spirit," she yelled over the noise. I chewed up the last bite and let her pull me to my feet. She was going to have me yelling for another reason if she tugged any harder.

I saw above the heads in front of me and through the shakers as a football player ran through a large paper banner that said WE ARE #1 in the middle of it and had players' names all over it. I couldn't tell who was who from here. They all looked alike to me.

Riley cupped her hands over her mouth and called out something I couldn't hear. Stomping started, and the players looked up at the crowd and did fist pumps.

"Number ten," Riley called out to me.

"What?"

"He's number ten," she repeated.

I knew who she meant, but I still asked. "Who?"

She rolled her eyes at me and laughed, then looked back out at the field.

After the other team came out, Mr. Presley, the music teacher, sang the national anthem. Then the crowd screamed again before we could all sit back down.

Once everyone was settled again, I searched for Krit's blond head. He had moved to the fence, closer to the players. He was okay.

Then I gave in to the urge and looked for number ten.

Covered in pads, he looked even more solid and massive. His helmet was in his hands as he sat on the bench. When the guys took the field and Rock was left behind, the crowd started booing. Rock didn't look back at the sound. He didn't encourage it. Just kept his attention on the field.

"PUT IN TAYLOR!" and "LET THE ROCK PLAY!" were just some of the things being shouted from the stands.

"Coach is going to make everyone angry. Wonder if he survives five minutes of playing time before he puts Rock in."

"LET MY BOY PLAY!" a voice called out, and I turned to see a balding man with a beer belly scowling at the field. He looked nothing like his son. He was shorter than Rock, and he looked like he didn't take care of himself. His hair needed washing, and his shirt was faded and stained.

Turning back around, I looked out at the field. That man reminded me of the kind of men Fandora brought home. Did Rock have a bad home life? Was this man a good dad?

"They say he missed practice Wednesday. Wonder why?" Riley said, stuffing her face with nachos.

"Krit missed the bus. He brought him home," I told her before I could stop myself. I just didn't want her to think he'd missed practice because he didn't care.

Riley stopped with a chip at her mouth and turned to look at me. "No way," she whispered.

I just nodded.

Her eyes were wide with amazement. "Ohmygod," she responded, before shoving the cheese-covered tortilla chip into her mouth.

Chapter Fifteen

ROCK

We won. By two touchdowns. One of those had been mine.

But none of that seemed to matter at the moment.

Since halftime, when we had run to the locker room and I'd looked up into the stands and seen Trisha's blond hair, I had been going on adrenaline. She was here. And I was taking her home. I'd beg Marcus or Dewayne for their car. I just couldn't let tonight end without seeing her.

My touchdown had been simply because I wanted to show off for her. Get her attention. She'd made me play better. I had come alive once I knew where to look when I turned around to see the crowd. Every time, she'd been there. In the same spot. And I had fucking loved it.

The guys were all heading to the field house, and that's

where I was supposed to be headed too. But she'd be gone before I got out of there. I couldn't chance this. Tonight was my night. I was on fire. No more playing games.

"Take this," I yelled at Preston, and tossed him my helmet.

"Go get her, tiger," he called after me with an amused tone.

His obnoxious comment only made me grin. I was riding on my high. She couldn't tell me no. This time I wouldn't let her.

Shoving through the crowd and nodding thanks to people telling me I had played a good game, I kept my eyes on Trisha. She didn't see me headed toward her. Good. I didn't want her to have time to run.

I got to the bottom of the bleachers just as Trisha's nerdy guy friend led the trio down the steps. His eyes locked on me and he frowned. I knew he wasn't a fan of me, but I could fix that. If he was Trisha's friend, I'd make sure he liked me.

"Trisha." When I called out her name, she stopped studying the steps. Her head jerked up and her baby blues showed her shock. Then her confusion. God, she was gorgeous. The crazy kind of gorgeous. "Let me take you home. Buy you dinner. Whatever, just don't leave. Stay. Wait for me to get done in the field house." It sounded like begging. I was desperate. The moving crowd stopped, and I felt all their eyes on me. I was drawing attention.

She glanced around at all the people who were now watching her. Waiting on her response. Maybe I was putting her on the spot, but I needed her to say yes. To give me a chance.

Just as she opened her mouth to say something, my dad appeared in front of me, blocking my view of her. I tried to step around him so I could watch her. She was about to say something. His hands grabbed my shoulders, and he shook me. He was pissed. "You're late for fucking practice and have to sit out for five minutes, and now you're out here instead of in the field house! What the hell, boy? Get your ass in there. Don't throw shit away for that." He waved his hand toward where Trisha was standing.

Rage pounded in my veins and I clenched my fists. "Give me a minute," I said, meeting his glare with one of my own.

"NO! Fuck that!" He grabbed my arm and tried to move me. I didn't budge. The old man forgot that I'd outgrown him a long time ago. He might catch me off guard and shake me in front of everyone, but hell if he'd get me to move at his command.

I jerked my arm free. "I said give me a minute," I repeated calmly, knowing people were watching me.

"You gonna throw this away? For a chick? Prove to everyone you're white trash like your momma? That what your plan is, boy? Because I won't keep you if that's what you're planning on." He spat, and his nasty onion-and-beer breath made me sick.

I ignored him. I wasn't fighting with my old man in front of the town. "Please, Trisha. Wait for me."

My dad was roaring dumb crap, and I blocked it out, waiting while she took in the scene in front of her. Then she nodded. It was a small nod, but she nodded.

My heart soared. I couldn't keep the grin off my face. "I'll be fast. Just don't leave. Please," I called out, and she nodded again, looking somewhere between horrified and surprised. I turned and headed for the field house. My old man was behind me, still bitching. I ignored him and jogged off.

Dewayne's dad was headed our way, and he looked even angrier than my dad. He patted me on the shoulder. "Good game, kid," Mr. Falco said, before walking past me. Then he said to my dad in a commanding voice, "That's enough. Stop yelling at the boy like that, or I'm calling the cops. He's done nothing wrong."

I hurried on inside, ready to get showered and changed. Trisha Corbin was waiting on me. Hot damn!

Dewayne was walking out of the showers with a towel around his waist. "You get what you wanted?" he asked, smirking.

"She said she'd wait for me. I need a car," I told him. "I thought about asking Dad, but he's pissed and yelling about me sitting out the beginning of the game and shit. Your dad is putting him in his place right now."

Dewayne opened his locker and pulled out his car keys. "Take it. I'll ride with Marcus to the party."

I caught the keys to his Mustang.

"Thank you. Seriously. Anything you need, tell me," I told him.

"Get your ass out there before she leaves," Dewayne replied, then started getting dressed. I headed for the showers.

It was the quickest shower of my life.

Chapter Sixteen

TRISHA

"Holy crap! That's Dewayne Falco's dad telling off Rock's dad," Riley whispered beside me.

"Forget that. Did you really nod your head yes at Rock?" Davey asked, looking horrified.

I had. I had told him yes. He'd run out here to see me. Gotten in trouble with his dad, and his dad was yelling mean, awful things about him. Rock's eyes had stayed on me, pleading with me to say yes. What was I supposed to do?

"He was . . . determined. And I was afraid his dad was going to take a swing at him," I admitted.

Davey scoffed. "What, and break his hand on his son's wall of muscle? Puh-lease."

"It was romantic," Riley said all dreamily. "I would have

jumped off a bridge for the man if he'd asked me. He was ignoring his nasty father and completely captivated by you."

"Shut that crap down, Riley," Davey muttered, annoyed. "It's Rock Taylor. When has he ever been serious about a girl?"

Riley shrugged. "He's never gone after one like he is going after Trisha. If she hadn't given in, she might have completely ruined his football career. He's missing practice for her, and now he's risking getting in trouble with his coach and dad by breaking the rules and running out here to get her to go out with him. I think she's different."

Why did I want to believe that so much? I was weakening.

"He was with Noah the skank today. What changed?" Davey asked.

"Don't know, but let her make her own decisions. Back off," Riley scolded.

Then she looked at me. "Want us to wait on you? Or are you really going to let him give you a ride?"

I had Krit and Green with me. "I can't leave Krit and Green," I reminded them. "I'll just stay and talk to him."

Davey sighed. "Great. We get to wait until this train wreck is over. Oh joy. I wanted a burger."

Riley glared at him. "Shut up, Davey." Then she looked at me. "I'll go get Krit and Green. You go wait on him outside the field house."

I did as I was told and walked slowly toward the field house.

What was I going to say to him? Why was he so determined to get me to talk to him? Davey was right, where was Noah? I assumed they'd be together tonight. Unless they really did finish things in a closet somewhere in the school.

The jealous burn in my gut frustrated me. I had nothing to be jealous of, but I was anyway.

The doors opened and Dewayne Falco stepped out with Marcus Hardy. Both of them looked over at me, and Dewayne nodded. Marcus smiled as if he knew a secret, and then they headed to the parking lot.

I fidgeted with my hands and finally stuck them in the front pockets of my jean shorts. I glanced back at Riley and Davey to see that my brother and Green were back with them. Krit's eyes were trained on me as he was talking. He liked Rock. I wondered how he would feel about this.

"You stayed." Rock's voice startled me, and I swung my gaze back around to see Rock walking toward me. His dark brown hair was damp, and it looked like he had run his hand through it to style it. His jeans hugged his hips and thighs just right. The way the black T-shirt he was wearing accented his muscles made the whole effect perfection. And he wanted me to go somewhere with him.

"I said I would," I replied.

He grinned. "Yeah, you did. But I wasn't sure."

I pointed back at Krit. "I have to go home with him. Make

sure he's okay and everything. I can't go anywhere with you."

His smile fell, but he didn't look angry. He was thinking. "I didn't know he had come too. I get that. Can I take you both home, then?"

"Why?" I asked. I didn't understand him at all. What did he get out of taking me and my brother home?

A crooked grin tugged at his lips. "Because I like to be near you."

I wasn't expecting that. My heart reacted like a girl and went all fluttery.

That same swoony girl inside me replied, "Okay."

Rock beamed, showing off his pretty white teeth. Dang it, he was nice to look at, and I was proving to be a weak female.

"There you are." Noah's sickeningly sweet voice reminded me of everything I was letting myself forget. "I've been waiting out by my car forever. I thought we'd go have some fun before we headed to the party and celebrate your win."

"Noah, I told you that was off." Rock's reply was laced with frustration.

"No, you didn't." She pouted, then ran her hand up his arm. "I didn't wear panties," she added.

Okay. I'd had enough. I was leaving now.

"Seriously, Noah. This isn't cool. I told you earlier today after the stunt you pulled in the cafeteria that this was off. I'm not going to the damn party." His tone was cold. Either she was lying or he was.

I took a step back, thinking I could sneak off. But Rock's gaze snapped back to mine, and his eyes were pleading with me. "Don't. Please just give me a minute."

He was asking me "please" again. It was really hard not to give in when he asked so nicely.

"Rock, stop playing with her. She's not going to give you what you need tonight. After a win like that you need a wild ride, and I'm ready to give you several rides before the night is over."

Yep, that was enough. "I need to go. They're waiting on me," I said in a rush, before hurrying off toward my friends and brother. All their eyes were trained on me.

"Trisha," Rock's voice called out.

I heard Noah saying something else, and then Rock raised his voice. I believed that he didn't want to be with her tonight. It was just that this was something he would always deal with. And I didn't want to be a part of it.

"Trisha, please!" he called out, and I realized his voice was closer. He was following me. And did he have to say please again?

I turned around and saw Rock coming after me and an angry Noah standing where he had left her. Her eyes were shooting daggers at me. Noah Miller was just one of many. She could make my life hell at school. And all the other girls would react the same way she was.

Rock was beautiful and strong and so damn hard to say no to. But I couldn't bring the drama into my life that would come with saying yes to him.

"Just let me go," I begged. "I can't do this. She's just one of many. Go to her. I've got bigger problems than fighting over a guy."

He flinched and I turned away.

Krit's arm came around my shoulder, and he was scowling at Rock. He didn't know what had happened. I'd have to explain to Krit that he didn't need to be mad at Rock. But right now I just wanted to go.

"Let's go get that burger," Davey said, breaking the silence.

Krit pulled me closer to him with the crook of his arm. "Yeah. I'm hungry," he agreed.

Rock didn't come after me again.

Chapter Seventeen

ROCK

Two weeks of trying to forget her. Trying not to look for her. Trying to ignore her when she smiled in the cafeteria. Two weeks of hell. Trisha Corbin was put on this earth to remind me there are some things I can't have. I would have thought having fucked-up parents would be enough of a reminder. But no . . . the universe had decided that Trisha was needed.

I hadn't gone with Noah that night after the game. I'd been crushed. Having been so close to getting Trisha for just a little bit and then having it snatched from me was too much. I had gone home and sulked.

After two weeks of sulking, I was determined to get Trisha out of my head. I wouldn't be using Noah to do it, though. Rose Mann, however, was hot and more than interested. I was going to hook up with her at the pool party at Marcus's house. His parents and little sister were out of town, so he was throwing a small get-together. Which meant most of the school would be there.

Dad was working days this week, which meant I had his truck. The last two Friday nights I had owned the field, so he was in a good mood. I was no longer on his shit list. As long as I was a star, he was happy. Once I would have done anything just to have his attention. But now I didn't give a shit. Except I really needed his truck.

Something up ahead caught my attention, and I turned on my high beams to see what looked like a girl walking. What the hell? It was dark outside, and this road wasn't a busy street. I turned off my brights and slowed down until I was beside her.

What happened next would haunt me for the rest of my life.

Trisha Corbin turned her head to look at me, and one of her eyes was swollen closed, her lip was busted, and there was blood on her face. She was limping and holding her arm funny. That pretty blond hair was pulled back in a ponytail that looked like it had been messed with. Hair was loose and sticking out in crazy directions. Motherfucker! I was going to murder someone.

Slamming on my breaks, I jumped out of the truck and ran around the front.

"Trisha" was all I could get out of my mouth. My heart was in my throat, and my damn hands were shaking.

She stared up at me through eyes wet from tears.

I was going to jail. Because whoever fucking did this was being put down. Slowly. And painfully.

"I need . . . I need to go to the . . . h-hospital." She said each word like it hurt.

"Yeah, sweetheart, you do. How can I help you get into the truck? I don't want to hurt you." It was a helpless feeling. Picking her up in my arms was what I wanted to do. And tuck her against my chest so no one could touch her. But I knew from the odd angle of her arm that touching her wasn't a good idea.

She inhaled sharply and held her breath a minute.

"Just stand . . . behind me in ca-case I lose my balance. I think my legs"—she paused and winced, then whispered—"are the only things that aren't broken."

"Shit, Trisha. Goddamn" was all I could say. I wanted to ask her who had done this, but it hurt her to talk. I would find that out later.

I opened the passenger side of the truck and watched as she limped, and listened to her whimpers. I had thought her rejection was hell. This was so much worse. I hated seeing her in pain. I would take her healthy and rejecting me any damn day over this nightmare.

When she started to lift a leg, she lost her balance and I dropped to my haunches and held her hips steady. "Can I lift you if I hold you here? Will this hurt?" I asked.

"That's not too bad," she said in another whisper.

I took her lower hips firmly and lifted her slowly until she was sitting safely in the seat. I moved her legs around to face her forward. "I'll drive slow and safe. The seat belt might be too much."

She nodded and mouthed, "Thanks."

I closed her door and ran back around to get in on my side.

If she was walking by herself, then Krit had to be somewhere safe. I didn't want to make her talk, but I also didn't want that kid left alone with whoever had done this to her.

"Where's Krit?" I asked as I pulled out slowly onto the road.

"Green's. I promised him," she said almost too quietly. "If he r-ran to Green's and stayed there . . . I'd call Davey to take . . . m-me to the hospital."

Instead she'd tried to walk the five miles from her house to the hospital. Stubborn female. But at least the kid was safe. "I'll get in touch with him as soon as we get to the hospital and let him know I'm with you and you're getting fixed up," I assured her.

"Thanks," she managed to say before wincing.

I wasn't going to make her say anything else.

We drove in silence while I pictured the many ways I was going to kill whoever had put their hands on her.

It took only seven minutes to get to the local hospital, but it felt like forever. Hearing her whimper and sniffle was doing me in. I hated this. I hated her being hurt. I hated not being able to stop this shit. Why couldn't she have let me be there for her? Why had she pushed me away?

I pulled up to the entrance and looked at her. "I'm getting you a wheelchair and helping you out. Stay put."

She gave me a little nod and a tight smile.

Never fucking again. She wouldn't get hurt again. I swore to God I'd make sure of it. I wanted to promise her that right then, but I didn't. She would just worry about how I intended to keep that from happening. I was going to show her.

Chapter Eighteen

TRISHA

Two fractured ribs, but then, I'd already known that. Luckily, my lungs weren't punctured. A dislocated elbow and a fracture in my radius bone, which meant that my wrist was broken. When Fandora's new boyfriend had grabbed my hand and slung me across the room, I'd heard the crack. So I already knew that too.

My nose wasn't broken, thank goodness. It had bled so badly I wasn't sure. I was just thankful Fandora had stood in front of Krit and kept him back. He had gotten slapped around a little, but she had put a stop to it fast. Krit had gone ballistic trying to get to me, but Fandora had stayed between him and her boyfriend, screaming at the guy not to touch her baby.

All of this because her disgusting boyfriend had grabbed my butt. I'd told him to stop, and then he had pinned me up against the wall and started telling me he wanted a taste of my pussy. Krit had walked in on it and gone apeshit. He'd started attacking the guy, and the man had used his weight to throw Krit off him and onto the floor.

Fandora had come running out of her bedroom and seen the mess in the living room, and of course blamed me. I had fought back, but when I kicked the greasy jerk in the nuts as hard as I could, he began to beat me instead of grope me.

When Gary Holmes, the older man who lived in the trailer beside ours, showed up at the door, Fandora and her sorry excuse for a man left. I had hidden in the bedroom, where Krit had followed me. The last thing I needed was for Mr. Holmes to call the police. I'd heard Fandora tell him that they were just having an argument. I had begged Krit to stay quiet.

In the end Krit had agreed to go to Green's if I went to the hospital. I told him if he didn't leave right then, I wouldn't call Davey and we would stay there all night. He'd battled with leaving me, but every time I breathed I whimpered in pain. So he finally left, making me swear to go to the hospital and call him as soon as I was there.

I couldn't let Davey or Riley know about this. They would want me to tell the cops. But I wasn't getting separated from Krit. He was safe here. Fandora had proved tonight that she didn't want anyone hurting him. I could survive.

Rock coming out of the darkness had made me want to

weep with relief. I had decided I was never going to make it to the hospital. Then he'd been there. And saved me.

The nurse had questioned me about Rock. They knew someone had done this to me, and their immediate response was to question the boyfriend. But I had sworn to them it wasn't him. He had saved me.

The fact that he didn't have a scratch on him helped.

Then they had started asking me who had done it. I had told them I'd fallen down the stairs outside my house and landed on a brick. It was the best I had been able to come up with. They didn't believe me. I kept swearing that that was what had happened, and I could see they were frustrated but they eventually backed off.

The nurse walked into the room with a kind smile. "We can't get your mother on the phone. I'm afraid you'll have to stay here until we can get her to sign the paperwork to release you. Do you know where she may be?"

Yes, at a bar somewhere. "No. My younger brother was staying the night at a friend's, and Mom went out on a date. Since my plan was to stay home tonight, she wouldn't think there would be any sort of emergency."

The nurse still didn't seem to be buying it, but she nodded. "Okay. Well, we have two very anxious boys outside waiting on you. Is it okay if I let them inside? One is your brother. I think the guy who brought you called him and he got a ride here."

Oh crap. What had Krit been saying in the waiting room for everyone to hear?

"Sure, yeah," I replied, with a smile I didn't feel.

She looked at me one last time with sadness in her eyes. I didn't need her to help me. She'd ruin everything. I wasn't being separated from Krit. I had less than two years before I was eighteen. I could save us both then.

Krit walked in first, with relief and worry both etched on his face. "You were walking! Seriously, Trisha. Walking? What if Rock hadn't driven by? You could have died out there. God! I'm never trusting you again. I won't leave next time."

"I couldn't let anyone know about this," I whispered, glancing behind him to see that it was Rock who was standing just inside the door, not the nurse.

Krit ran his hand through his shaggy hair, which he was refusing to cut. "You scare the shit out of me. I hate this. I hate living there. I hate her. I wish she wasn't my mother."

I hated seeing him like this. Knowing he hadn't been given a chance to be a kid. He had been trying to protect me all his life, even though it was really me who was protecting him. Even when we were little, he had held my hand after Fandora had beaten me, and promised he would keep me safe and that everything would be okay. I loved him. He was the only person I had ever loved and who had ever loved me. I would do anything for him. Didn't he get that?

"It won't happen again. I'm not going to let it." Rock's voice filled the room with a determination I almost believed.

Krit glanced back at him. "You can't stop it. This shit has been happening all our lives."

Rock walked over to stand at the foot of my bed. He kept his gaze locked on me. "Yeah, I can. Even if you don't want me to, I'm going to protect you, Trisha. I don't care what excuses you throw at me. I don't care if you ignore me. I will be there every damn time you need me."

Krit let out a hard laugh. "That's bullshit. You got a football career ahead of you. Don't make her promises you can't keep."

I was worried Krit was being too hard on Rock. I agreed with Krit, but he didn't have to throw angry words at Rock for trying to be nice.

"I'll gain your trust," Rock said. "Both of you."

Krit scowled, but behind his anger I could see the little boy who had hope. He wanted to trust in someone. He trusted me, but he needed more. We both did.

"What you did tonight was enough. Thank you," I told him before Krit could say any more.

Rock held my gaze, and he looked like he was about to say something when a commotion outside the door stopped him. I recognized the voice immediately.

Chapter Nineteen

ROCK

"Where are they? Did she hurt my baby?" a woman asked in a high-pitched voice as if she were panicked. "She always hurts him. I can't control her," she continued.

"No fucking way," Krit growled as he stalked past me toward the door.

He looked furious. I glanced back at Trisha. I didn't know if I should go after him.

"It's her. Our mother," she said softly.

"There's my baby! Are you okay? Did she hurt you again? Did y'all check him out?!"

Was this woman serious?

"That's enough, Mom. Trisha is beat to shit in there. No one believes your farce. She's too damn nice to hurt anyone.

Even you," Krit roared over his mother's voice.

"Honey, it's okay. You don't have to protect her," his mother started up.

"WOMAN, ARE YOU CRAZY?" Krit yelled.

"Oh God. Please go stop him," Trisha begged. "Please. If he tells them, we will be split up. He doesn't understand that foster homes could be worse."

I stared at her face, still beautiful though beaten and swollen. I realized she was right. At least where she was she knew what to expect, and Krit was there with her. The kid was bigger than her and loved her. He could also get in touch with me if they needed me.

Nurses were trying to calm them down, and security was walking up when I stepped outside the room.

"Krit," I called out.

He looked at me with a furious scowl. "This is it! You gonna fix it? Save her from this shit!" he challenged me.

It was time I started proving myself. I walked over to Krit and put my arm around his shoulders. "Your sister needs you. She's asking for you," I told him while glaring at the woman across from him.

He didn't move at first. Finally he nodded and walked back to his sister's room.

"Baby, don't go in there to her—"

"Leave him alone. He's going where he wants to be. With

the sister who loves him and got hurt tonight. And you need to calm down. Too many drinks have you saying shit no one around you believes. It's obvious Krit loves his sister and she loves him. If you want to keep your family, then you might want to act like a mother and not a drunk, deranged psycho."

Her eyes went wide as I told her exactly how things were going to go. The painted-on makeup didn't cover up her hard living. Her skin had seen better days. The stench on her was nauseating. Sour whiskey and cheap perfume.

"Now, you need to go sign the papers to release your daughter. She's been treated, and she needs to go home and rest. I'll be making sure that happens. If you fuck with her, I swear to God you'll lose everything. Do you understand me?"

The woman's bent shoulders snapped back as she looked at me hatefully. "Who the hell do you think you are? You don't tell me what to do. Did you hurt Trisha? Are you some loser who she's running wild and partying with?"

She was trying to twist it so I looked like the bad guy.

A security guard stepped up beside me. "No, ma'am. This here is Sea Breeze High's football star. He'll put us on the map one day. Good kid. Watch him play every Friday. This young man don't ever cause trouble."

I glanced over at the man beside me and recognized him as one of the security guards who worked the games. I owed him one.

"Y'all don't know what she's like," the woman started up again.

"Yeah, I do. She's the mother your son doesn't have in you," I replied.

The security guard beside me patted my back. "That's good, son. Why don't you go on back in there with the girl? We'll oversee her momma signing the release papers."

I shot her one more warning glare, then headed back to the room, where I found Krit watching me from the doorway.

There was surprise in his eyes. He hadn't expected me to stand up to her. I'd show them both over and over again I wasn't going anywhere. Trisha's pretty face had been what attracted me to her. I had watched her for a year, wanting to be the reason she smiled, and making her beam up at me had become a goal in life. Now that I had actually gotten to know her even a little, I wanted more.

It killed me that this beautiful girl who should be cherished and loved didn't have parents who protected and loved her. She deserved that.

"She's signing the papers," Krit whispered in disbelief as he watched his mother from the doorway. "You got her to fucking shut up and sign the papers," he repeated as he turned to look at me in awe.

It was a start. I had a long way to go to win their trust. But after tonight I was done waiting on Trisha Corbin to give me a chance. If she didn't want to, then fine. I wouldn't make her.

I'd just be the unwanted friend she couldn't get rid of. The girl needed someone to take care of her.

"Thank you." Her voice washed over me. She had claimed me with just a look.

"I'm taking you home. Then I'm staying there," I informed her. "I'll need to get my truck back to my dad for work in the morning, so I'll get Marcus or Dewayne to help me out. But I'm staying with you until Monday morning."

She had just started to say something when the nurse walked into the room, followed by that bitch Trisha lived with.

The nurse smiled at Trisha, then turned to me. "Will you be giving her a ride home?" the woman asked, but it sounded more like she telling me I was going to.

I smiled. "Yes ma'am. I'll be giving her and her brother a ride home."

"Rick is in the car waiting on me. Papers are signed. If he's giving y'all a ride, I'll see you at the house," the bitch said.

"Sure thing, *Mom*," Krit said with obvious annoyance.

"You drive safe with my baby in the car," the woman told me. I nodded that I had heard her, but I didn't give her a glance. I was too busy watching Trisha as they helped her adjust her arm sling. I saw the nurse's frown as she watched Fandora leave without a word to Trisha.

Trisha didn't need her stepmother. She had me. I would be enough from now on.

Chapter Twenty

TRISHA

When we had walked into the trailer, Fandora wasn't there. Her car was out front, but she'd said she was with her boyfriend, Randy. So apparently he had taken her back to whatever bar they had been at when Green's father had tracked her down. I hadn't known Green's dad was in the waiting room, aware of this whole mess.

"Let's get you to the bed," Rock said, coming in behind me. I didn't have it in me to push him away again. He was so sweet, and he had been there through all of this and none of it had scared him away. If he just wanted in my pants, then he sure wouldn't have faced down Fandora and stuck by me all night.

"If you need an extra pillow, you can have mine," Krit

offered, hovering around me like he was afraid I might break at any moment.

"I'll be fine with mine," I assured him.

"Are you sleeping in her room?" Krit asked Rock.

"She and I are going to talk about that. Why don't you go on and get some rest. Know I'm not leaving and she's safe," Rock told him.

I assumed Krit would argue, but he didn't.

"Yeah, okay," he replied, then leaned over and kissed my head. "Rest. I need you better," he said to me.

"I will," I told him.

He gave Rock one last look, then turned and headed for his room.

It hadn't taken him long to decide he trusted Rock. But then, after watching him at the hospital I was beginning to trust him too.

"Once you get comfortable I'm going to get you some water, and you need to take one of the pills the doctor sent home with you. It will help you rest easier."

"You don't have to stay," I told him. He had promised that he wasn't leaving me, but he had a life. I wasn't his responsibility.

"No, Trisha, I don't. But I want to stay," he replied. "I'm going to get you some water. Time for you to take this pill."

I didn't respond to that. He stared down at me, waiting on me to argue, before turning and heading to the kitchen. The determined gleam in his eyes confused me. Why was he so bent on staying here? I knew from hearing Rose Mann talk in the restrooms at school that he was supposed to be with her tonight at Marcus Hardy's party. He had also been talking to her by his locker, and I'd seen him kiss her in the hall earlier this week.

I had walked away from him, and he'd let me. From the looks of it, he had moved on. Now here he was again. I didn't understand him at all. There was a good guy under all that sexy. Not only had he wanted to help me get to the hospital, but then he had stayed and dealt with Fandora. Why would someone who had a future to think about waste time with me and this mess?

"No bottled water, and I wasn't sure the tap water was clean, so I poured milk. I've seen you drink it at lunch, so I thought that was a safe choice."

Rock was once again filling up my small bedroom with his presence, making everything seem less scary. Less hopeless. And he knew that I drank milk at lunch. My heart did a silly flutter.

"Milk is good," I told him. There weren't any other options but beer in the fridge. But he didn't point that out. I was also not supposed to drink the milk, but with Rock here I felt safe. Fandora couldn't get to me if Rock was standing between us.

He opened the two bottles of pills and shook my dosage out into his palm. "Always thought it was cute that you drank milk at lunch," he said, flashing me a grin that made me forget that my eye was swollen shut, my wrist was broken, and my ribs were fractured.

I drank milk at school because it was healthy, and I didn't get much of that at home. It was supposed to make your bones stronger, and I needed strong bones living in this house. I wasn't telling him that, though.

"Thanks," I said as he held the glass of milk and pills out to me. I quickly took my pills, being careful with my split lip. It had stopped bleeding and I wanted to keep it that way.

"Drink all the milk if you can," he instructed me.

I didn't argue with him.

Once the milk was gone, he took the glass from me and set it beside my bed. "Lay back," he said, and like with everything else, I did exactly as he said.

Rock then proceeded to tuck me in and make sure my wrist was propped up and my ribs were okay. Watching him work over me with a serious expression kept me from speaking.

When he was satisfied that I was comfortable, he stepped back. "I've got a beach towel in the truck and a duffel with a change of clothes. I'm going to grab those and get changed, and then tonight I'm sleeping on the floor in here. I won't get any sleep if you don't let me. So please don't tell me I can't."

The pleading look in his eyes combined with all that he had done tonight for Krit and me—I knew I couldn't tell him no about anything right now. The idea of Rock being in my room gave me peace. I never felt at peace in this trailer. Or anywhere. But Rock was giving me that. I wouldn't freak out now. I would just embrace it. I needed it right now.

"Okay," I whispered, and he smiled at me.

I wanted to smile back, but it would hurt my lip. He winked at me as if he knew that, and then he turned and left my room.

Krit had a comforter on his bed he didn't use. I'd get him to let Rock sleep on it so he didn't have to sleep on the worn carpet.

As if on cue, Krit's bedroom door opened and my little brother stepped into my room with a frown. "He coming back?" he asked.

"He's getting a towel and a change of clothes from his truck," I assured him.

Krit let out a noticeable sigh of relief. He wasn't up for dealing with his mother again. Rock had taken that weight off Krit's shoulders, which I always tried so hard to do.

"He's sleeping on the floor in here. Bring him that comforter you never use so he can sleep on it."

Krit nodded. "Yeah, I'll bring him a pillow, too. And he can have my blanket as well. I'll go grab a quilt out of Mom's room."

The door to the trailer closed as Rock came back inside. Krit walked into the hall, and I heard him speaking in low tones to Rock. I knew they were talking about me and Krit was needing reassurance from Rock. I didn't want Rock to make any promises to my brother that he couldn't keep. Krit didn't need that kind of disappointment in his life. He had enough.

Krit walked back into the room a few minutes later with a pillow, his comforter, and his blanket. "He said he didn't need anything and he was just going to sleep on his beach towel, but I ignored him. He's getting changed in the bathroom."

He was trying to make it easy on Rock so he would stay. But Rock couldn't stay forever. He was a kid too, with a football career in his future. He didn't have time to save us. "He can't stay forever, you know. He has a life and a future. We will be okay when he walks away. We have each other," I reminded him.

Krit didn't respond. He kept making Rock a bed on the floor beside my bed.

"You know that, right?" I asked again, needing Krit to acknowledge that this wasn't something he should get used to.

When Krit dropped his pillow on the makeshift bed, he turned his gaze to me. "No, Trisha, I don't know that. I think . . . I think you may be more important to him than football." Then he walked over and pressed a kiss to my forehead. "You're special. The kind of girl a guy does crazy shit for."

I started to say something, but Krit left my room before I could think of what to say.

Moments later Rock walked back in, wearing a pair of what looked like board shorts and a Sea Breeze Football T-shirt. His gaze landed on the spot Krit had made for him on the floor, and a small grin tugged at his lips. Then he turned his attention to me. "I think he likes me," he quipped.

I didn't smile. Not because my lip was hurt but because Rock didn't understand the truth in his comment. I had to protect Krit. Letting him trust in Rock was a bad idea.

"He thinks you're going to save us. I don't need you to encourage that idea. He's been let down too many times. I won't let you do that to him too."

Rock stared at me for a moment, and then he walked over to the bed. His finger traced the side of my head gently. "You're worried about me letting him down. What about you?"

What about me? I was sure it would break my heart when Rock walked away from this. But I was tough. I could deal with it. My brother had emotional issues that I didn't have. He lost it and became uncontrollably crazy when things were too much for him.

"I know you'll leave. I don't have any grand illusions. In real life there are no heroes."

Rock didn't reply at first. He continued to trace the side of my head and rub his thumb and forefinger over my ear in a caress that felt soothing. "One day, Trisha Corbin, you will call me your hero. And that day will be the most important moment in my life."

Chapter Twenty-One

ROCK

She hadn't woken up all night. Several times I had watched her chest to make sure she was breathing. Fandora hadn't come home, and Krit had already stuck his head in here once this morning to check on her.

Lying on my back, I had both my hands tucked under my head as I watched her sleep. Three hours ago I had heard Dewayne and his dad come get my dad's truck to take it back to the house. I had called Dewayne when I had gone out to my truck last night. I hadn't wanted Trisha to hear me.

Dewayne's dad had left me one of his work trucks he didn't use every day. The keys were hidden under the backseat. He wanted me to have some way to get around in case we needed to get Trisha back to the doctor or needed to escape. I hated telling Dewayne the truth, but I knew he'd help me.

Trisha's eyes began to flutter, and I was mesmerized. Slowly her one good eye opened. She focused on me and a smile touched her lips. It was a small smile. One that wouldn't hurt her split lip. I sat up and reached for the salve the doctor had suggested for her lip. "Your need some more of this," I told her as I stayed on my knees so I'd be at eye level with her.

"I can do it," she replied in a sleepy voice.

"I know you can. But I can see it better." It wasn't the best excuse, but I wanted to do this.

She lay there as I applied the soothing cream over her battered lip.

Last night after I'd told her she'd call me her hero one day, she hadn't said anything else. The room had gone silent until the soft sounds of her sleeping met my ears. I'd watched her sleep and reassured myself she was okay. I had found her, and everything was going to be okay now.

No more letting her push me away. She could push all she wanted, but I wasn't letting my damn ego and pride get in the way. Trisha wasn't trying to make me prove anything to her. She wasn't moved by jealousy. Those weren't games she played.

If I wanted her, and I did, I would have to do this on her terms. She didn't trust me. She was cautious and expected nothing from anyone. Being treated poorly was what she expected.

So if I acted like a jackass, she accepted it as fate. All the stupid shit I'd done trying to get her to give in had only pushed her further away from me.

"Is Krit awake?" she asked.

"Yeah, he's in the living room watching television," I told her.

She frowned. "Fandora?"

"Not here. Never came home last night."

She let out a sigh of relief. "Good. Do you have a way to get home?"

Here we go. She was now ready to kick me out. She was protecting Krit. I understood her now. "I have a truck that Dewayne left me. But I don't need it. I'm not leaving."

She didn't say anything at first, so I stood up and started folding up the comforter and blanket I'd used last night.

"Fandora will come home today. She will expect you to be gone, so she'll return," she said as if she were warning me away from something I didn't already know.

"It's her trailer. I expect she'll come back," I agreed.

I put my bedding in the corner neatly.

"She won't like you being here."

She'd be pissed. I expected that. But I wasn't scared of a crazy-ass evil bitch. "I'm sure she won't. But she'll have to get over it." I didn't wait for her to argue. "I got a Gatorade out of my truck last night and put it in the fridge. I'm going to go get that and let you take your pills. Then I'll fix you something to eat. What sounds good? You want something soft?"

"Uh, yeah," she replied, frowning at me.

"I'll see what I can find. You like eggs?"

"Fandora doesn't buy eggs. Toast and butter or cereal."

She wasn't arguing with me. I felt like I had won a prize.

"I'll bring both. We will see which one works best."

I left her in there before she could decide she needed to kick me out again.

Krit looked up at me when I walked into the living room. "She awake?" he asked.

"Yeah. She needs to eat. What's her favorite?"

Krit shrugged. "She doesn't have a favorite. We don't have a large selection. She's just happy when we get food. Lunch at school is the highlight of her day."

The kid didn't mean to say shit that sliced a fucking hole in my stomach, but goddamn, that was hard to swallow. Trisha liked the damn cafeteria food because she was hungry. Shit, that made me furious. What girl doesn't have a favorite food?

Preston getting excited about Mrs. T's cookies made a helluva lot more sense now. He always took some home to the boys and Daisy May now that she had teeth. He had this life too. But he had us. Trisha didn't have anyone.

She hadn't had anyone. She did now.

"We both like cereal. She won't admit it, but sugar flakes are her favorite. They're mine, too, but I lie and eat the cinnamon squares and leave the flakes for her. I know she likes them best."

I was wrong. She had Krit.

Chapter Twenty-Two

Present day . . .

TRISHA

Leaning against the door frame, I watched as Rock read a chapter of *Harry Potter and the Sorcerer's Stone* with Daisy May. It was their nightly ritual. Daisy May had come a long way since she became ours, but her reading level was still lower than most of the kids in her class. Each night Rock read a chapter with her from the book that she had checked out from the library. It was helping her tremendously.

Tonight watching them together reminded me of the moment I'd realized Rock Taylor was my hero. I had fought him every step of the way, not wanting to trust anyone but my brother. I was afraid of being hurt or rejected.

Rock hadn't given up on me, just like he wasn't giving up on Daisy May. He believed in her, and I knew that was going to be enough to help her conquer this. When Rock Taylor believed in you, then you believed in yourself.

"Night, Daddy," Daisy May said sleepily.

"Night, baby girl," he replied as he put the book on the table beside her bed and stood up over her.

"Night, Mommy," she said as she shifted her gaze over to me.

I walked into the room and stood beside Rock. "Good night, sweetheart. You read that whole last page all by yourself and didn't miss a word. You're going to be the top reader in your class one day," I told her.

Daisy May grinned and looked from me to Rock. He nodded in agreement, and she beamed. All it took from Rock was a nod of encouragement to make her smile like she owned the world. He did that to girls.

I bent down over her and kissed her sweet little cheek. "I love you," I whispered against her soft skin. Those were words she hadn't heard enough in her short life. Rock and I had agreed to tell all three of our kids we loved them every morning and every night and every chance we got during the day.

"Love you too," she said with a happiness in her voice that I cherished.

Rock dropped to his haunches so he was at eye level with her. "You're my princess. Love you no matter what. Always." It was something he had started saying to Daisy May a little over a year ago when she had broken a lamp by accident and burst into tears, afraid we wouldn't love her anymore.

"Love you no matter what," she repeated.

I walked out of the room and headed into the hallway to wait on Rock. It was time we went to check on our boys. They were getting their showers and finishing up their homework while Rock and Daisy May read.

Rock closed her door after making sure she had her night-light on.

His arm slid around my waist, and he pulled me against him. "You smell really good," he said in a deep, husky voice as he ran his nose up the side of my exposed neck.

"Don't start yet." I winked at him as I pulled away. "We have to get the boys in bed first."

Rock chuckled as his hand cupped my ass. "Then don't look so damn sexy."

I rolled my eyes at him. My hair was in a bun on the top of my head. I was wearing a pair of cutoff sweats and one of his old T-shirts, which I had also cut off so it didn't hang to my knees. Nothing about my appearance was sexy. I even had the spaghetti sauce from dinner splashed on me from letting it overheat on the stove.

The bathroom door opened, and Jimmy walked out in his pajama pants and T-shirt. He was letting his hair grow. He wanted it like Preston's. Right now it was damp and tucked behind his ears. Life with a teenager was supposed to be more difficult than this. Jimmy was thirteen now, but he never once gave us a moment's trouble. It worried Rock. He was afraid Jimmy was being too good because he feared losing us.

"Ready for bed?" I asked him.

His smile, so much like his brother's, tugged at his lips. "Yeah. I'm ready. But y'all didn't have to wait on me. You could have put Brent to bed without me."

"I tuck all my kids even. I'll be doing it as long as you live under this roof," Rock replied with a teasing tone. "Even when you're eighteen."

Jimmy knew Rock was teasing him and rolled his eyes with a laugh. "Yeah. Sure you will."

Jimmy walked into the room he shared with Brent, who was now ten. Brent was already in bed, looking at the newest sports magazine he had gotten in the mail. The kid was obsessed with football. Which Rock loved. It was their connection. They talked football for hours.

His eyes lifted and he looked up at us. Of the three kids, he was the most serious and cautious. He trusted Preston, but it had taken months before he trusted us. This past year had been so much easier. He had started to believe that we wanted him and that we were a family. One he could feel safe in.

"You should read this. The draft predictions are ridiculous," Brent said, tossing the magazine at Rock, who caught it.

"I'll do that. We'll discuss it tomorrow," Rock replied, walking over to him. "You ready for the math test tomorrow?"

Brent nodded. "Yep. I'm gonna kill it."

Rock bent down and kissed the top of his head. "That's what I like to hear."

Once Jimmy was in bed, I went to his side and ruffled his hair. Sometimes I felt like I was raising a good version of Preston. I remembered the wild child Preston was in high school, and Jimmy was nothing like that. But his facial expressions and mannerisms were so much like Preston's. "Sleep tight," I told him, and kissed his forehead. "Love you."

"Love you, too," he said in a whisper. That was new too. He'd just been replying with his own "I love you" the past few months.

Once we had both boys tucked in, we cut the lights and closed the door.

Rock stood there with his hand on the doorknob once we were in the hallway. "That never gets old," he said in a whisper.

He didn't have to explain. I understood. Two years ago we were told that we could never have children. Having a family was something we both wanted. We wanted to create a world we ourselves had been cheated out of. We wanted to have a house full of love and safety to give to our kids—what we had always dreamed of having ourselves.

We had that now. We were not only able to have a family

filled with all those things we had longed for, but we were able to give it to kids who had been living a life of hell much like the ones we had been raised in. They were here now, though, and they were ours. And never again would they suffer or fear or go hungry. We would love them always.

"We're very blessed," I agreed quietly.

Rock smiled at me. "Yeah, we are."

Chapter Twenty-Three

TRISHA

It was three days before Fandora came home. I had a doctor's note for missing school, while Rock made Krit go every day while he stayed home with me. No matter how much I begged him to go to school, he just ignored me and acted like I hadn't spoken. He was missing football practice, and he didn't have an excuse for all the classes he was missing.

I was selfish to enjoy sleeping without fear and feeling safe. But Rock being there gave me both those things. Relying on that scared me. I didn't know why he was doing this or when he was going to grow tired of it.

When Fandora had come into the house to find me on the sofa tucked in with a blanket watching television, and Rock sitting in the recliner, she had been furious. The shades of purple her face turned were impressive. I didn't move. I just lay there in horror, waiting for her to lose it.

"You need to go buy groceries," Rock informed her as he stayed relaxed in the chair beside me.

I stopped breathing. What was he doing? Did he not know this woman was crazy?

"*Get out of my house, or I'm calling the cops*," Fandora screamed at him.

Rock didn't move. He didn't even flinch. He couldn't stay there forever, and at some point I would be left alone with this woman again. She would take this out on me.

"Rock, don't—"

"I'm not going anywhere. You call the cops, and I'll be sure that they know you haven't been home to check on your kids for three days. They're running out of food. Trisha can't take care of herself right now. So please, Fandora, call the motherfucking cops. I'd love to talk to them."

Fandora was frozen. She was furious, but she was also unsure how to handle this. No one had ever been here to correct her or demand anything of her before. As for threats, she wasn't used to those, either. Except for Krit threatening to run away if she kicked me out.

"You will not stay in this house," she hissed.

Rock shrugged. "Don't see how I can leave. I leave and you will end up killing Trisha, and I won't let that happen. 'Cause

I swear to God if something happens to her, I'm going to the cops. And let me warn you, they love me. This town loves me. I think you got a taste of that at the hospital."

Fandora looked at me and pointed at the door. "Out. Get out. I'm done letting you mooch off me. I've let you stay too long. Krit won't leave me—he can't, he's a minor. But you get your ass out of my house. I'm done with you."

Rock moved then. He was up so fast Fandora flinched. "You kick her out and Krit will leave too. Don't fucking kid yourself, woman. That boy adores her and you know it. He hates you, though. He'll leave too, and when they're both gone you won't get that monthly check from the state."

Fandora threw her purse on the floor and screamed. "I hate her! She's a slut, and I want her out of my house!"

Rock scowled at her, then just looked disgusted. His gaze turned to me and softened. There was reassurance in his eyes. "I'll go pack your clothes. You rest."

Where was I going to go? What about Krit? Rock was right that he would leave. He'd demand to be where I was, and I didn't know where I was going to be.

"Don't speak to her. Don't touch her. I'll have you behind bars so damn fast you won't know what hit you. When Krit leaves too, I won't have anything keeping me from having your sorry ass locked up. I can get both your kids to go to the police and incriminate you enough to get you put away for a while."

"You can't do anything!" Fandora yelled at him. "I've given them food and a roof over their heads. They are both lazy and won't work! I should be given a fucking award for keeping her trashy ass as long as I have."

Rock stalked toward her, and I watched as she backed up. Her eyes were finally showing fear.

"You call her one more name and I'll deal with this shit myself. She's the sweetest, kindest, most amazing girl I've ever met. So shut your filthy fucking mouth."

The door opened behind her, and I moved to sit up. Krit was standing there, taking in Rock in his mother's face looking ready to murder her.

"What's going on? What did you do?" he asked, glaring at Fandora. "Did you touch Trisha?" His voice raised in a panicked tone.

"No. She's just kicking your sister out. I'm going to pack her things," Rock replied calmly.

Krit looked at me, and I tried to plead silently with him not to say or do anything stupid. I didn't think she'd really hurt him, but she might start if I wasn't here.

"I'll go pack my things too," Krit said, not even looking at his mother.

"You can't leave. You're my son," Fandora screeched.

"The hell I can't. I go where Trisha goes," Krit informed her.

"NO! You can't leave. I won't allow it," she continued.

Krit let out a hard laugh. "I don't give a FUCK what you allow."

Then he walked to his bedroom. Crap. He was packing to leave too. Where were we going to go? I had seen Rock's dad. We sure wouldn't be welcome there.

Rock shifted his attention to me. "Don't get up. I'll get everything you need."

But where was I going?

Chapter Twenty-Four

ROCK

I was almost to Trisha's bedroom when Fandora's words stopped me.

"FINE! She can stay." She wasn't happy about it, but she was giving in.

I turned back to look at her. "You going to touch her? Because I'll be checking in all the damn time. One finger on her and I swear I'll call the cops."

Krit slammed his door open and walked out looking ready to kill someone. "You ever touch her again and I will go to jail for life because I'm going to kill whoever puts their hands on her. Including you," he warned in a tone that most kids his age couldn't pull off.

The kid was growing up fast. He had to.

Fandora's eyes went large. "Are you threatening to kill me?" she asked in disbelief.

"I will kill *anyone* who touches Trisha. I am done letting shit happen to her. She doesn't deserve it. No one deserves it. I won't let you anymore."

"I won't be attacked in my own house. If she hadn't been flirting with my boyfriend, this wouldn't have happened. He got angry and made her shut up and stop touching him. That's why she's laid up right now. I didn't touch her."

Krit let out a hard, furious laugh. "What the fuck ever! He had his hands all over Trisha, and she was fighting him off. She doesn't want your sick, disgusting men. She's got him." Krit pointed at me. "What would she want with greasy, fat old men?"

Fandora stared at her son like she'd never seen him before. I expected this side of him was a first for her. He was a man now. She'd forced her little boy to become a man because of her actions. He was going to protect his sister no matter what.

"Krit, don't. Just . . . go to your room and work on your homework. Okay?" Trisha's soft voice broke through the tension in the room.

Krit looked at her, and a tenderness in his eyes replaced the hatred that had been there. "I love you. And because I love you I am done doing what you tell me to do. I won't let you protect me anymore. I'm bigger than you, Sis. It's time I kept you safe."

I really liked that kid.

Trisha's eyes filled with unshed tears as she looked at her little brother. "I'm okay. Just don't do this to yourself. Go calm down and focus on your homework."

"Oh, for fuck's sake. I'm done with this bullshit. I'm going to bed. Don't bother me," Fandora snarled as she walked to the hallway and toward her bedroom door. As she passed Krit and me, she stopped and shoved something at Krit. "Here's a fifty. Go get whatever food you need." Then she slammed her door.

Krit held the fifty in his hand and looked at me, then Trisha. "We leaving or staying?"

"We don't have anywhere to go. We need to stay. I'm just going to focus on figuring out where we can go sooner rather than later. I need to get a job as soon as I can."

Krit frowned. "You don't have a license or a car."

Trisha shrugged. "I will figure it out. You just worry about your homework. I'll also get the groceries."

Like hell. She wasn't going to go do anything. She needed to heal.

I took the money from Krit. "I'll go get the groceries. You watch over her until I get back."

He nodded and headed back into the living room. "I'll do homework in here," he told both of us.

"Rock, you have to go home. You need to get caught up with school and get to football practice," Trisha said, sounding worried.

She was right. I did need to do those things if I wanted to survive going back to my house. My dad was going to be furious. But she was more important than any of that. "I have it under control," I reassured her, which was sort of the truth. Dewayne had been getting my work every day, and his dad had written me an excuse for missing school. I had the flu as far as anyone else knew.

Trisha sighed and leaned back on her pillows. "Why are you doing this?"

"Because you need me," I replied, then headed for the door. I wasn't telling her anything more than that.

"Get milk," Krit called out to me.

Chapter Twenty-Five

TRISHA

After missing a week of school, I was ready to go back. Fandora ignored me completely, treating me as if I didn't exist, and this was a wonderful thing. She hadn't been at the trailer much. She stayed gone most of the time. Rock left school and came home to check on me at lunch every day and after practice. He was pleased Fandora was staying away. He'd also bought so many groceries I knew it wasn't just fifty dollars' worth. He'd added money to that. When I had tried to argue with him about it, he just blew me off like I wasn't talking.

When Krit had been so excited over corn dogs and grapes, I decided to forgive Rock for spending his money on us.

This morning Rock was coming to get me for school. Krit wanted to ride the bus with Green, but he was insistent I ride with Rock to school. I was also not to carry my book bag or my books. Rock was planning on doing that until my ribs healed. The idea of walking through Sea Breeze High with Rock Taylor at my side all the time was exciting and intimidating. I knew girls wouldn't see me as a reason to stay away from him.

"Bus is here. See you after school!" Krit called as he ran out the front door. Fandora hadn't come home last night. So luckily she wasn't here for us to worry about. Krit had carried my book bag to the living room and made me swear not to pick it up, to wait on Rock till he arrived.

I felt helpless, and I hated that.

When the gravel crunched beneath tires outside, my heart fluttered. Silly heart.

I walked over to the window to see Rock open his truck door and step out. He was dressed in jeans and his practice football jersey. They wore them on Mondays after winning Friday night's game.

It looked real good on him.

He knocked once and walked inside. Having him in the trailer made me remember how safe I felt when he had stayed with me. I liked that feeling. I liked him being here.

"Morning," he said in a sexy drawl.

"Good morning," I replied, feeling my face heat. I had to get control of this. Rock was my friend. He hadn't flirted with me again after the night he'd picked me up on the side of the road. Our whole dynamic had changed. We were . . . friends. Just friends. That thought made me sad.

Shaking it off, I knew this was all we would ever be. I needed to be thankful for that. He was a great person to have as a friend. His protective nature was a major plus.

"You ready to go back?" he asked, picking up my book bag.

Not really, but it was better than being here. "Yeah. I have to catch up."

He nodded, then held open the door. "I'll help you."

He was always helping me. It was going to get old for him soon enough. I was going to become a burden.

"You've got your own work to catch up on. I'll be fine," I assured him.

Rock just chuckled behind me. I didn't glance back at him. My cheeks were warm and I wasn't even sure why.

He stepped around me and opened the truck door for me, then held out his hand. I glanced down at his hand and frowned.

"Take my hand. I need to help you up so you don't strain yourself," he explained, clearly amused.

I wasn't sure touching his hand was a good idea. My heart was already all fluttery and my face was warm. Rock was suddenly causing my body to react in crazy ways. "Okay," I said almost too softly.

When I placed my hand in his much larger one, his closed

around mine, sending warm shivers through my body from the contact. I was losing it.

"You good?" he asked me when I still hadn't moved my hand from his once I was seated in his truck.

I jerked my hand away, feeling like an idiot, and nodded. "Yeah, thanks," I muttered, and didn't look at him.

He didn't move right away, and I was finding it hard to breathe knowing he was looking at me. Finally I turned my gaze to see him staring at my legs. I glanced down and realized that my shorts had ridden up even shorter than they were. I had to get some bigger shorts. Not getting exercise was not helping me lose weight. I tried to tug on them. Rock cleared his throat and closed my door.

I took several calming breaths before he opened his door and climbed inside. I didn't have a shirt loose enough to cover the fact that my ribs were wrapped either. My clothes seemed to be shrinking.

He started the truck and Tim McGraw's voice filled the space. Rock grinned and reached over to turn down the music. "I blare music to wake up in the morning," he explained.

I nodded. "Good idea."

He looked at me a moment longer than necessary, but I wouldn't meet his gaze. I was afraid my feelings were all over my face, and I needed to figure this out and protect that. Rock wasn't asking for something more with me. He wanted to be friends, and I had said yes. I needed to respect that.

"Did you sleep good?" he asked.

I had. The pain medicine I had to take at night to rest knocked me out. "Yeah. I slept good. You?" I asked.

He shrugged. "I guess. I sleep better in your room."

Oh. I wasn't sure what to say to that. So I studied my hands in my lap.

He didn't say anything more. We rode in uncomfortable silence the rest of the way to school. Miraculously, there was a parking spot empty near the front. It was where he always parked. To the right of us was Marcus Hardy's truck, and to the left was Dewayne Falco's Mustang. It was like the three of them had parking spots that had been assigned. No one ever parked here but them.

"We're here," he said, stating the obvious. "Stay put. I'm helping you down."

I did as I was told.

Rock opened my door and reached for my book bag, then slung it over his shoulder before holding out his hand for me.

Once again I slipped my hand in his, and he held on to me tightly as he eased me down from the truck. I only winced once, and Rock's hand squeezed mine when I did. "You okay?" he asked, sounding concerned.

"Yes. I'm fine. Thank you," I replied.

He didn't let go of my hand as he closed the truck door. I waited for him to release me, but he didn't. Instead his fingers threaded through mine. "Let's go," he said, and we headed for the entrance.

Excitement and confusion were battling inside me. Why was he holding my hand like this? He knew I didn't need his help walking.

A whistle startled me, and I looked up to see Preston Drake grinning from ear to ear as his eyes zeroed in on our hands. I loosened my grasp, preparing for Rock to drop my hand like it was on fire. Instead he squeezed it tightly. "He's a bitch-face sometimes. Ignore him. He means well," Rock said, leaning down to me. Then he winked.

Rock winked at me.

What was going on?

"Finally got the girl. 'Bout damn time. You've worked hard enough for it," Preston said with a smug grin on his face.

"Shut it, you shithead," Rock grumbled. Preston only laughed in response.

"I'm . . . we aren't . . ." I wasn't sure if I was supposed to be explaining this or not.

"Yeah, we aren't," Rock finished for me, glaring at Preston. Then his hand released mine and I felt cold. And alone.

"Let's get you to first period," Rock said in a strained voice.

Something was wrong with him. His tone was hard, and I wasn't used to that from him. At least not since we'd become friends.

"Okay," I replied.

Chapter Twenty-Six

ROCK

I stood at my locker, trying not to grab my books and start throwing shit. I was in the fucking friend zone with Trisha, and I was seeing now that I was stuck there. She didn't see us any other way. I'd tested it this morning by holding her hand. She'd been blushing when I'd picked her up, and then she'd shivered when I'd touched her hand. For the first time I'd thought maybe I had gotten under that thick skin of hers.

I was wrong. Dammit.

Slamming my locker door, I took one more deep breath. I had to get control of this. Fact was, I wasn't going anywhere. She needed me, and my infatuation with her was something deeper now. Stopping it seemed impossible. But if I was going to survive this, maybe I needed to shield my heart.

Hands slid up my back and nails scratched at my neck.

"Missed you this weekend at the party," Rose said from behind me. She was pursuing me like her life depended on it.

"I was busy," I replied, moving back a step out of her reach, then heading for my first-period class.

She fell into step beside me. "I heard you brought Trisha Corbin to school this morning. Are you two a thing now?"

No. But not for lack of trying to get her to trust me. "We're just friends," I said, hating the way it tasted. I wanted to claim her as mine.

"Oh, well, that's good. My parents are out of town this week. I was hoping you could come over tonight and stay . . . all night."

I knew if I went, I'd get laid. Hell, I'd probably get several blow jobs too. Rose was known for her killer blow jobs. But I wasn't even slightly interested. Not in the fucking least. Which only told me I was too far gone with Trisha.

"Can't. Got plans," I told her, then stepped into my literature class.

Marcus was already there, sitting at his desk and flirting with some new girl I didn't recognize. I didn't pay any attention to her as I sat down beside him.

Marcus didn't look away from the blonde he was flirting with. He was a man on a mission, and I had no doubt he'd succeed.

"You up for some fun tonight?" Marcus asked me, and I turned my head to look at him.

"What?" I asked, confused. I hadn't been listening to his conversation with the girl, so I had no idea what he was talking about.

"Hillary here has a friend named Chandise who has a thing for you. They want to know if we're up for a good time tonight. I told her we are always up for a good time." Marcus was grinning like he'd already gotten laid.

I hated to cock block him, but I wasn't going with them. "Sorry. I got plans. Ask Preston instead." Who we all knew was always up for a good time.

Marcus frowned. "Her friend hates Preston."

No one hated Preston unless he'd fucked them and left them. Oh. That was it.

"I see. Then Dewayne," I replied.

Marcus sighed. "Yeah, but she wants you."

I wanted Trisha. We all fucking wanted something. Didn't always get what we wanted. "Can't," I replied, and opened my notebook.

Marcus got the message and dropped it.

I let him work out his plans with the girl, and I went back to trying to figure out what to do about Trisha.

Present day . . .

Trisha stood in the bedroom undressing. It was something I had seen a million times before, but it never got old. I could watch this with complete fascination over and over again. With each year I somehow managed to love this woman more.

Seeing her mother our kids only made that love stronger.

When she wiggled her hips to make her shorts fall to the ground, leaving her in nothing but the black satin panties covering her sweet ass, I gave up my restraint.

I pressed my chest against her back and slid my hands around to rest on her flat stomach. "You're so damn gorgeous," I whispered in her ear before nibbling on her earlobe.

She shivered in my arms and melted back against me. "Mmmm" was her only response.

I cupped both her breasts in my hands and let their heaviness rest in my palms before tugging on her aroused nipples. Her breathing grew heavy as she pressed her chest into my hands, her way of silently begging for more.

Until Trisha, I had been a leg man. But after seeing her naked the first time, I became a tits, ass, *and* leg man. She was so damn perfect I couldn't decide what I loved more on her body.

"Bend over and put your hands on the bed," I said, placing a hand on her back and pushing her forward. Over time Trisha had come to love it when I was demanding with sex. It made her hotter when I told her what to do. In the beginning it hadn't been like this. I'd been as delicate with her as possible and treated her like the treasure she was.

Trisha bent over and put both her palms on the bed, then spread her legs as she arched her back. She knew she looked like a fucking wet dream, and she worked it. "God, I love your ass," I said, running my hand over it lovingly before jerking her panties down and having her step out of them.

"Wet for me yet?" I asked her, knowing the answer already. I slipped a hand up between her legs and teased her inner thighs as she panted and whimpered. Then I slipped my fingers between the tender pink flesh.

"Fuck yeah," I growled as her arousal coated my hand.

"Rock, don't play with me. I need you to fuck me. Now. We can play later," Trisha said on a pleading moan.

When my woman wanted to be fucked, I fucked. With one hand still pleasing her, I used my other to unsnap my jeans and shove them down, along with my boxers. "You just want it tonight? Is that it?" I teased her.

"Yes," she panted. "Yes, please."

"Can I lick my sweet pussy first?" I asked her, bending over her to lay a kiss on the small of her back.

"*Ah*, Rock, please." She was begging now, and wiggling her ass in my face.

I'd have to kiss her pussy later. Right now I was needed inside her. With one hard thrust I filled her up, and she pressed her face in the mattress to smother her cry. We were on the other side of the house from the kids, but we still tried to be careful when they were home. While they were at school, I often came home to fuck my woman until she screamed so loud the neighbors could hear her.

Chapter Twenty-Seven

Eight years ago . . .

TRISHA

Carrying my own book bag would keep me from healing and possibly make my fracture worse. However, after three days of Rock walking beside me and carrying it to each class while girls flirted with him and he didn't stop them, I was ready to get myself a wagon to pull. Anything to put some distance between me and Rock and his adoring crowd.

He didn't say much to me except to ask politely if I was okay or if I needed anything. With everyone else he joked and laughed. He winked at a few girls and chuckled at their attempts to hang on him. It was just too much.

I was like his little sister who needed help but he wished he didn't have the obligation. Rock was a good guy. I knew that much. He had signed on to help me, and even though this was obviously holding him back, he didn't complain. The only answer to this was to get someone else to carry my book bag. I was more than positive he'd gladly hand over the responsibility.

"Rock," a redhead I didn't know said in a sickeningly sweet voice. Rock paused and glanced at the girl, then grinned.

"Hey, Ginger. What's up?"

Hey, Ginger. What's up? I repeated in my head, and then mentally vomited. I had to get away from this.

"Tonight there's a party at my place. You're coming, right? I have a special new bikini I bought just for you."

My mental vomit was about to become actual vomit. This was ridiculous. In desperation I began to scan the crowded halls for someone to rescue me from this. Anyone.

"I heard about the party. Not sure I'll be able to make it, though," he replied. He wasn't amused by her or even disgusted. He sounded almost disappointed he was going to miss the special bikini. *Ugh.*

I saw Riley and Davey talking, and Davey's eyes met mine. They were talking about me. I hadn't told them much at lunch each day, although they had asked about Rock after he had deposited me and my tray at their table before going to his table. I just did my best to change the subject each time.

Right now, however, I was ready to ask my friends to rescue me. "Help," I mouthed at Davey, and he was instantly moving through the crowd toward me.

Rock and Ginger were still chatting about the party, and the things she could do to him, while I kept my focus on Davey. When he finally approached, I wanted to sag in relief.

"Hey," he said, looking up at Rock, then back at me.

"Hey, you're headed my way to the next class. Would you mind carrying my bag?" I asked him in a lower voice so as to not draw attention to myself. Rock was listening to Ginger talk right now.

"No," Rock replied before Davey could say anything. He slipped his arm around my hips, careful not to touch my waist, and rested a hand on my hip. "Don't need your help. I got this," he told Davey.

Well, crap. I was trying to get him free of me. He was not helping at all.

"You can stay and talk to, uh . . . Ginger," I replied, motioning to her, "about her bathing suit choices. And I'll go with Davey. There's some stuff I'm having problems with in trig that he can help me with."

"No," Rock repeated in a more firm tone. "You can ask him later. I'll get you to class. Let's go."

And then he started to walk, gently guiding me along with him. What the heck? I looked back at Davey and shrugged. I'd talk to Davey today at lunch when Rock dropped me off. Because apparently, Rock wasn't going to allow that at the moment.

His hand stayed firmly on my hip as he moved us up through

the hallway. It never ceased to amaze me how the crowd just split for him as he moved through it. I hated to admit that I felt secure at his side, tucked in safely.

"You were trying to get rid of me," he finally said as we got closer to my next class.

"You looked like you'd rather be alone and have more time to discuss her special bikini. I was trying to help you out," I snapped, without meaning to. Cringing, I mentally slapped myself for being an idiot.

"Don't care about her bikini," he replied in a hard tone.

Instead of nodding and letting this go, I moved away from him and turned to glare up at his too-handsome-to-be-fair face. "I am not your responsibility. I hate feeling like I'm this burden on you that you can't get rid of. I have other friends who can help me. I don't like putting a kink in your social life."

Rock stared at me as if he didn't understand a word I was saying, and then he frowned. "What?"

What? Was that seriously his response? I hadn't spoken another language. He had to have understood the words that just came out of my mouth.

"I didn't stutter," I told him.

A smirk tugged at the corner of his mouth. "No, you didn't," he agreed, then took a step toward me and lowered his head close to my ear. "But you look hot as hell when you're jealous."

It was my turn to be confused. "What?" I asked, backing up.

He reached out and grabbed my hip and pulled me closer to him while glaring at someone behind me. "Careful," he snarled to someone. "You almost ran into her."

"She was the one walking into me," a male voice argued.

Rock's eyes flared and he tucked me close to his side. "Then move the fuck out of her way next time."

The guy was Felix Hardgrove. He had a 4.0 GPA and was about the size of my brother two years ago. He backed up and scurried away.

"It was my fault. You didn't have to scare him," I said, tilting my head back to look up at Rock.

He was clenching his jaw as he stared straight ahead. "I never wanted to go to her party. I don't want to go to any fucking party you aren't at. Accept the fact that all I see is you, Trisha Corbin. Then decide what you want to do about it." Rock walked past me into the room and put my bag beside the desk where I sat every day.

I stood there and watched as he got out my books and a pen, then placed them on my desk. He always did that, too. He didn't want me bending over. When he finally turned to leave, his gaze locked with mine. It wasn't a teasing grin or a flirty wink. It was intense, and somehow it was as if he was pleading with me.

Chapter Twenty-Eight

ROCK

I had taken a chance. I knew girls pretty well, and from her sudden sass I was almost positive Trisha was jealous of Ginger. It was the only reason I let Ginger keep going on and on about her bikini. Anything to get Trisha's attention. I'd almost missed the fact that her spunky ass had signaled her friend over to get away from me. Hell no was that happening. No one else was carrying Trisha's books. That was all me. I was taking care of her.

Getting through the next class wasn't easy. I couldn't focus on anything the teacher was saying. I was planning out how I was going to fix this with Trisha. My being her friend was over. I wasn't taking her to that damn lunch table she sits at with her friends and leaving her today. She was going to sit with me. She was mine, and she needed to admit that shit now.

Before she drove me crazy.

I was at the door to her classroom when the bell rang, and I made my way inside to pack her books back into her bag.

She sighed when I took the first book from her hands. "I can do this, Rock. I'm not completely helpless."

I didn't respond. I tossed the backpack over my shoulder, then held out my other hand to Trisha. "It's lunchtime."

She looked at my outstretched hand and then back at me before finally slipping her hand into mine.

I helped her up and tugged her close to my side. "Wasn't so hard, was it?" I said with a smirk, then led us out of the room.

I nodded at Preston, who called out my name. Dewayne cocked an eyebrow at me and then grinned when he saw my hand grasping Trisha's. I didn't take us near him. He would only say something stupid and make Trisha feel uncomfortable.

Stopping at Trisha's locker, I put the bag inside. Then, instead of taking her hand again, I placed my hand on her lower back and moved her toward the cafeteria.

"You don't have to carry my tray," she said.

"But I am."

"Why? I know you're tired of this. You don't have to take care of me."

I tried not to get frustrated, but damn, was she that clueless?

"Davey and Riley will help me carry my books. You've been doing it all week and having me as a burden—"

That was it. I grabbed her hand and pulled her into the empty art room we were passing and slammed the door.

"What?" she asked, looking between me and the door.

I had tried words with her. I had tried actions. I had tried everything to get her to realize that I wanted her. That I wanted to be near her. That I wanted her to be mine.

She was making me lose my mind.

I stalked toward her, and she backed up against the wall as she watched me, wide eyed and confused.

Dammit, she was too sexy to be fucking cute, too. That was shit guys couldn't shake off. Girls like her weren't supposed to exist. They made men weak. She had me so fucking tangled in knots it was painful.

I placed my palms on the brick wall on either side of her head and stopped only an inch from our bodies touching. "What do I have to do to get you to get this? What, Trisha? Fuck, you're all I can think about," I said softly as my gaze dropped from her eyes to those plump lips I played with in my fantasies.

The tip of her pink tongue wet her bottom lip, and I was lost.

My mouth covered hers, and the small gasp that broke from her lips was the only chance I needed to slide my tongue onto the sweet heat of hers. I had kissed a lot of girls. But never had I felt like my world was being completely rocked.

Trisha's hands slipped over my shoulders and she held on to me. And that was fucking perfect. She wasn't pushing me away. She was holding on to the ride and, damn, it was one hell of a ride.

The softness of her lips moved under mine, and then she began to join in on the kiss. It took all my willpower to keep from pressing her against the wall. I had to be careful with her ribs. But I wanted my hands on her. I wanted to get lost in how wonderful she felt.

When she leaned into me and whimpered, I broke the kiss and moved back instantly. "Are you okay?" I asked, looking down at her ribs.

She didn't respond, and panic that I'd hurt her started to grip me. I found her eyes and saw the same arousal in them that I had been feeling until that whimper had scared me.

I started to lower my mouth again, needing to taste her more.

"No, wait," she breathed, pressing both her hands on my chest this time.

"Did I hurt you?" I asked her.

She shook her head. "No, it's just . . . I . . . We shouldn't . . . Why did you do that?"

I closed my eyes and forced myself to be patient with her. Trisha had her issues, and trust was one of them.

"Because I'm crazy about you. Because your lips are the prettiest damn lips I've ever seen. Because you think you're a burden to me when I just want to keep you close to me all the time. Because you are making me lose my mind. Because I don't want to be your friend, Trisha. I want to be yours."

Her mouth fell slightly open as her blue eyes stared up at me in surprise. How did she not already know all this? It wasn't like I have been subtle.

"You're . . . you're crazy about me?" she asked.

I held back a laugh. "Yeah, and everyone seems to see it but you."

She frowned and bit her bottom lip. I wanted to pull it out and suck on it. She looked away from me for a moment and I gave her time.

"What about Ginger's bikini?" she asked, not looking at me.

This time I did laugh. "I could not give a rat's ass about Ginger."

Slowly Trisha looked back at me. "But the others. All of them. You can have a different girl every night. They line up to get your attention. Why me?"

I cupped her face in both my hands and took in the beautiful features she seemed to be blind to. Inside and out she was beautiful. "I can't see anyone past you. I haven't been able to for a long time. Hell, Trisha, you've been in my head, taunting me, since the first day I laid eyes on you."

"Oh," she said in a whisper.

"Yeah, oh," I repeated.

Chapter Twenty-Nine

TRISHA

My heart was racing and my lips were still tingling when Rock led me into the cafeteria. He had kissed me. Like, a mind-blowing kind of kiss that made my knees weak. I had even gone light-headed for a moment.

Rock's hand was holding onto mine as he walked us through the lunch line. When he picked up my tray, he looked at his table with his friends and then looked at my table where my friends sat. "Today I want you to myself. We can figure out where we are going to sit later. Right now I don't want to share you."

How had this changed so fast? Just this morning he was barely talking to me. Now he wanted me all to himself.

"Okay," I said, still unsure how I was supposed to respond to that.

Rock led us to the far corner of the room where a table sat empty. I could feel the eyes of everyone following us. It was like pricks of heat on my skin. I wanted to run out of the room. I hated attention, and this was by far the most attention I had ever gotten.

When he set our trays down, he pulled his chair over to sit right up against mine. His thigh was brushing mine as we took our seats.

"Eat," he said close to my ear when I didn't make a move to touch my food.

"I can't eat with everyone watching me," I explained, afraid to confirm the fact that we had drawn attention.

"They are getting over it. Most of them aren't looking anymore," he replied with a smile in his voice.

I cut my eyes to look up at him, and he winked at me.

"Please eat for me," he said, reaching up to cup my chin. His thumb brushed my bottom lip.

"Well, ain't this sweet. Damn more interesting over here than the usual place," Dewayne Falco said as he pulled out the chair across from us and sat down.

"Dewayne," Rock growled at him, startling me.

"Trisha don't care if I sit here. Do you, Trisha?" Dewayne said, turning his amused smile to me.

"Uh," I started to say, when Preston Drake sat down beside me with an extra milk carton in his teeth. He dropped it in his hand and set it down, then flashed me a crooked grin.

"The party has moved. I missed the memo," he drawled, then opened his milk and took a drink.

"I don't think Rock wants us here," Dewayne said as he took a drink of his soda. "Not that we give a shit."

Rock had gone solid beside me. He was angry. These were his closest friends. I didn't want to be a reason they fought.

"No sweet tea today. What the hell is up with that?" Marcus Hardy said by way of greeting as he plopped beside Dewayne and put his tray down. "I need some sweet tea to get through the next class. Dead poets bore me."

"Shit," Rock muttered beside me.

"Rock ain't being very welcoming, Marcus. He's being kinda shitty," Dewayne said, still looking completely amused by the whole thing.

Marcus gave me an apologetic smile, then moved his focus to Rock. "With us sitting here, y'all aren't the afternoon's entertainment," he explained with a shrug. He was right. They were blocking a lot of the crowd.

"You good with them eating with us?" Rock asked me.

I nodded. I wasn't ready to talk yet. Sitting with these four was a little overwhelming. I didn't want to say something stupid, and I wasn't sure I had anything to say to them, anyway.

"Guys, y'all know Trisha," Rock said.

"It's hard not to know her. You've been panting after her for over a year. We're kinda tired of watching it. Thanks for giving him a break. We all appreciate it," Dewayne said.

Preston chuckled beside me but didn't pipe up. I had a feeling the only one out of these four who wasn't scared of Rock was Dewayne. They were close to the same size.

"Dewayne," Rock said in a warning tone.

Dewayne only smirked. "Am I lying?"

"Seriously, D. Shut up," Marcus said, shooting him a disapproving glare.

Dewayne shrugged and took a bite of his burger.

Rock's hand slid over my knee and stayed there. "I swear they aren't that bad," he assured me.

Smiling, I reached for a French fry. "I think they're nice," I told him.

They all four started to chuckle, and then Preston burst out laughing. I glanced at all of them, then looked up at Rock, who was smiling down at me with something warm in his eyes that made my heart flutter.

Chapter Thirty

ROCK

Trisha didn't miss another football game. Once the season was over, I had my Friday nights free to spend with her. I never thought I'd look forward to football season ending. Any time I could have her alone were the best hours of my day. She hadn't completely melted on me immediately, but over time she slowly began to trust me.

Now when I walked up to her in the hallways at school and wrapped her up in my arms, she came to me willingly. Kissing her sweet lips whenever I wanted to was also my favorite addiction. She not only let me have that mouth when I wanted it, but she kissed me back.

Life was fucking close to perfect. If I didn't have to worry about her going back to that damn trailer every night, then it really would be perfect. Krit was dealing with some issues lately that worried Trisha. When the last guy his mother had brought home had hit on Trisha, Krit had lost it and almost beat the man to death. Trisha had called me screaming and crying. My heart had almost stopped at the sound of her panic.

When I got there the dude was on the ground, unconscious and covered in blood, and Trisha had Krit in a corner talking him down while he glared at the man as if possessed. There was broken furniture everywhere, and even Fandora had a busted lip.

Apparently, he had backhanded his mother to get her away from Trisha. The kid was like a loaded gun. Trisha wanted him checked out. She was worried that he had some emotional damage from growing up the way they had. I was afraid the kid had a personality disorder. I'd been angry before, and if I'd seen the man touch Trisha I'd have beat his ass too. It was the glazed-over look in Krit's eyes that concerned me.

Tonight Krit was going to spend the night with Green, and his band was going to practice. They weren't getting actual gigs yet, but they were practicing enough for someone to think they were. Surprisingly, they were good, too. Krit could sing. It had been a shock the first time I'd heard them practice.

So I had Trisha all to myself. All night. I was saving every penny I had to get us an apartment the moment I turned eighteen. But I wanted to do something special for Trisha tonight.

I had let her take it slow. I hadn't said shit that I wanted to because I was afraid she'd freak out.

Last week I had worked nights for the first time, stocking at the local grocery store. With that money I was getting us a hotel room in the next town over. I wanted to hold Trisha all night in a bed. Because I was saving my money, this was all I could afford. I wouldn't be able to take her out to eat too. So I'd made us sandwiches and bought some of the chocolate chip cookies she loved. I also bought her favorite soda and got a bag of chips and dip.

I had checked in earlier and set the cooler in the room with the sandwiches and dip. Dewayne had snagged me some candles from his house that his mother wouldn't miss. After setting them around the room, I had left a lighter by the bed so I could light them later.

The reason I hadn't told Trisha what we were doing was because I wanted to surprise her with a night somewhere she didn't have to worry about Krit or Fandora coming home. I wanted to hold her while she slept and know she was safe in my arms. What I hadn't thought about was how Trisha would read into this. Until I parked the truck and glanced over at her.

The wide-eyed look on her as she stared up at the hotel in front of us told me I had made a serious mistake. She didn't get why I had done this. She was thinking something completely different. We hadn't done anything more than kiss. I'd wanted to do more, but I was afraid to with her. I didn't want to lose her or scare her. I'd been a fucking saint with her.

Then I go and do something like this.

Dammit.

"Trisha, babe, this isn't what you think. I didn't bring you here . . . for that. I just wanted us to have a night we could sleep with no fear or worry. I wanted to hold you. Nothing more. I swear, baby."

She didn't look at me. She continued to stare at the building in front of us. Shit!

"I swear to God I would never have brought you here expecting anything. I wasn't thinking about that. I just wanted us to have a place that was ours. Where we didn't have to worry about anyone else coming along or coming home. Just us."

She nodded slightly, but she didn't look at me yet. So I waited. I gave her a moment to process what I was saying to her. I was about to tell her I'd sleep on the floor, although I really wanted to hold her all night, when she finally turned her head and met my gaze.

"Okay," she whispered.

She didn't look like she meant it.

I reached over and pulled her up against me. "Listen to me," I pleaded, taking her face in my hands and tilting it so she had to look at me. "If all we ever do is kiss, then I'll be the luckiest fucking man on the planet. Because I have you. I . . . I love you, Trisha Corbin. I love you like crazy. You've got me so obsessed with you I can't see anything or anyone beyond you. Every plan I make is because of you. Every morning when I wake up all I think about is seeing you. Every night when I go to sleep all I think about is how much I want to be holding you in my arms as you fall asleep. You are it. You're my gift. You. Just you. This hotel room was to give us a place that was just ours. I have something to eat up there and I even rented us a couple movies. This isn't about sex, baby. I swear to you."

She blinked slowly, and her eyes misted over. I wasn't sure what I had said to make her cry. I started to replay my ramblings in my head, and then her full lips moved. "You love me?"

I had been scared to say it before tonight. It had come out in my panic to reassure her. But it was true. I'd never love anyone else the way I loved Trisha.

"I think you may be the only person who doesn't know that already," I said, smiling at her surprise. She was so damn adorable sometimes.

A slow smile played on her lips before she leaned toward me. "I love you, too," she said softly, before kissing me.

I could've died right then and known I had lived.

Chapter Thirty-One

TRISHA

Rock opened the door to the hotel room he had gotten us for the night. My heart was still so full from hearing him tell me he loved me that I couldn't stop smiling. I had been in love with Rock for months now. I wouldn't tell him because I wasn't sure he had wanted to hear that.

He had said it to me. And he had also said a lot of other beautiful things that had made me love him even more, and I hadn't thought that was possible.

"Cooler has our food in it. You hungry now?" he asked as I stepped inside the room. There was one big bed in the middle of the room and a television on the wall across from it. I could see the sink and mirror straight ahead, and then a door to the bathroom. It was the nicest place I'd ever stayed. Until last month when I went to the party at Marcus Hardy's house, it would have been the nicest place I had ever been. But Marcus Hardy's house had blown my mind. It was like nothing I had ever imagined.

This, however, was ours. For the night.

"I got you a grape soda. Several, actually," Rock said, slipping his hand around my waist and kissing my temple.

I loved grape soda, and once he had found that out, he made sure I had it often. Another thing I loved about him.

Normally, I would want a grape soda. But I didn't want that right now. I had been daydreaming for so long about the moment I would tell Rock I loved him. I had known how I wanted it to happen. I had fantasized about it so many times I wasn't even nervous when I turned to face him. I couldn't say the words because in my daydreams he just knew. I had never prepared words for this.

I kissed him.

It only took him a moment to respond. His hands were on my hips, pulling me up against him tightly as his mouth began to work its magic on me. His minty taste always excited me. I slipped my arms up as high as I could and stood on my tiptoes so that my fingers could slide into his short hair. My breasts pressed against his chest, and the ache in them only intensified. Since the first time Rock's hands had settled under my breasts and his thumb had grazed the undersides of them, they had started getting very excited when he got anywhere near them.

Not begging him to touch them was hard. It scared me and excited me to think about it. I had seen him looking at my boobs a lot. He liked them. It made wearing shirts that were too small bearable, knowing he liked the view.

When his hands slid up my sides and stopped just below my breasts again, I let out a frustrated whimper. He stopped kissing me for a moment, but his mouth stayed hovering over mine. His warm breath bathed my lips, and I wasn't sure I could breathe.

His hands slowly began to move, and I opened my eyes to look up at his warm ones. He was watching me closely as he inched his hands up until he was touching the undersides of my breasts. So close to the centers, which ached for attention.

The moment he moved higher and his fingers ran over my sensitive nipples, I sucked in a breath and grabbed on to his shoulders. This was what I wanted. What I had wanted for a while.

"Can I take your shirt off?" Rock asked, his voice raspy and low.

I nodded. I couldn't form words.

He closed his eyes for a minute, and his nostrils flared before he reached down and pulled my T-shirt up my body. I lifted my arms, and he moved the shirt up and then tossed it aside. I wanted to close my eyes now. But I also needed to see him look at me. I would see the disappointment in them if he didn't like what he saw.

His eyes flashed and he swallowed so hard I could see his

Adam's apple move in his muscular neck. "Damn," he whispered reverently. "So perfect."

My body hummed with pleasure from his words. The fear that I'd been holding on to about this drifted away, and I wanted more. I was ready for Rock Taylor to make me feel good. His large hands covered the satin bra I was wearing. It wasn't anything special, but it worked. It was one Fandora had given me after she no longer wanted it. It was one of the few things she'd ever given to me.

"Can I take off the bra?" he asked me. He was breathing hard.

"Yes," I managed to say.

His hands slid around the back of me and undid the hook with ease. I closed my eyes this time. I was about to be bare to him, and I wanted that but I was also not sure how to handle looking at him while he looked at me.

"Oh, fuck, Trisha. God, I'm so fucking ruined," he said as his hands grabbed my waist. I wanted his hands somewhere else. My now bare breasts throbbed, in need of attention.

"Come here," he said as he began to move me. I opened my eyes as he backed me up against the bed. "Lie down."

I was ready to do whatever he asked of me. I scooted back and lay my head on the pillow. He pulled his shirt off with one fluid movement, and I had only a moment to process the perfect view of his chest before he was moving over me.

He held himself over me and kissed me less gently this time. There was a hunger to his kiss that made my heart pound. I lifted my body and grabbed his head to pull him against me. I wanted to feel his chest against mine. But he held himself off, then pulled back, breaking the kiss.

His eyes were on my breasts. "If I do something you don't like, tell me. I'll stop. I swear it."

I didn't believe he could do anything that I wouldn't like. But I nodded. "Okay."

He didn't move to touch me, and the throb in my breasts had made its way to between my legs, too. The ache was making me feel frantic.

"Please, Rock. Touch me." Those words came out before I could stop them. I was getting desperate.

A low growl vibrated in his chest, and he swore under his breath before his hands slid up and covered my breasts. Then he squeezed them, making me squirm at the pleasure that came with it. "Ah," I cried out.

Rock's eyes burned with a brightness I'd never seen before as he looked from my chest to my eyes. His thumbs brushed over my nipples and I bit my bottom lip to keep from making any more embarrassing noises.

Then I watched as Rock lowered his head to my chest while his eyes stayed locked on mine. When his tongue flicked out and over my right nipple, I let my bottom lip go as a soundless gasp came from my mouth, which was now wide open in wonder.

When he pulled my nipple into his mouth and sucked, I had to close my eyes to ride the wave of pleasure. Seeing him do this and feeling it at the same time was too much. I wasn't sure I could handle any more. My body felt so tightly strung, humming with a delicious ache that would drive me mad if it lasted too long.

"Not only are they the prettiest, most perfect titties on earth, but they taste like honey. And I fucking love honey," Rock said before licking my tips again.

Hearing him talk like that made me shiver. He was going to have to stop, but if he did, I was afraid I would attack him and demand he soothe this ache.

He continued to play with my breasts, molding them in his hands, then kissing them and causing me to squirm and moan. Every time I accidentally made a sound, he would groan and get greedier. It was like a fire was being lit between my legs. I had to press my legs together to keep from crying out in pain.

When his mouth began to move down my stomach and then over each rib, I held my breath. I shifted some and squeezed my legs together as the throb between them got worse at the excitement of Rock's mouth getting closer.

His hands moved over my waist, and then he slipped a finger under the waistline of my jeans. He stared at it for a moment, and I waited, unable to take a deep breath, to see what he would do.

Then his eyes lifted to meet mine. "I want to take them off."

Yes. Oh God, yes. "Yes," I panted.

His nostrils flared again as he began unfastening my jeans. I lifted my bottom off the bed so he could pull them down. The panties I was wearing didn't cover much. They were too small, like most of my clothing. They were also faded and the pink almost looked white.

Rock's hands moved up my legs slowly, as if he were memorizing them. When he got to my knees he stopped, and I was just about to plead that he do something before I combusted when he pushed my legs open. I let him, unable to tell him no about anything at this point.

He took a sharp breath and swore again as he stared at the crotch of my panties. The cool air that hit them alerted me to what he was seeing. I was wet. Oh God. I was wet. I started to press my legs together, embarrassed. Rock's kissing always made my panties wet. I couldn't help it. And from the way the cold air touching me felt, I knew I had to be soaking.

"No. God, no, Trisha. Don't hide this from me," he said in a desperation I recognized. Opening my eyes only a little, I peeked at him and let him push my legs open again. He looked mesmerized. "Fuck, baby. That's hot."

It was?

He moved a hand up the inside of my leg, and my thigh tingled. He was going to touch me there. He wanted to even though he could see I was wet.

One single finger ran over the center of my achy, needy core, and I grabbed the sheets under me and cried out. The shots of intense pleasure that went through every cell in my body made me feel like I was about to explode.

His hands were whipping my panties off before I could focus again. I opened my eyes to see his head as it lowered to settle between my legs.

The first hot contact with his magical tongue made me lose my mind. I wasn't sure what I said or begged or promised, but I was panting and begging. That much I knew. Rock's mouth kissed and licked the achy need, making it worse and better all at once.

I grabbed his shoulders, and my nails bit into his flesh. I couldn't stop myself. I was about to explode and I didn't know how to control myself. I wanted this and I was terrified of it.

"Never wanted to taste pussy before, Trisha, but I swear to God you taste like sunshine and sugar. I could eat you for hours and not get enough." Rock swore before sliding his tongue inside me. I bucked against him and my world blew up. Light sent off a million colors behind my eyelids, and I was screaming Rock's name while the bed and everything else spun away from me. I was riding a wave of perfection that I never wanted to get off of.

I heard Rock saying something in the distance, but my body was jerking as those aches and throbs reached a point where they exploded, just like I'd feared. Except it was beautiful. So beautiful I wanted this feeling forever.

It began to fade, and my mind was slowly processing the fact that I had lost myself for a moment and I wasn't sure what I had done or said while I was lost.

Rock was staring down at me as I opened my eyes, and the first thing I realized was that his hips were settled between my legs and he was naked. The hardness I had felt through his jeans many times was now pressing against my oversensitive center, which was already getting excited over another round.

"That was the most gorgeous thing I've ever seen. I swear, Trisha, nothing will ever compare to the look on your face just now," he said, an intensity in his eyes that warmed my heart. "I want inside you. I want to make love to you. I want to be so deep inside you that you're a part of me."

Yes. All of that. Yes.

I nodded, and he closed his eyes and whispered what sounded like "Thank God." When he opened his eyes again, he ran his lips across my collarbone, then up my neck, before he kissed the area behind my ear. "It'll hurt at first. But I swear I'll make sure you feel that sweet place again. Trust me."

"I love you," was my response.

"Fuck, baby," he whispered as his hard tip entered me, stretching me in a way that felt right.

I let my legs fall open all the way, and his body shuddered over me. Then he eased in farther until the tight sharpness bit me just before I felt him break through the barrier. I grabbed his arms and held back the cry in my throat. I didn't want him to stop.

He froze once he was completely inside me. I felt full as the sharp pain throbbed, until it began to ease.

"I'm okay," I told him, and he inhaled sharply.

Then he moved and a slow burn began in me. With each move of his hips I lost my breath and made a noise.

"I love you. I love you so damn much. You make me crazy. You're mine, Trisha. You'll always be mine."

His words warmed me. I slid my legs up the back of his and locked them around his waist.

"Fuuuuuck," he groaned, and buried his face in my neck. "Them long legs of yours. Just damn, baby. I'm the luckiest son of a bitch in the world."

Smiling only for a moment, I enjoyed knowing I had the power to bring this big man to this. He wanted me, and I had him as insanely wrapped up in me as I was in him.

The build that I had felt before began to grow again with each rock of his hips. I craved that feeling. Pressing into him,

I let the pleasure rise in me. Just before it claimed me again, I begged for it.

"GAAAAHHHHH!" Rock's roar and trembling and jerking of his body sent me spiraling off again.

"Trisha! Fuck!" he cried out, just before I lost my grasp on reality.

Chapter Thirty-Two

Six years ago . . .

ROCK

Standing inside the one-bedroom apartment I had just paid a year's worth of rent on in order to get approved for the lease, I realized I had done it. Working nights wasn't easy, but it was worth it. I had all the money I needed to move Trisha in with me. Telling my dad that I wasn't signing with any of the four SEC football teams that were trying to get me was the last thing I had to face. He'd be furious and he'd kick me out. But that didn't matter now.

I had a truck of my own and an apartment. I had a job that I was going to be able to work at more once I graduated in six months. Trisha wasn't going to be left in that shithole with her wicked stepmother anymore. Once I rescued Trisha, I knew Krit would be gone too. He would have left already if it weren't for Trisha.

Krit had already said he was moving in with Legend, an older guy in his band, the moment I got Trisha out of his mom's trailer. Trisha didn't like that idea, but her little brother was sixteen now. He was also six foot two and had grown into that tall lankiness. He could take care of himself. Convincing her of that was difficult, though.

Dewayne and his dad were bringing me some furniture Mrs. T said she didn't need anymore and insisted I should take. Dewayne had told me that she was also sending me towels, pots and pans, dishes, rugs, and even a quilt. I didn't argue with her, although I had a feeling she was giving me stuff she was going to have to replace in her own house.

Marcus was giving me his old bed and dresser. His mother had said she wanted to redo his room and I could have his old stuff. He was bringing it over later today. With their help, I didn't think we would need anything. I was waiting until I had it set up and ready before I showed Trisha. I was also talking to Krit and making sure he was set up to move out too.

Fandora had gotten better about not letting the men in her life hit Trisha. But when they went for Krit, who was capable of beating the shit out of the fuckers himself, Trisha always jumped in and ended up hurt, if only a little, before Krit put a serious whipping on them.

I was ready to be able to sleep with Trisha tucked safely in my arms. Two years of sleeping with a phone in my hand and often sleeping on the floor of her room had been tough. I hated leaving her in that house. If Krit wasn't a badass crazy shit, I wouldn't have been able to do it. But the boy had a temper, and anyone who pissed him off needed to get the hell out of his way. And his sister was the only person he loved on earth. I knew he'd kill someone before he let them hurt her.

"So this is it?" Preston asked. I hadn't heard him walk in. My thoughts had been elsewhere.

"Yeah," I replied, glancing back at him as he stood in the doorway checking the place out.

"You did good."

I thought I had. I just wanted Trisha to think so too. She was all that mattered here.

"I think so," I agreed.

He sauntered in and nodded toward the two doors to the left. One was the bathroom and the other was the bedroom. The rest of the apartment was right here. Living room and kitchen all together. "There's only one bedroom. Where will I sleep?" he asked.

I chuckled. "Not here."

"Damn. And we were supposed to be best friends. I'm wounded."

"Sure you are."

"You told your dad yet?"

I wasn't telling my old man until I had my things ready to move out. Because he was going to lose it. My plan was to get everything in that house that I wanted to keep out first because my dad was likely to throw it all in the yard and light it on fire. The man talked nonstop about my college choices. He wanted me to go to Florida State. He was driving me crazy about choosing. I knew I wasn't choosing any of them. I couldn't take any scholarship that required me playing football. If I played ball, I wouldn't be able to work as much. I needed to work and take care of Trisha.

"I'll tell him once I have everything moved in," I told him.

"Smart," Preston agreed.

Two knocks on the door and then a "This ain't shit. I'm impressed."

We both turned to see Dewayne walking in the door with a grin on his face, followed by Marcus.

"Y'all aren't allowed to have parties here unless I'm home from school. No fun allowed while I'm away," Marcus said.

Marcus was leaving for the University of Alabama next year. He was the only one of us leaving town. We tried not to think about it often. Preston had a baseball scholarship at the local junior college. He had gotten scholarships to bigger schools, but he wouldn't leave town. His siblings needed him.

"Shit. We're throwing a Marcus-has-left-town party," Dewayne drawled.

Marcus laughed and rolled his eyes.

"I always knew you'd be the first one to move out. When

you admitted that you loved Trisha Corbin, I knew this was it. You'd move into your own place first and get married first. Hell, if you're fast you might have a family before Preston," Marcus said, smirking.

"What? I ain't having no family," Preston said, snapping his attention back to Marcus, who looked amused.

"Dude. You can only sleep with so many hundreds of women before you knock one up. It'll happen," he replied.

Preston scowled. "Don't speak that shit. I'm always gloved."

Everyone laughed at that. Getting smiling, happy Preston to scowl was always fun.

In a few months our lives would all change. We didn't know what the future held, but we had each other. This was my family. The one I had leaned on since I was a kid. I could have taken a much different road in life, growing up the way I did, but having these three guys who gave a shit about me changed that. Somehow we had stayed out of real trouble. Marcus had always been there to remind us to keep it clean and stay out of jail.

I was going to miss times like this. But I had Trisha, and my future would always have her in it. That made the future exciting instead of terrifying. Since the moment she sat at that lunch table, laughing with the three people in the world who I considered family, I had known she was it.

She was my future.

Chapter Thirty-Three

TRISHA

Krit pulled up to an apartment complex and put Fandora's car in park before looking at me. "Before we get out, I want to talk to you," he said.

When he had woken me up this morning and asked me to get dressed and go somewhere with him, I hadn't imagined this was where we would be going. I knew he wanted to move in with Legend, who was a year older than me and seemed to have a good head on his shoulders. But if he was showing me the place to talk me into letting him move out, he didn't have to do that.

If he wanted out, then I was ready to let him go. I'd survive somehow. I was sure Fandora would kick me out, but I could figure somewhere else to go. I didn't want to hold Krit back because of me. He hated living there. He hated her.

He didn't deserve to live in hell to keep me safe. He looked like a man, but he was just a boy with so much potential. "Yes. If you want to move in with Legend, then yes. I want that for you," I told him before he tried to sell me on the idea.

Krit frowned and tilted his head to look at me. I waited on him to say something. When he finally looked pissed, I wondered if I had said the wrong thing. "You mean that shit." He shook his head and let out a hard laugh. "Dammit, Trisha. Do you think I'd do that to you?"

I realized I had made a mistake. Crap. I had to fix this.

"I just meant . . . I just want you to be happy, Krit. I thought bringing me here to an apartment meant you were going to try to talk me into letting you move out. I don't want to hold you back. I want you to have it all. You deserve happiness."

He ran his hands through his shoulder-length hair and slammed them on the steering wheel. "What about you? You've sacrificed more than anyone. You took fucking beatings to keep me safe as a kid. If I moved out and left you to that bitch, what would that say about me? It would make me a motherfucking asshole who didn't deserve to live. So, no, Sis, I'm not asking you to let me desert you. I would sacrifice my soul to protect you. Don't you know that? I only love you. I have never and nor will I ever love anyone else. Bitches can't be trusted. You're the only woman on earth I could love."

Tears burned my eyes and I blinked them away. "I'm sorry. I

thought . . . I just . . . I was wrong. I know you want to keep me safe. We're family. We have each other. Always."

Krit nodded. "But you have Rock now. And I am thankful you have him. He's a big dude with scary-as-hell arms and a chest like a wall. He can keep my sister safe, and he loves you. Like I've never seen a man love, ever. That makes him worthy of you. He has the world's finest treasure and he knows it." He let out a laugh and shrugged. "I might need to correct something I said before. I think I love him, too. I love him for loving you the way you deserve to be loved."

This time I let the tears burning my eyes free. I sniffled, then brushed the tears off my face. "I'm sorry," I said, smiling. "You just don't normally say things like that, so I wasn't prepared for it emotionally."

He smirked. "Before we can get any mushier in here, I just want to tell you that I am thrilled about what you're going to see in a minute. It's every dream and wish I've ever had. It makes me so fucking happy. Not just for you but for me, too. So know that when you start worrying about me." He opened the car door and stepped out before giving me a chance to ask him what the heck he was talking about.

Krit closed the door and walked up to the entryway to the stairs, then looked back and waved for me to come on. I had no idea what he wanted to show me, and my mind was envisioning a million different scenarios. I made my way up to him, but he didn't say anything. He just nodded and turned to the stairs. "Second floor."

We walked up the one flight of stairs, then turned right and walked down three doors. Krit stopped outside 204. Then he knocked.

We were meeting someone?

The door opened, and Rock filled the doorway. He gave Krit a nod, and then he turned to look at me. "Welcome home," he said with a smile, and held out his hand for me.

"About moving in with Legend, yeah, I'm doing that tonight. Love you, Sis. Go live your happily ever after you deserve." Then Krit bent down and kissed my cheek and whispered, "This man moved heaven and earth to make this happen. It's one of the reasons I know he deserves you. Be happy."

I started to say something, but Krit straightened and walked off the way we had come.

I watched him walk away, then turned to look back at Rock.

"I'm confused," I finally said, still trying to piece everything together.

Rock stepped out, scooped me up in his arms, and carried me inside before putting me back down and closing the door behind him. I took in my surroundings. The sofa I remembered from the Falcos' living room sat against the left wall with their coffee table and a black recliner I didn't recognize. A small television sat on a table in front of them. I shifted my gaze to the other side of the room to see a small Formica table with fresh flowers in a vase in the middle and four matching chairs around it.

On the wall in a frame was a picture taken by Tabby Falco after a football game one night. Rock was standing behind me with his pads still on and his arms wrapped around me as we both smiled at the camera.

"This is ours." I said the words just as a sob broke free and the realization sank in.

Rock had talked about getting a place of our own, but I thought it was a dream to help us get through the tough times. I never imagined it would happen so soon. Or at all. I had only hoped we would get this one day.

"Yes, it is," he said, pulling me into his arms and kissing the top of my head as I continued to take in everything.

"How?" I asked in awe.

"Lots of nights and overtime," he said with pride in his voice. "It's paid up for the year."

The year? Oh my God. This was real. We had a home.

Krit's words in the car came back to me, and I burst into tears as I realized what he had been trying to tell me.

"What's wrong, baby?" Rock asked, turning me to look at him. His big hands cupped my face. "I'll fix it. Just tell me what's wrong."

I shook my head. "Nothing," I said on a sob. "Nothing is wrong. It's perfect. Rock Taylor . . . you're my hero."

Chapter Thirty-Four

ROCK

I watched as Trisha slept in my arms. The early morning light was slowly filling the room. We had slept our first night in our new home. Krit had brought over all Trisha's things just before nine. He had moved him and her out after leaving her here with me. He said Fandora had been more than happy to get them out of there.

He had left here after giving his new address to his sister and kissing her cheek, telling her they were both free now. She had cried on me again. Yesterday had been a day of happy tears for her. Knowing I had made her this happy made me feel like a fucking king.

Her eyelids slowly began to flutter open and I watched, entranced by the perfect beauty that was all mine. Once she had them both open and those baby blues were focused on me, she smiled. That smile that made my heart stutter and my knees weak. Only this woman could do that to me. She'd be the only one who ever had that power. I didn't question that. She was my forever.

"Good morning," she said softly.

"Morning," I replied, bending my head down to kiss the tip of her nose. "Did you sleep well?" I asked already, knowing she had.

She grinned. "Yeah. I managed." The teasing glint in her eyes made me hard. But then, Trisha could yawn and I'd get hard. Didn't take much.

We had made love twice last night before falling asleep naked, wrapped up in each other. My woman was easily turned on too. She had made me pull off to the side of the road more than once, her mouth doing things to me that kept me from driving. She was my own personal piece of perfection. It was hard to keep her sated. Not that I was complaining, ever.

Her hand slid down to wrap around my arousal. "Mmmm . . . someone is excited this morning."

I pushed my hips toward her and she tightened her grip on me. Fuck, that was good. "You're naked in my arms. Hell yes, I'm excited. If this is what the rest of our life is going to be like, I'm worried we may never leave the bedroom."

She giggled and began sliding down me until her big lips

were wrapped around my cock. I threw the covers off us and to the floor as I rolled onto my back and slipped a hand into her long blond hair. "Ah, Trisha. That's so fucking good," I groaned. Waking up to my horny woman locking her lips around my dick was what dreams were made of.

She hummed her reply and I jerked in her mouth. She knew I loved it when she did that. "I'm licking that sweet pussy next. Spread your legs and let me see you touch it. But don't get off. I want you doing that on my face."

Trisha's eyes went wide, and she moaned as she pulled her knees up and stuck her round ass in the air, then spread her legs before slipping a hand between them. When she ran her finger through the wet slit she moaned again, and my dick fucking loved that.

"That's it, baby. Play with that pretty pussy," I said as I shifted my gaze from her pink lips wrapped around me to her fingers getting coated with her arousal.

It turned her on for me to watch her masturbate. I never managed to let her finish it before I pushed her hand away and either ate her up or sank into her. I had tried more than once to let her do it all, but it drove me wild. I couldn't.

"I'm gonna come," I panted as my balls tightened. "I want it on your titties," I told her. I loved it when she swallowed, but I also loved watching my release on her body. Her ass and tits were tied for my favorite places. She took her hand away from between her legs and moved between mine, taking me down her throat. When she gagged, I felt the heat lick through me. "Now, baby. I'm fucking coming," I warned her, and she pulled my cock from her swollen lips and aimed my release to shoot all over her tits as she held them out to make sure they got every shot.

When I was done, she lifted her gaze up from her tits to grin at me wickedly.

"Damn, that's sexy," I said, looking at her. "So fucking sexy," I repeated. My cock was already stirring, even though the head was still tender. Seeing her tits covered in me was enough to have me ready for round two, fast.

I was breathing hard, and my body was humming with pleasure. I grabbed a T-shirt from the side of the bed and sat up and slowly cleaned myself off her tits, then played with her nipples before slipping my hand between her legs. "Lie back, baby. It's time I ate breakfast," I told her.

She laughed, then moved up on the bed and lay down, letting her long legs fall open, revealing her bare pussy. When she'd first waxed it, I had been like a dog in heat for weeks. I had already been obsessed with her pussy, but seeing it bare had made me lose it. I wanted it all the time. I'd once pushed her into a janitor's closet and went down on my knees between her spread-open legs and eaten her out with her panties shoved aside. From that day on, if she wore a skirt she knew what would happen. I had no control.

When I lowered my head to lick her tight little clit, she cried out my name, and that was all it took for my cock to make a full comeback.

Kissing her candy-coated pussy was one of my favorite things to do. I loved the way her legs trembled and how she clawed at my shoulders and pleaded things that made no sense.

When her body tightened, I stopped and slid into her in one move.

"OH GOD!" she cried out, and her body tensed and shuddered under me. When Trisha had an orgasm, it was like she was lost for a moment as her body squeezed me tightly and milked me so damn sweetly I always followed right behind her.

"I love you," I said against her neck as my release filled her.

She was my home. Not this apartment, but her. As long as I was with her, I was home.

Chapter Thirty-Five

Present day . . .

TRISHA

Today was one of those rare days I was home from work while the kids were at school. Rock had left for work and taken the kids to drop them off. I was supposed to relax and enjoy my day. At least, that was what my husband had informed me before kissing me good-bye.

I wasn't sure what that was, exactly. My life was full and busy, and I loved that. Being a mom and a wife were the two things I had always wanted to be. When the kids went to stay with Preston and Amanda, I spent that time with my husband.

I had taken an extra-long shower this morning, then made myself an omelet for breakfast. I was about to call Willow, who I knew would be home with Eli, who was almost three now and very busy. Smiling, I thought about the last time we had gone shopping and how Low had run after him once he had unbuckled himself from the stroller. She had caught up to him in the window with the mannequin, where he was trying to pull the shoes off it. She had scooped him up just before the mannequin tumbled to its demise.

I reached for my phone at the same time my doorbell rang. Putting my cell down, I walked to the front door to find a wide-eyed Amanda Hardy. "What's wrong?" I asked, reaching for her hand. If Preston Drake had done something stupid, I was going to slap him myself. He hadn't gone through all the craziness to make this woman his only to mess it up weeks before the wedding.

"Sadie. She just called me," Amanda said, looking ready to cry. "She's coming home. Or here. She's . . . Jax broke off the engagement."

Jax Stone was the biggest thing in rock music, and each year he just got bigger. Sadie White had been a young girl from Sea Breeze High when he first met her and fell completely in love with her. It had been fun to watch a rock god fall for a girl I knew.

"What?" I asked, confused. The last time I had seen them, he was just as infatuated with her as I remembered. That was only a couple of months ago. Rock's cousin Jess was engaged to Jax Stone's brother, Jason. Jess was pregnant with a Stone kid. We had thrown them a baby shower and Jax and Sadie had come.

Amanda sank down onto my sofa and shook her head in a daze. "She sounded hollow. She wasn't sobbing like I would expect with this kind of news. She was just . . . empty. Void of emotion. I don't . . . I've never known Sadie to be so . . ." She trailed off.

Jax wasn't a player. He had fought to make Sadie his, and, unlike other celebrities, they had a healthy, happy relationship. Heck, if you googled Jax, then a million pictures of them showed up on the Internet. The world loved them.

"She didn't tell you why?" I asked.

"She . . . No. She . . . just said Jax ended things, and she was coming home. That's it."

I went to get my cell and dialed Jess's number. She'd know something.

Jax Stone and Sadie White were the kind that you expected forever for. The way he looked at her was the way Rock looked at me. Something was terribly wrong.

Epilogues

SADIE

Jessica, my mother, was coming to get me. When I had called her to tell her my plane arrived at ten at Pensacola International Airport, the closest major airport to Sea Breeze, she said she'd be there. We would have plenty of time to get back to Sea Breeze in time to get Sam, my little brother, from school. He was in kindergarten this year.

I put my hands on my stomach and closed my eyes. I wasn't ready to tell Jessica anything yet. She'd want to know. Jessica was nosy, and although she had grown up a lot from the woman who had raised me, and had become a good mom to my little brother, she was still not someone I wanted to talk to about this. I wasn't ready to talk to Amanda about it yet either, and she was my best friend.

I needed to process everything first. This wasn't just about me now. If I had told him, maybe he would have changed his mind and listened to me. But I didn't want the fact that I was pregnant to control his decision. I wanted him to listen to me and trust me because he loved me.

We had been through so much together over the past five years. Until yesterday I thought that we were rock solid. That nothing could penetrate what we had built. Then he had pulled the rug out from under me and walked away. It hadn't been my Jax who had done that. It was Jax, but he was different. It was a side of him I'd never seen.

It had also shown me I couldn't trust someone that way ever again. I'd fallen in love with him so easily. I had stars in my eyes the moment he leveled that blue gaze at me. He hadn't stolen my heart—I had laid it down at his feet after only knowing him a few months. And I had never taken it back. It was his.

Until now. When he had walked out of our house—or his house now—and not listened to me or asked me about what had really happened, my heart had shattered.

This morning, after I had stayed up all night crying and waiting on him to return, I had picked up the pieces of my heart and taken them back with me before stepping out of the mansion in Beverly Hills that had become my home.

It was his home. It had never been mine. And it never would be again.

The plane touched down and I looked out at the airport I wasn't familiar with. We normally flew into Sea Breeze in a private jet. But I had used the money that I had saved in my bank account to get a plane ticket. All I had brought with me were the clothes I could fit into the only luggage I had: a Louis Vuitton set that Jax had given me for Christmas two years ago. Everything else I had I left there. Most of it he had bought for me anyway, and I didn't want it.

There were some things, like my books and my pictures of Sam and Jessica, that I wanted. And there were some photos of Amanda and me at Marcus's wedding that I kept on the mantel. I asked Barbara, the head of the house staff, to get it packed up for me, and I left her money and my mom's address to ship it to me. She had hugged me tightly and told me that he'd come around. That she loved me and believed I'd be back soon.

I hadn't had the heart to tell her that I'd never be back. I had squeezed back just as tightly and promised to call and check in soon. Then I had walked out of the house, leaving my memories and dreams behind.

When I walked off the plane and headed for baggage claim, the numbness that had settled over me remained. I wasn't feeling anything. Nothing at all. Although I knew this was actually happening, I wasn't processing it well.

When I stepped off the escalator, Jessica was standing there, looking entirely too beautiful to have a child my age. The look in her eyes, so full of pity and pain for me, did something. It flipped a switch. Tears filled my eyes and I walked straight to her and dropped my carry-on at her feet, then threw myself into my mother's arms and began to sob.

"Oh, baby girl," she whispered. "I'm so sorry."

I knew I had to get a grip on myself. But seeing my mother had brought all the pain back. It was like I was reliving Jax walking out last night after telling me it was over.

"He's an idiot. I'm going to put a hit out on him," my mother said as she ran her hand over my hair. If I weren't hurting so much, I would laugh. Leave it to Jessica to threaten to have someone murdered.

I swallowed the next sob and took a deep breath. Then I pulled back, ducking my head as I wiped my face. Once I was sure I had it under control, I lifted my gaze back up to meet my mother's. "Hey."

She frowned and cupped the back of my head. "Hey, you. Let's go get those expensive-ass bags of yours and go home. Sam will be thrilled to see you when he gets home."

Being reminded that I would see Sam soon made this all easier. I nodded and picked up the duffel bag that matched the rest of my luggage and headed for the baggage carousel.

My bags came out eventually, and then we headed for the car. Mom was driving a newer Honda. She had finished school last year, and she was now a labor and delivery nurse.

Her income was good and she gave Sam a good home. I was proud of her.

We put my luggage in the trunk and the backseat. I had four bags with me, including my carry-on duffel, which I'd put all my underclothes and accessories in. I had made it out of the airport without anyone noticing me and approaching me. But I had also gone without makeup, my eyes were swollen from crying all night, and I had my hair in a ponytail with a baseball cap over it. A trick that Jax often tried, but it never worked for him.

My fame came from being Jax Stone's girlfriend, and then fiancée, over the past five years. Once he was seen with new girls, I was sure that would end. People would soon forget I existed. My hand went back to my stomach and I remembered that maybe I wouldn't be able to fade away. If the media ever found out that this baby was Jax Stone's, I'd have to go into hiding.

That is, if I ever told Jax. He may have been able to brush me away with ease, but I knew him well enough to be sure he'd want to know his kid. But could I trust him to protect me, too? And not let the media eat my life up?

JAX

Sadie's red Mercedes Roadster that I had given her just two months ago was still parked in the garage space that was designated for her. The Jaguar I had given her last year was parked in the next space over. The other seven were also full as I pulled my Escalade ESV into the last space. She wasn't gone.

I hadn't told her to leave. I had, however, ended things. Pain sliced through me as the idea of losing Sadie sank in. My head pounded from the hangover from hell I had woken up with in the penthouse at the Wilshire. I wasn't sure how I had even gotten there. After I had downed an entire bottle of vodka, things had started to fade away.

Sadie's betrayal and the pain of having my heart ripped from my chest had numbed me, keeping me from drinking my weight in alcohol. It had been a reprieve until I woke up in my own vomit this morning, feeling like I'd been run over by a truck several times.

I stepped out of the Escalade and closed the door. I had to face her again. She'd had all night to decide what to do. When I had gotten a shower this morning and slowly started to sober up, the fear that she'd be gone when I got home had claimed me, and it had been hard to breathe.

She had been making out with my drummer behind my back. Seeing it from my publicist before it was going to hit the media today had been as painful as having my body sliced open slowly with a blunt knife. I had beat my drummer to the point that he was hospitalized, then I'd come home and finished unleashing my fury by yelling at Sadie.

Never had I ever imagined my sweet Sadie could do

something like this. Just watching her try to explain it infuriated me and broke my heart at the same time. I didn't want her lies. I had seen the proof. She'd gotten jaded by this life, and somehow I had missed it. Just like I had feared it would, it had gotten to her. People devoting websites to what she wore and where she went had gone to her head. It had changed her. The girl I had fallen in love with was now gone.

I had lost her, and it was all my fault. Bringing her into this world had ruined her. I never should have touched her. My selfishness had turned the most beautiful woman inside and out into what I despised.

She would have to leave. She wasn't gone now, and she was probably ready to beg me so she wouldn't lose this life I had given her. If she wasn't Jax Stone's fiancée, she was no one. She loved that life, apparently, and she wouldn't go easily. Remembering that the girl I had fallen in love with was now gone would be hard. Forcing Sadie out of my house was going to destroy me.

This was a hell that I would never overcome. That I never wanted to repeat. No woman would own me again. Ever.

I was done.

I opened the door leading into the house from the garage and stepped inside. She wasn't waiting on me. At least I would have a moment before her groveling started and I had to stomach seeing the woman I had loved turned into a greedy monster that this world had created.

I dropped my keys onto the table, knowing someone would put them where they were meant to go, and headed to the hallway that led to the back side of the house. I didn't hear anyone, but I knew there were at least six employees here at the moment.

When I finally made it to the hallway that led to our bedroom, I stopped and took a deep breath. If she was in there asleep, I had to be tough. Hard. I couldn't let the vision of her sleeping in the bed where we'd had the best moments of my life get to me. Sadie would destroy me completely if I didn't do this. She had already ruined me. My soul was gone. She'd taken that and killed it. If I was going to get over this and move on, she had to leave.

I had to be the one to make her.

The door to our room opened, and Barbara walked out with a box in her hands. She paused when she saw me, and then her face hardened. What the hell? Had Sadie lied to her? Had the woman not seen the entertainment channels or looked at the paper today? Hell, we were going to be on the evening news before this was over. I wasn't the one she should be pissed at. But then, Sadie's sweet face could charm a damn snake. Beauty like hers blinded people.

"Is she in there?" I asked, angry that Sadie had turned my staff against me so easily.

Barbara scowled at me and shook her head. "No, sir. She's gone. I'm finished packing up all her things, although she asked that I not send her the clothes she left behind. She didn't want the things you had bought her. She had to take some of it because you've been her life for the past five years. But she wanted her pictures and some of the things she brought with her. I told her I would ship them to her mother's. The things she left are still in her closet. I figured you could decide what you wanted done with them."

My breath stopped and my chest tightened. "She's gone?" I asked, already knowing the answer.

Barbara nodded. "Yes, sir." She didn't elaborate. She nodded again and walked past me as if she couldn't get away from me fast enough.

I stared at the room, unable to move. She was gone. She'd left. She hadn't begged me to forgive her or made up excuses and lies. Last night she'd begged me to let her explain, but when I had yelled at her to shut up, she had, and she'd not said another word.

Not wanting to walk into the room I'd shared with Sadie, but knowing I had to face it, I moved toward it, preparing myself for her to be gone. The room felt cold as I entered it. Like any warmth or heat it had once had was gone.

I let my gaze travel over the room. The pictures of us were all gone, as were the pictures Sadie had of Jessica and Sam. The walls felt bare now.

The table on her side of the bed was now bare. Her lip gloss she kept by the bed and the book she had been reading were gone. The photo of the two of us on the night of our engagement party was also missing.

Had she taken that?

I knew opening her closet was going to rip me wide open. Her smell would be there still. Was I ready to face that? No. I wasn't. I headed to the master bathroom instead. Seeing all her lotions and perfumes and random jewelry no longer scattering the marble counter made the room seem dull and lifeless.

I'd made love to her on the counter so many times. Memories flashed in my head, making the pain so severe I had to bend over to get through it. My knees started to give out and I turned and walked away. I had to get out of there. I could smell her as I passed the closet, and I inhaled deeply.

How was I going to live my life without that smell again? Without hearing her cry out my name and cling to me while I filled her? What I'd had with Sadie wasn't something a man can forget. Pushing open her closet door, I stood there and let the scent of her engulf me. The purses I had bought her still lined the shelves, along with every pair of designer heels I had ever bought her. The outfits she'd worn to concerts, music awards shows, and to all the events we had attended still hung in the bags they were stored in. The only things missing were the Sadie clothes. The things that made her my Sadie. Her jeans, shorts, and T-shirts. She hadn't taken the expensive clothing.

She'd left all that. Did she even have a purse now? Did she have enough clothes?

Was she going back to her mom? In Sea Breeze? Where would she work? She had a degree in education that she hadn't used yet because we didn't have time for her to get tied down to a job. She had gone on tours with me, and when I had to travel she went too. Would she teach school now?

She would need money. Fuck!

I turned to look at the drawers that I knew held all her jewelry. Maybe she had taken that. She could sell it and live for years. I stalked over and jerked open the top drawer to see it completely full. I knew without looking that the others would be just as full. Reaching down, I picked up the five-carat diamond I had put on her finger when I asked her to spend forever with me. She'd cried and nodded before throwing herself into my arms.

Now it was nestled safely in this drawer. No longer on her slender finger, telling the world she was mine. She wasn't mine now.

Giving in to the devastation, I fell to my knees and dropped my head into my hands as the sobs broke through me.

I'd lost my world.

SADIE

Sam was cuddled up at my side, sound asleep, as I sat on the sofa in my mother's house, which was bought and paid for by

Jax Stone. It was a small three-bedroom house in a nice, safe neighborhood in Sea Breeze. I hadn't allowed him to put her in anything bigger than this. There was no point. It was just her and Sam. She kept the third bedroom fixed up for the times Jax and I visited her, although we rarely stayed the night here.

I had left my phone with Barbara. It was one more thing that Jax Stone had given me. I wasn't keeping a phone he paid for. I would call Amanda tomorrow when I was strong enough. Right now I needed to just let Sam distract me. He had shown me how he could write his ABC's, and he had sung the national anthem for me. We had colored several pages from the Teenage Mutant Ninja Turtles coloring book that I had sent him last week in the mail.

He had asked several times when Jax was coming. It had been like a knife to the heart every time he said his name. Jessica had explained to him the first few times that we wouldn't be seeing Jax anymore, but he had been concerned and kept asking me. He loved Jax.

I finally forced myself to look at my little brother and explain that Jax and I had broken up and weren't friends anymore. Then I had eased that blow by telling him that it meant I was moving into this house with him and Mommy. He had been upset over not seeing Jax and he kept bringing him up. But he was very excited about me staying here with them.

"I need to get him in bed. He has to be up bright and

early for school," Jessica said as she walked up to scoop him into her arms.

"Okay. Thanks for letting him stay up and keep my mind off things. I missed him."

She smiled. "He's the best medicine around," she said, kissing his forehead before walking back to the hallway that led to the bedrooms.

Sam's entrance into the world had been dramatic and destructive, but my mother had gotten it together and gotten medical help, thanks to Jax. She had become the mother I had never had. When I saw her with Sam, it warmed me. I loved seeing them both happy.

I pulled the throw off the back of the sofa and wrapped myself up in it before leaning back and closing my eyes. I hadn't slept last night, and the events of the last forty-eight hours were starting to weigh on me. I hadn't turned on the television all day. I wasn't sure when the news would hit that we were broken up. I figured it would be when a picture of him with someone new was plastered all over the media. I wasn't ready to see that.

Jessica had understood that.

"How you feeling? Ready for bed?" she asked, walking back into the room.

I nodded and forced my eyes back open. "Yeah. I am."

Jessica walked over and sank down beside me, then pulled

me into her arms. "I hate seeing my girl so broken," she whispered into my hair as I curled into her arms.

"Momma," I said in a whisper. I hadn't been going to tell her about the baby, but I needed someone to know.

"Yes, sweetheart," she said, holding me close.

"I'm pregnant."

She stopped petting my head, and I heard her inhale sharply, then exhale. "Does he know?"

I had been going to tell him. "I was surprising him with the news yesterday. I had it all planned out. I had had Barbara make us a picnic in the den downstairs where we have that amazing view at night of the lights outside on the hills. I had even set up candles everywhere that Barbara helped me light. I didn't tell her what I was doing all this for. I wanted to tell him first. But then he didn't come home or answer his phone. Three hours later I had blown out the candles and left the picnic downstairs and headed up to our room. That was where he found me." I stopped and closed my eyes. I wasn't ready to repeat what he had said.

"He yelled at me. Told me I was like all of 'them' and I used him to get things. Then he called me a liar and told me it was over before he left."

Jessica's body had gotten tense. I knew she was getting upset over this. "Did he explain why?"

I shook my head. "No. When I asked, he said I knew.

Then he told me to shut up. He's never told me to shut up. So I did."

My mother's arms tightened around me. "Oh, baby. I am so sorry. He's going to regret this, though. You mark my words, he will regret this. It will haunt him and he will figure out he's made a mistake and come back groveling. You make him beg at your feet for a long time before you give in. You hear me? Don't forgive him easily for this. But do forgive him. Because he's made a horrible mistake."

Relationship advice was something I would never take to heart from my mother. Jessica wasn't the smartest female when it came to men. Although, Sam had changed her on that, too. But still, she'd made so many mistakes in her life. I was one of her first mistakes.

"I can't. I won't ever trust a man that much again. Especially him," I whispered.

Momma sighed and rested her chin on my head. "He's really fucked, then, isn't he?" she said in a sad tone.

JAX

Sleep never came. All damn night. I had even gotten up and gone to another bedroom and tried to sleep in there. It didn't work. All I could see was Sadie's tearstained face as she begged me to tell her what was wrong. Never once had understanding flashed in her eyes. She had been so good at acting innocent.

How fucking long had my Sadie been a manipulative liar?

I made my way to the kitchen because I wasn't eating in the dining room alone only to remember every good memory with Sadie I had in there. I would grab some food and then get out of this house. Barbara came walking out of the kitchen with a frown on her face. She didn't smile when she saw me. Had the woman forgotten who she worked for?

"Excuse me, Master Jax," she replied formally. "I need to finish cleaning up the picnic Sadie had prepared for you downstairs that you never showed up for."

Picnic? "What?" I asked, annoyed by the fact that my staff was taking Sadie's side after I'd been the one who was burned.

"The picnic she had prepared with candles and such for you the other night. She was so excited about it too. She'd spent days preparing for it. She wouldn't tell me what it was about, though. I didn't have to ask her, really. I already knew. The silly girl forgets I am aware of everything in this house. I know what's in her trash can."

Confused, I stood there as Barbara stalked past me, seeming even angrier than before.

"What the hell are you talking about?" I yelled, causing her back to snap straight before she turned around to shoot daggers at me with her eyes.

"I'm talking about the surprise Sadie had for you, sir."

"What surprise?" I asked, furious that she was making me play this stupid game.

Barbara cocked one of her white eyebrows and tilted her head as she studied me. "It isn't for me to tell you, sir. It was Sadie's surprise. Not mine."

Fuck this! I wasn't living in a house with people who didn't respect the fact that I signed their fucking paychecks. "You are aware you don't work for Sadie, aren't you, Barbara? You work for me."

She frowned and then shrugged. "I've decided I'm not sure I want to work for you, sir. If you want to let me go, I will pack my bags and leave."

The anger boiled over and I met her glare with one of my own. "Did you watch the news yesterday? Pick up a paper? Get on the fucking Internet at all?"

Barbara snarled, then looked disgusted with me. "Yes, sir, I did. And I am sure Sadie did as well. Yet she never called you. Even though her phone is here in the office, I am sure she could have found another phone to call you. The thing is, sir, she didn't do that. My opinion on this is that if Sadie was guilty of what that photo is accusing her of and she was trying to manipulate you, then she'd have woven an excuse and called you, begging you to listen to her. She would have been willing to hear you yell at her and lash out at her if there was hope she could get you back." Barbara paused and pointed a finger at me. "But she didn't. Did she? She didn't call you, not once. Because you told her to leave. You yelled at her and called her names I never in my life imagine that sweet girl has been called. You broke her. She won't trust you again, and she will never give you another chance. So no, she wouldn't call and try to explain. She doesn't think you deserve an explanation."

Barbara untied the apron around her waist, then walked over and handed it to me. "I've decided I am done here. I realize I'm right and the beautiful soul you destroyed won't ever come back here. She's gone. And I don't think I can bear to stay here and watch your life spiral out of control. Because it will. You've lost your light."

Barbara turned and left. I stood there and listened as she spoke to the employees, and then I heard her giving her keys to someone. I didn't move. I wasn't sure I could. Because what she said made sense.

What the fuck was I missing?

When I finally moved, I didn't go to the kitchen. My appetite was gone. I went to the office instead. And sure enough, there was Sadie's new iPhone. The newest version had just come out last week, and I'd had it waiting for her when she woke up that day. She had said she'd just figured out the last one and wasn't ready for the new one, but she had laughed at me.

Then we had spent an hour in the shower together.

Without her my life meant nothing. This emptiness wasn't ever going away. What had Sadie wanted to tell me? Had she gotten a job? I wasn't sure what else would be important enough for her to make plans for a big night to surprise me.

Unless . . .

Holy hell . . . no.

She would have told me. She wouldn't have left.

"You broke her. She won't trust you again. . . ." Barbara's words came back to me.

I pulled my phone out of my pocket and dialed Jessica's number. It rang three times before Sadie's mother answered. "You have five seconds" was her greeting.

"Is she there?" I asked.

"Where else do you think she'd be?" she snapped back.

"Is she . . . is she . . . pregnant?" I asked, feeling a mixture of hope and fear battling in my chest.

Jessica let out a hard laugh. "Sorry, fucker. Your five seconds are up. Figure this shit out on your own."

Then she hung up on me.

I stared down at the phone in my hand and thought about calling back. But what good would that do? Jessica wasn't going to answer my question. Which made me think I was right.

I walked to the back of the house, where I knew I'd find someone who knew. My staff knew something. Jean-Claude, the butler, gave me an annoyed glance. Even he was mad at me.

"Is she pregnant?" I asked him.

He shrugged. "What's it matter to you? Could be anyone's,

anyway. Right?" he snarled, as if the idea disgusted him and he was disappointed in me for thinking badly of Sadie.

Then he walked away. I slammed through the kitchen doors and no one was there. I wondered if Barbara had fired everyone before she left. I wouldn't be surprised at this point.

SADIE

I woke up to the smell of coffee and my mother sitting on the edge of the bed. "I have coffee. You can't sleep all day. I'll even consider making pancakes if you'll eat them."

I stretched and covered my eyes from the light streaming in through the windows. "Morning, now go away," I mumbled, then closed my eyes again.

She pulled the covers back to let the chill in the room hit me. "Nope. We have shit to deal with, and I need you up and alert so we can face it and be prepared for the onslaught. Because, baby, it's coming."

That didn't sound good. I sat up and reached for the coffee cup in her hand. "The media knows," I said, before taking a sip and letting the heat of the coffee warm me up.

"Actually, they don't know shit. That's the problem. They think something happened, which I am trying to figure out myself. However, it does explain why Jax lost his mind."

Jessica reached behind her and pulled out the morning paper. "It's already in the local news. Entertainment section, first page.

Prepare yourself," she said, handing me the paper and taking the cup away from me.

I snatched the paper out of her hands, and in the center of the full-colored page was a photo of Nave Anikin, Jax's drummer and longtime friend, kissing me. That night Nave had been high as a kite and had taken me by surprise. He'd slammed his slimy mouth to mine, and I had been shocked frozen for a moment until it hit me what was happening and I kicked him in the balls. He had fallen backward and moaned in pain.

More than once I had almost told Jax about it, but I had hated to end their friendship. I was positive that Nave didn't remember it. He never acted weird around me or anything. I let it go and kept my distance from all the band members at parties. They got trashed and did stupid stuff.

When I felt guilty for not telling Jax, I remembered how guilty I would feel when Nave was without a job and Jax had lost his friend. I didn't think the outcome was worth telling anyone about this. It was two years ago. After all that time, I'd forgotten about it.

But someone had seen it and had waited until now to share the photo.

"Gonna tell me why the world thinks 'Jax Stone's fiancée is playing the band now'?" Jessica asked, repeating the headline of the article.

I dropped the paper and looked out the window. Jax had

seen this before it hit the media. He had seen it, and instead of asking me about it, he had attacked me.

"You didn't read it," Jessica said.

"Don't want to. It's all lies," I said, hating the realization that Jax hadn't trusted me.

"Not all of it. The fact that Nave Anikin is in the hospital with his jaw wired shut and several broken body parts is a fact. It is believed Jax Stone beat him within an inch of his life, but he isn't talking. He refuses to press charges."

I dropped my head into my hands and sighed. "What did you do, Jax?" I muttered to myself.

"You gonna call him and explain this?" Jessica asked me.

No, I wasn't. I should have been given that option before Jax beat Nave to a bloody pulp and tossed me out. Now it was too late.

I shook my head. "If he wants to believe the media, then let him. He doesn't want me to explain. If he did, he'd have let me before he ended things."

Jessica handed me the cup of coffee. "You're right, of course, but you love him, Sadie, and you're pregnant with his baby."

I would have to tell him eventually. But I needed my space first.

"I'll probably always love him. Doesn't mean I can ever trust him again. That doesn't make a relationship."

Jessica's shoulders fell. "Yeah. I guess that's true. But it still sucks."

"I need some alone time. I'll be out in a little bit. Let me know if we get media outside. I don't know how I'll handle it without Jax's help, but we will figure something out."

She nodded and stood up. "I'll go kick their asses. I don't need no stinking Jax Stone to keep my girl safe," she said, before walking out of the room and closing my door behind her.

By the time I had finished my coffee, I heard the first car doors. Peeking out my window, I saw a representative from every news channel in Alabama and the surrounding states, and national ones too. They knocked on the door and rang the doorbell. I was thankful Sam was already at school. This madness would have to end, though. Even if I had to go get a hotel room to move the focus off my mom's house.

I changed into some jeans and a long-sleeved shirt, then brushed my hair and pulled it into a ponytail before opening my bedroom door. Mom was in the kitchen, looking out the window with the phone to her ear. "Yes, she's here. Get your asses here and get them off my property before I have them all thrown in jail for trespassing. Y'all don't have enough room in your jail for all this shit. Do something about this now."

She was talking to the police. That would help some and for a while. But this would be an ongoing battle. I wasn't sure how to defuse the situation.

Mom hung up and turned to look at me. "It's started," she said, with an apologetic frown.

"Yeah, it has," I replied, sinking into the kitchen chair and wondering how my life had gone so wrong.

JAX

When my jet landed at the Sea Breeze private airport, there was security everywhere. I stepped out of the plane and was immediately surrounded by large guards. "Evening, sir. Most of the media is camped out at Miss White's mother's house, but we do have some hanging out like scum around the property line here. We wanted to get you to the car and out of the vicinity safely," one of the men waiting for me explained.

Shit. They were already after Sadie. She didn't have me there to help.

"Get them away from Jessica White's house. Now," I demanded, stalking toward the waiting black SUV.

"Yes, sir," the man replied.

"Where's my usual driver?" I asked when a man I didn't recognize opened the door for me.

"He, uh, quit, sir," the guy replied.

"What?"

"He quit, sir. This morning," he repeated.

I didn't have to ask why. It was because of Sadie. Even though there was a photo of her kissing my fucking drummer all over the news, they still took her side. The fear that I was the only idiot who hadn't trusted her and believed in her was growing worse.

Why hadn't I given her a chance to explain? Because the image of Nave's hands on her and his lips on hers had made me so crazy I lost my mind. I couldn't think straight from the anger and pain pumping through my veins.

I got into the SUV and glared straight ahead. "Take me to Sadie."

He had music playing, and one of the songs I had written for Sadie came on the radio. "Turn off the radio," I barked.

He quickly shut it off, and I leaned back in my seat, trying to figure out how I would handle it if she had an explanation for this. If I had been wrong and jumped to conclusions. Even if she didn't have an explanation . . . what if she was pregnant? With my baby? What the hell would I do then? I wasn't going to leave her and let her figure it out. As much as I hated that picture, I loved her. God, I'd always fucking love her.

The driver pulled us into the driveway of the house I'd bought for Jessica and Sam. Jessica's Honda was parked outside, and so were several police cruisers. My army of protection pulled in around us, and I didn't wait for them to secure things before I slung open the door and stalked to the house.

I didn't even knock before Jessica opened the door and her eyes shot hot daggers of hate at me. "What the hell are you doing here? You don't think you've done enough? You tossed her out like trash, and she's done with you. So go back to your fancy house and fancy life, and leave my baby girl the fuck alone!"

Never had Jessica ever spoken to me this way. I was shocked, but her reaction only made my fear that I'd completely messed up more real. But with that fear was a hope that my Sadie was still the same girl I had thought she was until I'd seen that picture.

"I need to talk to her," I said, ready to push past Jessica if I had to in order to get into the house.

"It's Jax," Sam's little voice said excitedly as he came running around Jessica's legs. "Sadie said he wasn't coming back and he wasn't her friend anymore. But he changed his mind!" Sam cheered and clapped his hands. "Want to come play Teenage Mutant Ninja Turtles with me and Sadie?" he asked, staring up at me.

She was in there. She was playing with her little brother. Fuck. That didn't sound like the woman I had accused her of becoming. God, what had I done?

"Go back to your sister. I'm sending Jax away. He makes Sadie sad," Jessica told him, and Sam's smile fell.

"Is he why she keeps crying?"

His question was my last straw. "I need to see her now," I said. I moved Jessica out of my way, then patted Sam on the head as I walked through the house looking for Sadie.

When I walked into the living room, she stood up from her spot on the floor with an army of turtles around her and backed away from me. "What are you doing here?" she asked, fear and pain shining all over her face.

Her eyes were swollen and red. She wasn't wearing any makeup, and her clothing was stuff she had bought for herself. The hardest thing to see was her bare hand. I'd grown accustomed to seeing my ring on her finger.

"Please go. You've said enough. I don't want Sam to hear this. Just go. I didn't take anything that was yours, or at least, I tried not to."

She wasn't making excuses. She was worried about Sam.

"Did you do it?" I asked her straight-out. What I should have done first.

Her back stiffened, and she lifted her chin in pride. "You don't get to ask me that now. The time for that is over. You need to leave."

Dread settled in my stomach. A sickness began to churn. "Sadie." I took a step toward her. "I should have given you a chance to explain. I messed up. But I'm asking you now. Did you do it?"

She backed away, putting more space between us. "Will you leave and not come back if I tell you?" she asked.

Not if she didn't fucking do anything wrong! Not if she hadn't been making out with my damn drummer. I was going to beg like a damn dog if that's what had to be done, but I wasn't leaving her if what I now suspected was true.

"No," I replied.

She frowned and moved her gaze to settle on something

else across the room. She didn't want to look at me. "The things you said . . . You'll need to leave. Regardless of my answer, what we had is over."

She hadn't kissed him. I could see it in the pain shining in her eyes as she stared at the spot across the room that wasn't me. "He was high. He doesn't even remember it, I don't think. He never mentioned it. But two years ago at an afterparty . . . he grabbed me and kissed me. I kneed him between the legs after it sank in what was happening. I should have told you, but I was sure he'd never have touched me had he not been trashed and out of his mind. I decided that it would save your friendship and that since nothing happened, it was pointless to tell you. I see now it was a mistake."

Nave had been in rehab eighteen months ago after he had hit an all-time low and almost killed himself with an overdose. He had been into heavy drugs back then. I didn't doubt a word she had just said. It made complete sense.

"I'm sorry." The words fell from my mouth, and even I knew it wasn't enough. It never would be enough.

"Me too," she replied, and finally shifted her focus back to me. "But you need to leave. It's over, Jax."

No. It wasn't over. I wasn't letting her fucking go because I'd made a jackass mistake. "I didn't mean for you to leave. I thought I'd come home the next day and you'd be there. I thought—"

"You turned on me. You didn't trust me. And I never want

to go through that again. I can't live in fear that something will happen again and you'll toss me away without asking me for my side. I don't trust you anymore." She said the words and tears filled her eyes. "I'm sorry. But you need to leave."

I wasn't leaving. I had to figure out how to save this. To save us. "Are you pregnant?" I asked, praying to God she was.

She stiffened, and her hands went to her stomach, answering my question without her saying a word. Finally she nodded. "Nine weeks."

When the breath went out of me, I had to grab my knees to hold myself up. The relief and joy were spun with pain and fear. She was pregnant with our baby. But she wanted me to leave her. I could never leave her.

"If you believe it is yours and want a part in its life, I won't punish the baby by withholding a relationship with its father. You will get to be as big a part of our baby's life as you want to be. But we won't be a family. That is a dream I can't trust now."

If I believed it was mine . . . Motherfucker, she thought I still didn't believe her about Nave. "Sadie, I know it's mine. I should have listened to you and let you explain about Nave. I was just so damn hurt I let the picture and the note that came with it rip me open. I acted on jealousy and heartbreak. I was shredded by the belief that you had changed because of the life we live. I couldn't think straight."

"And when things like that happen, you have to trust the

people you love. Not assume the worst of them. If you loved me the way I loved you, then you would have trusted me. You didn't trust me. So you didn't love me enough. I need more than that, Jax. I can't let you destroy me. I have another life to take care of now. This isn't about me anymore. It's about the child inside me."

"I love you more than life. I lost my mind because I love you so damn much. You're wrong about that, baby. So wrong."

She shook her head. "It doesn't matter. We are over. Except for the child we share, that is all that will be between us. Now please leave."

If it weren't for the unshed tears in her eyes and the heart-break all over her face, I would believe she really had closed me out. But I knew her too well. This wasn't over. We would never be over. I just had to figure out a way to prove it to her. Words weren't going to be enough. Actions had ruined us, and actions would have to save us.

SADIE

The next morning I woke up to my mother sitting beside my bed again with another cup of coffee and another newspaper. "Good morning, sunshine. Today I am the bearer of good news. The media is no longer stalking us, and Jax Stone has made a statement."

I sat up and took the paper she was holding out to me. "You really should google it and watch the video of it, or just turn on the news. He does a fantastic job. But here is the print version."

There was a photo of Jax with a microphone in his face, looking directly at the camera. "Jax Stone explains the rumors surrounding Sadie White's betrayal. It's false."

I dropped the paper onto the bed, slung the covers off me, and headed for my MacBook. Opening it up, I googled "Jax Stone," and it was the first thing that came up.

I clicked the YouTube link and watched.

"The rumors that came along with a photo of my drummer, Nave Anikin, kissing my fiancée, Sadie White, are false. Nave wasn't in his right mind two years ago. You all already know that he's gone through rehab since then and is in a better place now. But at that time he did things he wouldn't normally do.

"Kissing my Sadie was one of them. She pushed him off her, and they never spoke of it again. What you see here is a surprised Sadie White being accosted by an out-of-his-mind Nave Anikin. Not a lover's thing. Nothing romantic. Sadie is innocent of all the incriminations surrounding her, and I would appreciate it if my fans would stand behind her and support her through this cruel media stunt. Thank you." Jax stepped away from the microphone, and reporters were yelling questions at him as the bodyguards surrounded him and they walked off. Toward his jet.

"Looks like he's gone and so are the vultures," Jessica said, standing behind me.

"Yeah, it does." I had told him to leave and he had left. This was his apology to me, and I knew I forgave him. Even without this, I had forgiven him yesterday when he apologized. But I was so scared of being hurt by him that my fear hadn't allowed me to give him a chance to fix this. Instead I had pushed him away and he had let me.

"Are you going to be okay? Maybe since the road and driveway are clear you can go visit Amanda. She's called several times the past two days."

I needed to visit Amanda. I had to get out of this house and clear my head. I nodded, then reached for the cup of coffee in Jessica's hands and took a long drink.

"FYI, this is decaf. You can't have the real thing now that you're pregnant."

I hadn't thought about that. "Thanks."

"Hey, you took care of me when I was pregnant with Sam, so it's my turn to return the favor," she teased.

If I could still smile, I would have.

Two hours later Amanda Hardy opened her apartment door and threw herself at me. "Ohmygod, I've been so worried about you," she said as her arms wrapped around me.

"I'm sorry. I should have called. I just needed some time once I got here," I said, and she pulled back from me, holding on to my shoulders.

"He was in town yesterday, wasn't he? That speech he made that's gone viral was outside the Sea Breeze airport."

I nodded.

"Did y'all talk?" she asked almost cautiously.

"Yes," I replied.

A sadness touched her face. "So it's really over, then?"

I nodded again.

She grabbed my hands and pulled me into her apartment, then closed the door. "We need ice cream. I have cookies and cream and birthday cake. Which one?" she asked, walking toward her kitchen.

I followed her. "I'm not hungry," I said.

"You don't have to be hungry to eat ice cream," she informed me. She stopped at the window and froze. Then she turned back slowly to me. "Are you sure he's gone?"

"What?" I asked, confused.

She pointed out the window. "That's an expensive SUV parked out front, with one of the large men who follow him around standing outside of it. I don't know anyone other than Jax Stone who gets around Sea Breeze that way."

The doorbell rang and we stared at each other. It was Jax. I knew it without going to the door. What was he doing here?

"You want me to get it?" Amanda asked with a look of hopefulness.

I could say no and we could sit here while Jax stood outside the door, but that might draw a crowd. I didn't want more media attention. And if I admitted the truth to myself, I wanted to see if it was really him.

"I'll get it," I told her.

"Okay, um . . . I'll just stay here. Unless you need me."

I went to the door and opened it slowly, preparing myself for the fact that this might be Jason or just one of Jax's message boys. But when Jax filled the doorway, my heart squeezed. He hadn't left.

"I went to your mom's and she said you were here," he said, his gaze locked on me like he was trying to memorize my every feature.

"I thought you left," I said before I could stop myself.

"You're here, Sadie. I don't belong anywhere else."

I didn't know what to say to that. "Why are you here? Now?"

A sad smile curved his lips. "You don't have your phone. And I wanted to know if you've gotten an OBGYN here, and if so, when your next appointment is."

He had come to Amanda's to ask me about my doctor's appointment. . . .

"Oh, um . . . no. I have to apply for Medicaid first. I don't have insurance anymore, I guess." I stopped there. Jax had paid for me to have Blue Cross and Blue Shield. I didn't know what I was supposed to do now. I didn't expect him to keep paying for it. Even if I was pregnant with his baby.

He scowled. "Even if I didn't love you with every fiber of my fucking being, I would still make sure you had health insurance, Sadie. I know you think I'm some evil monster now, and I damn well deserve it, but I'm not. You will have the best and so will our baby. I love you both. You're my life even if I'm no longer yours."

My heart twisted at his words and I gripped the doorknob tightly in my hand. "I don't think you're an evil monster." Because I didn't. I wasn't sure what I thought anymore, in all honesty.

"I called and got the name of the best OBGYN in this area. I can get us a private meeting with him at any time so you can decide if you like him. Just tell me what you want or need."

He had been searching out the best doctor for me and the baby. My heart twisted some more.

"I'd like that. I need to see someone," I told him. "Dr. Andredai confirmed the pregnancy, so I would need to get my records sent to the new doctor from his office."

Jax nodded. "I'll call him and have that done as soon as you're sure what doctor you want here."

He was talking like he was staying here. He couldn't stay here permanently. "Jax, you're not done recording the new album. You need to go back to LA," I reminded him.

He let out a hard laugh. "Yeah, well, they can all fuck off. I can't finish it now. I've got more important things in my life."

"Your tour is in four months. The record has to release

before then," I argued. I had been with him through five album releases and tours. I knew how this worked.

"Tour needs to be canceled anyway. I can't leave with you pregnant. I'm not going anywhere you can't go," he said as if this made complete sense.

"Jax," I started, and he reached out and took my hand in his, stopping my train of thought.

"Sadie, you're it. My life. My world. Even if you don't want me or can't trust me, you are still my reason for living. And our baby—I won't miss one minute of that. I want to be by your side through the whole thing. We created a life together. I fucked up, and I'll live with that my entire life, but I won't leave you. I'll be here for whatever you allow me to be here for."

"You can't throw away your music career. That's insane. You're not thinking clearly," I started to argue, but the lump in my throat was growing and I had to push it down.

"Nothing matters if you're not in my life. Nothing," he said, and took a step toward me. "You and our baby are all that will ever matter to me."

At first I thought he was going to kiss me, and I was trying to decide if that was a good idea, when he dropped his hand, then turned and walked away.

What was I going to do with him?

"Please tell me you're going to forgive him," Amanda said from behind me. I figured she would have listened in.

"How can I? What if he hurts me like that again? How can I trust him?"

Amanda sighed and wrapped an arm around my waist. "I understand. I thought after finding out my boyfriend got paid to sleep with women that I'd never be able to trust him again either. That was a lie I never imagined I could forgive. But I did. Because he loved me enough for both of us when I didn't think I could love him anymore. Right now Jax is loving enough for you, him, the baby—which, I might add, I am ecstatic about that news. God, that man is pitiful. Come on, Sadie, give him a break." She laid her head on my shoulder. "You're gonna be Jax freaking Stone's baby momma." She giggled.

A smile tugged at my lips at her ridiculous description. Maybe she was right. Jax had never done anything like this before. We had fought, but that had always ended in really hot sex in crazy locations. This had been our first big one. And my emotions were so raw right now I wasn't dealing with things right.

"I don't want to love him. But I do. So much."

Amanda sighed. "Join the club. He has several major fan clubs all over the world. And women offer to have his baby millions of times a day online."

She was making a joke, but she was right. I laughed this time. It wasn't a full laugh, but it was a laugh.

"I'm going to go home and talk to Jessica, and then I think

I'll go to his house and see him. Now that we've both had time to think and process, we need to talk."

"Yes, you do," she agreed.

JAX

When the doorbell chimed through the house, I knew it was her. No one else would come looking for me here. I hadn't told a soul where I was. But Sadie would know. I ran down the stairs and headed for the front doors, unlatching them and jerking one open before the first chime ended.

She was standing there, dressed in the same jeans and thermal shirt she'd had on earlier today. Her eyes met mine, and I could see she was nervous. I hated to think of Sadie ever being nervous to come to me. I wanted to reach out and grab her and hold on for dear life. But she didn't look like that was what she was hoping for. I stepped back and motioned for her to come inside.

"Opening your own doors?" she asked me, and I wasn't sure if she was teasing or not.

"There isn't any staff here. They left earlier this evening when I told them they could go," I explained. Although even if someone had been here, no one would have beaten me to the door tonight.

"Oh, well, that's probably best. We don't need anyone listening to us talk about this."

I agreed. I wanted Sadie alone and to myself.

"You hungry? Did you eat a good dinner?" I asked her, thinking about the fact that she needed to eat for not only her health but our baby's as well.

"Jessica made me pasta salad and baked chicken," she said with a small smile. That little smile gave me hope. I hadn't seen a smile on her face since the morning before I'd lost my mind.

"Good. Want dessert?" I asked. "Mrs. Mary left chocolate cake."

She shook her head. "No. I'm still too full."

Then we could talk. "Let's go to the great room. More comfortable seating in there, and I've got a fire going."

"Okay," she replied.

Before I turned to lead the way, I held out my hand to her like I always did before we went anywhere. It was a habit and one I loved. She always came to me so willingly. This time her eyes went from me to my hand and she froze. Yet another thing I had ruined. My girl didn't come to me anymore with ease.

"You don't want to touch me anymore?" I asked, unable to keep my mouth shut and be patient with her.

She jerked her gaze back up to meet mine. "I . . . Of course I do. I just . . . God, Jax, this is so confusing."

I stepped toward her, reached down, and took her hand, threading her fingers through mine. "Not this part. This," I said, holding our joined hands up, "is never confusing."

She let me take her to the great room without moving her hand away.

I took her to the butter-leather sofa facing the fire and reluctantly let her hand go so she could sit down. I wasn't moving across the room from her, though. We were going to talk, but we were going to be close to do it.

I sat down beside her and turned my body to face hers while draping an arm along the back of the sofa. "You came to see me. Not going to lie, Sadie, I'm really damn hopeful right now."

She clasped her hands together in her lap and looked at them instead of me. "Can you promise me that you'll never do that again? Never assume something of me without asking me first?" she asked, and then slowly turned her gaze to look at me.

She was here to give me a second chance. "Baby, I swear to God, I'll never hurt you like that again. I would have to hear it straight from you before I believed anything bad of you ever again. And even then I don't think I'd believe it. My girl is still as perfect as she was when I fell in love with her. I questioned that, and it will eat me up for a really long time. I can't forgive myself, but I really want you to. I'll do anything you ask. Just love me again, Sadie. Please."

She inhaled deeply and kept her eyes fixed on me. "If I hadn't been pregnant, would you have come for me?"

I had asked myself this same question already. The answer was yes. I wouldn't have been able to make it another night without seeing her and making sure she was okay. "Yes. Even when I believed that bullshit, I was worried about you. I missed you. I never stopped loving you."

She studied me for a moment, and then she nodded. "I believe you."

I was ready to pull her in my arms now. "Can you love me? After all this . . . can you love me again?" I asked her, needing to know if her heart was going to be closed off to me forever.

She smiled. "I never stopped loving you. I wanted to. It would have been easier. But I can't turn it off with a switch. I've loved you for five years, and I'll love you for a hundred more."

I held out my hand again. "Come here." I waited to see if she would. Her small hand lifted, then slipped into mine. I tugged her over to me and grabbed her waist, then deposited her in my lap.

"I'm gonna need you now," I told her as I pulled her mouth to mine.

"M'kay," was her response just before my mouth covered hers.

SADIE

Jax broke our kiss just long enough to pull my shirt up over my head and toss it aside. He got my bra off next, before easing me back onto the sofa while kissing the tops of my breasts and circling each areola with his tongue. When he bit each pebbled nipple, I cried out. But then, he knew I would.

I loved the tight sting from his teeth.

"We'll be sweet later. Right now I need you," he said as his hands started working on my jeans and tugging them down my body. Once he had me completely naked, he stood up and stripped.

It was a sight that the majority of the female world fantasized about but that I got daily. The Jax Stone strip show. Nothing was better than that.

He kissed his fingertips, then touched his side, where my name was tattooed in the shape of an infinity sign.

"If you'd never believed me . . . would you have removed that?" I asked.

Jax lowered his body over mine and kissed a path up my stomach, through the valley between my breasts, then along my collarbone. "I was hurt, Sadie. But once I came out of my pain haze, I would have realized it didn't fucking matter if you'd done it or not. I can't live without you, baby."

"I'd never hurt you like that. I don't want you to believe I could do that to you," I told him.

"Mmmm," he murmured in my ear. "Well then, make my ache feel better right now. Stand up for me and stick out that sweet ass."

My body was already tingling, but those words made the tingles burst into flames. He moved off me, and I stood up and bent over to grab the back of the sofa.

His hands circled my waist and he groaned. "Fuck, Sadie. This ass is amazing." He put his hand between my legs. "Spread them wider."

I did as I was told and waited anxiously for him to fill me. This was normally how we ended fights. In one thrust he was inside me. I cried out his name and held on to the sofa as he moved his hips so that he slid in and out of me. "My sweet ass," he said as he slapped one of my butt cheeks.

Whenever we fought, Jax needed sex that reminded him that I was his. It eased his mind. This was part of it. Claiming my body. The good part for me was that his words made me hotter.

"No one else gets to touch this. Just me. It's always just been mine," he said in a reverent tone as he caressed the spot he had spanked. "Tell me it's mine, Sadie."

Biting my lip, I kept from smiling, but I didn't say anything. When I didn't tell him he got more demanding, and I loved that. His hand slapped my other butt cheek. "Tell me," he repeated, and I pressed back against him with my bottom and he growled.

His hand slid down to my swollen clit, and he stopped moving. I was panting now, needing him to take me over the edge. "Tell me," he repeated in a deep, demanding voice.

"It's yours. I'm yours," I said, desperate for him to take me there.

"Fucking right I am," he growled, and slammed into me as his thumb played with my tenderness between my legs.

I started to tremble as my orgasm built. "Now, Sadie," he said, and just like that I exploded as his arms wrapped around me to hold me up, and he emptied his release inside me.

We both shuddered and cried each other's name. Then we were on the sofa and I was curled up at Jax's side as he pulled a cashmere blanket over us. I laid my head on his chest and traced the infinity with my name on his side.

"Thank you. You always know when I need it like that, and you make it fucking amazing," he said as he kissed the top of my head.

"You're welcome, but I enjoyed that mind-blowing orgasm at the end, so it wasn't all for you," I teased him.

He chuckled and pulled me closer. "I'm gonna want you again in a few minutes. I'll be sweet this time," he said.

I wasn't sure I needed sweet right now. "Maybe we could do sweet tomorrow. I kind of like the idea of you fucking me against the wall next."

"God, I love you," he said as his thumb slipped under my chin and he tilted my head back so that I was looking at him. "You tell me you want to be fucked, and I'm hard instantly. You ready to deal with the reaction you created?"

Laughing, I moved on top of him. "I think I can handle it."

He reached for his jeans on the floor and reached into the pocket. "First, this needs to go back where it belongs. Where it will always belong. For fucking ever," he said as he slipped my engagement ring back on my finger. Then he kissed it. "Don't ever leave me again, baby. Even if I act like a shit. Slap me or get naked. Either will get my attention."

I grinned, bent down over him, and kissed his nose. "Why didn't I think of that the first time?"

He chuckled and reached back to squeeze my bottom in his hands. "There won't ever be a next time. I know how it feels to walk into our room and have you not be there. I never want to fucking feel that again."

I kissed his forehead, then trailed kisses down the side of his face to meet his lips. "Good," I said before I sank into a kiss that would get me pushed up against a wall, full of Jax Stone, within minutes.

Marcus and Willow from *Because of Low*

WILLOW

Eli was standing on a stool beside me, helping me roll up cookie dough, then pat it flat. His preschool class was having a party tomorrow, and he was assigned to bring the cookies. This was all he had talked about all week. To a three-year-old little boy, cookies were of upmost importance.

"Can we save one for Daddy?" he asked as he rolled the dough more than it actually needed, then pounded it down with his little palm.

"I think he'd love that. Why don't you give him that one?" I suggested.

Eli beamed up at me. "Okay! I will," he replied. "But he won't want to eat it alone. Maybe I should make one for me, too."

Leave it to my little boy to reason out how he could get a

cookie tonight. Grinning, I pretended to think about it. "Okay, I guess that makes sense."

Marcus was over at Trisha and Rock's, helping Rock build a basketball court in their backyard. They had said the project would only take a few days. It had taken two weeks so far. Trisha said if they'd stop playing ball themselves, they could finish the court.

I heard the front door open. Eli stopped what he was doing and jumped from his chair, then took off running toward the door for his father. Every day Eli looked more like Marcus. I touched my stomach and wondered if the baby girl in there was going to look like me or have more of her father's beautiful features. I certainly wouldn't mind if she did look like him.

"Larissa!" Eli cheered, and I stopped rolling cookie dough and went to wash my hands. If Larissa was here, then something was up. My sister hadn't called me to tell me my niece was coming over.

"Take Larissa to your room, buddy. Y'all play for a bit while I talk to Mommy," Marcus told him. That was another major flag. He never sent Eli to play when he hadn't seen him all day. He normally kept Eli attached to him until we tucked him into bed.

I headed for the hallway just as Marcus appeared in the doorway of the kitchen. His face was etched with concern.

"What's wrong?" I asked, not even needing to ask if something was wrong. I could tell from his face.

"Tawny's gone. Her clothes and things are gone. She's left,"

Marcus said, looking at me with pain in his eyes. He didn't want to have to tell me this. The fact that my sister was the awful woman who had ended his parents' marriage and was now married to Marcus's father while they raised their daughter—that was something we had accepted and dealt with.

"What do you mean?" I asked, having a hard time believing my sister had just left her daughter. She was a lot of things, but surely she wasn't this selfish. She loved Larissa. At least, I thought she did. I knew she at least loved Jefferson Hardy, Larissa and Marcus's father.

"Dad got a call from Larissa's school. It was three thirty, and no one had come to get her. Tawny wasn't answering their calls. Dad said he went and got Larissa and then headed home to see if Tawny had fallen asleep or something. Her car was gone, and so were her things. She's left them. She's also had her phone turned off and sold her car for cash. It was found already at a sleazy dealership in Mississippi. Dad's making phone calls and trying to track her down. He didn't want Larissa to hear this. She's asked about her momma twice now."

I grabbed a chair at the table and sank into it. "Oh God."

Deep down I had always worried that the happily-ever-after life Tawny had wanted wasn't going to work for her. I just hadn't imagined *this* scenario. I never thought she'd leave her daughter. Without a word.

Marcus pulled out the chair beside me, sat down, and slid

his hands over my knees. "I need to tell Mom before someone else does. She needs to hear this from me and not a nosy friend of hers. I don't want to call her and tell her over the phone. And I need to let Amanda know too."

"Yes, go tell them. I'll get the kids in bed. We still have cookies left to make, and then we can read a book. Don't worry about us. Just call me and keep me updated if your dad hears anything. I'll think of anyone who might know where to find her, and I'll make some calls once the kids are in bed."

Marcus nodded and slipped his hand into my hair, then pulled my head to him so he could claim my mouth in a kiss. "I love you," he told me, then kissed me harder.

I enjoyed the taste of my husband but pulled back after a few seconds because he wasn't letting up. "You need to go," I reminded him.

He nodded. "Yeah. I'll hurry. Tell Eli I promise to make it up to him tomorrow. I'll keep him home from preschool and he can go to work with me."

I laughed and shook my head. "Tomorrow is party day, and he's taking the cookies."

Marcus grinned. "Okay then, movie night tomorrow night," he said.

"Much better," I agreed.

He kissed me one more time, quickly. "God, you're sexy as hell. It's hard to come home to this and then run off again."

"Hurry back," I told him, then slapped his tight ass.

He winked at me, then headed for the door. I waited until it closed behind him to go check on the kids. I wanted to hug Larissa close to me and let her know I loved her. She needed some extra love right now. Tawny wasn't the best mom, but she did love Larissa. Her father wasn't the most affectionate man in the world, though.

Eli's little head turned when I walked into the room. He had Larissa helping him put together his newest Lego set.

"Where's Daddy?" he asked, looking perplexed. He had thought Marcus would be the one to come get them.

"He had to run to Grana's. He'll be back soon," I assured him. Then I turned my attention to Larissa. "Hey, princess, got some hugs for me?" I asked Tawny's Mini-Me.

"Hey, Lowlow," she said as she stood up. She ran over to me and threw herself into my arms. She held on extra tight and I squeezed back. She was six now, and she knew something was wrong. "I love you bunches," I told her.

"I love you more bunches," she said, and my heart broke a little more. How could Tawny leave her? More than once in my life I had hated my sister. This was one of those times.

"We're making cookies. You want to help Eli and me finish them up?" I asked her. She pulled back and nodded excitedly.

"YAY!" Eli cheered, and ran from the room back toward the kitchen.

Larissa giggled, and I stood up. Her little hand reached up and slipped into mine. Her little grasp was tight, and I held on to her just as tightly as we followed Eli back into the kitchen.

MARCUS

When I pulled into my mother's driveway, my father's truck was already there. What was he doing? The jackass comes running to my mom for help when his current wife leaves him? Dammit!

I jumped out of my truck and slammed the door before stalking up to the house. I didn't knock. I just opened the door and walked inside. I could hear their voices from the living room, so I headed that way. My dad better have had a fucking good reason for coming over here. And when I say good reason, it better be because Tawny's sorry ass was here hiding in the garage. If that wasn't the reason, then he was getting my fist in his face.

My mother didn't need this bullshit.

"I thought she said it was fine. She was good with the divorce," I heard my mother say. I stopped walking.

"I heard the door. Wait," my dad demanded, before appearing in the hallway. Our gazes locked.

"I need an explanation. *Now*," I commanded.

Dad let out a sigh and ran his hand through his short hair. "I shoulda figured you would be coming over here."

"That ain't an answer, Dad," I snapped.

Mother stepped out into the hall, saw me, and sighed. "Hello, honey. Come on in and sit down, you two. Might as well tell him everything, Jeff," she said as if this was all normal.

Nothing about my parents talking calmly in the same house was normal. He had ripped my mother's life apart and sent Amanda into a depression when he'd gotten Tawny pregnant and run off with her. Now, four years later, he's hanging out in the house I grew up in like this was totally okay. It wasn't fucking okay.

"Fine," he replied, and turned to follow my mother back into the living room.

I watched as my dad did exactly as my mother said.

Beyond confused, I went into the living room.

"Sit down, Marcus," my mother said, pointing to the sofa across from the one she and my father had sat down on.

"No, Mom, I think I'll stand," I replied, shoving my hands into my pockets and staring at my parents like they were aliens. Which was how they were currently acting.

"Jeff, you start," Mother said, and leaned back, crossing her legs. She was completely composed.

"Tawny and I were getting a divorce. She had . . ." He stopped and looked at my mother, who nodded for him to continue. Then he turned his attention back to me. "She had found out I was coming here the nights I got home late. I admitted to her that she was a mistake I had made during a hard time in my marriage. I wasn't in love with her. Larissa was the only reason we were together." Dad held up his hands and shrugged like this was okay. "She took it well. She said she hated being married and trying to live up to the expectations set by your mother. Not that she ever came close. She wanted out too. She agreed to joint custody of Larissa. She was thrilled over it, although she tried to hide it. I had the paperwork drawn up and everything was going smoothly. Until she found out yesterday that the prenup she had signed said that if we have joint custody of Larissa, she will not get child support. I will take care of all Larissa's needs, but I won't give Tawny money. It also states that she doesn't get anything—no money at all from me. I told her that I would leave her the house in Mobile because I wanted Larissa to have a safe home when she was with her mother. Tawny screamed that she needed more than that and didn't want to be stuck in that house in Mobile." When he stopped, my mother reached over and wrapped one of her perfectly manicured hands around his. As if this were some insane dream, my father opened his palm and threaded his fingers through my mother's. What the fuck?

I pointed at him, then at my mother. "Are you saying . . . that you've been here like BEEN here?" I asked, my voice raised.

Mother looked almost guilty, and my father squeezed her hand. "Yes, Marcus. That's what I mean. I've been in love with your mother for the largest portion of my life. When work stress got to me and I was working more than I was at home, I made a mistake that would have destroyed most families. But your mother was there for you kids. She kept the three of you together and helped you heal."

I stared at my mother. "And you're just . . . letting him back in?" I asked, remembering the days I had held her while she cried and I swore I would hate my father for the rest of my life.

"I didn't let him in easily, if that's what you're thinking. He worked for it for a while. But I love your father. A small portion of what happened was my fault too. I had neglected his needs and put my organizations above him. I'm not giving him an excuse, because what he did wasn't excusable, and I swore I'd never forgive him. But I have found that when you love someone, you can forgive just about anything. Eventually."

This time I sat down. I needed a minute.

"This isn't how we wanted you or Amanda to find out. We were going to go through with the divorce and slowly ease you both into having family dinners where I attended. We intended to be careful with your emotions and let you accept it over time. However, Tawny decided to run off, so everything changed."

"So you're still married to her?" I asked, looking at my parents' hands still joined.

"No. She left the signed divorce papers on the kitchen table with a note that she couldn't take Larissa. And that was it. Nothing else."

Shit. How was the woman I adored more than life related to this heartless bitch? It was a question I had asked myself more than once over the years.

"Larissa is going to come stay here. With us," my mother said, snapping me out of my thoughts.

"What?" I asked, again thrown into shock.

Mother tilted her head and leveled her eyes at me. "You know I love that child. Once I got over everything, I started letting Amanda bring Larissa around. I've grown attached. She needs a mother right now, and I intend to give her the love she needs. If Amanda is okay with it, I'm going to turn her room into Larissa's. My hope is Tawny will grow up and come back to be a part of her daughter's life. But until that day comes, I will be this little girl's mother. She laughs like my own baby girl did once, and when she smiles she looks just like the daughter-in-law I love dearly. She even has Willow's mannerisms. And then I see your father in her too. Nothing about that little girl isn't lovable."

Larissa was charming. But my mother was willing take her in? And love her? Holy shit, the woman really was a saint. I'd always put my mother on a pedestal, but now I saw that she deserved it. Shaking my head, I stood up. I needed to go home and talk to Low. She would help me deal with all this.

"I can't . . . I just . . . I need to go," I said, then turned and walked to the door.

"I'm sorry I hurt you. I'm sorry that I lost myself and that I put too much on you as you were growing up. I messed up, Marcus. I'm sorry, Son. But I do love you, and I am so damn proud of the man you've become. You have a wonderful mother."

I stopped and turned to look at him. I needed to say this, and I needed to say it now before I let this fester until I blew up.

"Cherish her, then. For the rest of your goddamn life you'd better cherish that woman. If you ever hurt her again, you won't get a third chance. I'll make sure you don't get much of anything. I was a kid when you left her last time. I'm a grown man now, and you'd better not fuck this up."

I didn't wait for him to speak. I left the house.

WILLOW

Larissa was tucked in tight on the bottom bunk of Eli's bunk bed. She had been asleep for the past ten minutes. Eli, on the other hand, was just now finally giving up and closing his little eyes. I knew he was waiting on Marcus, and I tried everything I could to get him to go on to sleep. But he was determined to kiss his daddy good night.

The front door opened and closed, and Eli's little eyes snapped back open. He looked at me with a sleepy smile. "Daddy's home?"

I nodded. "Yeah, baby, he is," I whispered.

Marcus filled the doorway, then walked into the dark room.

He pulled me to him and kissed my head. Something was wrong. I could feel it in the way he was holding on to me. Like I was his lifeline.

"Daddy," Eli whispered, and Marcus's head turned. He let me go and went to stand by the top bunk as Eli rubbed his eyes and sat up.

"You still awake, buddy?" he asked.

"Waiting on you," Eli said, as if that made complete sense and Marcus should know this.

"I'm sorry, dude. I had to go see Grana and help her with something. Tomorrow it's movie night. Me and you," he told him, ruffling his hair, then kissing him on the forehead.

"Can Momma and Larissa watch it with us?" he asked.

Marcus paused a minute. I wondered if Tawny had returned. "Larissa is going to go visit with Grana tomorrow and stay there a little bit. But Momma can watch it with us. I bet she'll even make us popcorn," Marcus told him.

Why on earth was Larissa going to my mother-in-law's? To swim with Amanda? It just seemed odd. I mean, she'd been there before, but still, why now?

"Will you, Momma?" Eli asked.

I smiled quickly and nodded. "Yes, sir. I might even make brownies, too."

Eli did a small whoop and gave his dad a high five.

"Shh, you two. Larissa is asleep," I reminded them.

247

Marcus leaned over and kissed Eli's cheek. Eli lay back down while Marcus pulled his covers back up. "Sleep tight, buddy," he said. "I love you."

"Love you too, Daddy," Eli replied.

Marcus bent down and brushed Larissa's curls off her face, then kissed her forehead. "My princess has some hard days ahead. But I think things are going to be okay," he said quietly as he stood back up.

His hand slipped into mine and he led me out of the room.

He kept going until we got to our bedroom. Closing the door, he locked it, which was a habit most nights. Eli had once walked in on us doing things we'd had a hard time explaining. We were more careful now.

"My parents are together. Tawny and Dad were getting a divorce because of this. Tawny split when she found out that with joint custody of Larissa, she didn't get child support. Dad offered to give her the house in Mobile, but she said she didn't want that. She also left a note, with the signed divorce papers, saying she couldn't take Larissa."

I sank down onto the edge of the bed, letting his words sink in.

My sister had left a note. She had really left Larissa. Oh God. And Marcus's parents? I glanced up and looked at my husband as he paced back and forth, running his hand through his hair.

"He was at my mother's house. My dad was there like he belonged there. Like he hadn't broken her heart. Like he hadn't thrown her aside like she meant nothing to him. But she was holding his hand, Low. Holding his fucking hand."

Wow. Just . . . wow.

He stopped pacing and looked at me. "He's moving back in. Mom is going to raise Larissa and give her the motherly affection she needs until Tawny decides she can be a mother. I swear, Low, my mother is some saint. The Catholic church needs to take note of this fucking madness."

My man was a swirl of emotions, and I was just sitting here letting him lose it. Standing up, I wrapped my arms around his waist and held on to him. "Take a deep breath," I told him. "Your mother has always been a saint. We already knew that. This shouldn't surprise you so much. She's accepted Larissa and been nothing but sweet to her. You've seen it. I've seen it. She's a good woman. The best. She raised you, didn't she?"

Marcus sighed and pressed a kiss to my ear. "My mother is a wonderful woman, but she isn't the best," he said, before kissing my cheek. "I got the best right here in my arms."

Smiling, I slipped my arms up his chest and latched them around his neck. "They're adults, Marcus. If they are ready to fix what was broken, it's their decision. Your mother is a smart woman. She wouldn't agree to anything lightly. I have no doubt in my mind that man had to beg and prove himself. As for Larissa, that's a really good place to grow up. If my stupid, selfish sister doesn't come back, Larissa will have a life that she deserves. She'll get to see what real princesses have in life. A mother like yours and a father who wants to be at home with his family. Not hiding from the raging, crazy woman he's married to." I ran my hands through the hair at the base of his neck and smiled up at the man who owned my soul. "Things will be okay. Believe that."

Marcus lowered his head and kissed my lips gently. I opened to him immediately, and his tongue slipped inside my mouth, tasting me as if I was his last meal on earth. I enjoyed having my mouth ravished by my husband.

When he pulled back, he gave me that intense look I loved. It excited me. "You are my center. You keep me grounded. You calm me down. You help me see things in a better light. What I feel for you is so much more than love, Willow Hardy, that I don't have a name for it."

I loved it when he said things like this. I had a very romantic man. "Then show me," I whispered, stepping back and slipping my T-shirt off. "You get a bonus tonight. I smell like cookies," I teased him.

A predatory gleam lit his eyes as he loosened his tie and jerked it off, then began unbuttoning his shirt as I slipped off my shorts and panties under his watchful eyes.

"You can smell like cookies, but that pussy better smell like my sweet pussy is supposed to smell. I've been thinking about it all damn day. Especially with the naughty little teasing text you sent me at lunch."

Laughing, I backed up and crawled to the center of the bed. I sat on my bottom, then let my legs fall open. Marcus's eyes turned into hot, smoldering flames as he swore, then yanked his slacks off along with his boxers and came at me.

His head went directly between my legs, and I fell back, gasping for air. He didn't take time to tease me tonight. His tongue ran directly over my clit before he fucked me with his mouth.

MARCUS

Low always tasted so amazing. The more turned on she was, the sweeter she tasted. I kept her legs open with both my hands until she was crying out and gasping for breath after coming down from her first orgasm. She tried to push me away and I didn't let her. I loved licking her while she went crazy from how sensitive the release had left her clit.

When she started panting and begging me, I grinned, then let her have a moment. She gave me a sleepy smile that said she loved it when I was bad. While she got her breath back, I slid my hands over her swollen stomach. My daughter was safely tucked inside there. We had a couple more months before Crimson Joy Hardy was due to enter our lives.

The third bedroom had already been painted a sky blue with purple polka dots. Every weekend Willow had something else for us to work on in Crimson's room. I knew how quickly it all went. It seemed just like yesterday my little boy was born. I wanted to soak up every minute of it. Not waste a moment.

Willow was biting her bottom lip and watching me closely when I looked back up at her. "It's big," she said.

I nodded. Her stomach was getting bigger. But she knew I loved that she was carrying my baby in there. I moved my hands up to cup her breasts. "And these are bigger."

Willow started to laugh, but it became a moan as I pulled one of her perfect pink nipples into my mouth.

After lavishing both her breasts with attention, I moved up to kiss the spot on her neck that made her squirm. Then I grabbed Willow's waist as I rolled onto my back and pulled her on top so that she was straddling me. "Take it, baby," I told her, moving her hips back until the tip of my erection pressed into her.

"M'kay," she breathed out, then lifted her hips and sank down on me. "AAAAAH!" she cried.

Another beautiful thing about pregnancy was that she always felt swollen inside, too. It was incredible. "So good," I told her, reaching up to grab her breasts in my hands as she began to ride me.

Her soft moans and sweet little cries made it hard for me

to lie back and let her control this. I didn't give her this control often, but sometimes I needed her to take the reins.

Letting go of her breasts, I slipped my hands around to grab her ass while my eyes stayed glued to the sight of her tits bouncing in my face. Fucking gorgeous.

"I love this ass," I said, squeezing it. She fell forward on both her hands, and her tits were in my face. My mouth went to work eating them up while Willow said my name and told me how good it felt. When she sat back up, the hard tips were wet from my kisses, and my cock throbbed at the sight.

"I'm gonna come," she said, looking at me as her eyes began rolling back in her head. "I'm . . . coming," she wailed, and the silky walls encasing my dick squeezed and spasmed, pulling me right into the release with her. I jerked my hips and met her thrust as I spilled inside her. Marking what was mine.

WILLOW

Three days after my sister had decided to run off and leave her daughter, Larissa moved into Amanda Hardy's old bedroom. With the help of Amanda, Margaret, and me, Larissa made the room her own. She even seemed clingy with Margaret, like she knew that this was the woman who was going to take care of her. Who was going to love her. She trusted her already. My sister had denied her so much.

Margaret Hardy would fix that, though. She would love with

that big heart of hers, and everything would be okay. Marcus had even calmed down and accepted that his parents were back together.

Amanda had reacted very differently from her brother. She had squealed and jumped up and down. She had been upset about Tawny leaving Larissa like she had, but she was beyond thrilled that her dad was moving back in to be with her mother. Marcus didn't understand it at all. Since I hadn't really had a life like the one Amanda had grown up in, I didn't understand it completely. But I told Marcus my guess was that after growing up with two parents you love, it's never something you give up on. She was a little girl who had lived a fairy tale, and then it was jerked away from her. She had just been handed that life back. A week before her wedding, too.

I couldn't imagine there was a bride-to-be as happy as Amanda Hardy was right now.

"Still hard to believe they're back together," Marcus said, walking up behind me and slipping his hands around to rest on my stomach. "But I'll admit, deep down it feels good. Even if it scares me because I'm not ready to trust Dad, seeing my parents together makes things seem right again. I just wish Larissa had that."

I thought about my sister, who had never been happy about being a mother. Even when Jefferson Hardy had decided to give her the family life, she had only stayed happy for a short time.

She didn't like playing house. And she didn't like being stuck with an "old man." I know because she told me that just a few weeks ago when I went to visit Larissa.

I wasn't sure anything could make Tawny happy. And Larissa deserved a life with love from her parents. Tawny and I hadn't gotten that kind of home life. Maybe that was why she was so screwed up. But I wanted Larissa to have a chance for more. I didn't want her to end up like her mother. I wanted her to love life and not live always searching for something.

"Larissa really likes your mom. She's her little shadow. I think she knows Tawny is gone. Margaret said the last time she asked about her mother was the first night she spent here. When Jefferson was here to tuck her in, she seemed content. She hasn't asked again."

Marcus sighed and rested his chin on the top of my head. "Mom loves her. I haven't seen her this happy since Amanda and I were living at home. She's baking cookies and making cakes with Larissa just like she used to do with us. I think it's going to be good for both of them. If Tawny comes back, then she's going to have to fight Dad for Larissa. He already said he's not agreeing to joint custody. He's filed abandonment charges against Tawny and gotten full custody of Larissa. He said he'll allow Tawny every other weekend, but that is it. He doesn't trust her not to come back into Larissa's life and turn it upside down and leave again."

"Good. Because that's what she'll do. I think deep down, in her own weird way, she loves Larissa. But having a child isn't something Tawny ever wanted."

I turned around in his arms and kissed the man who gave me my fairy tale. I had never expected a Marcus Hardy in my life. I'd had a friend in Cage York and I had thought that was all I would need. Cage had been my protector. But I had found out that I needed all-consuming, wild, magical love. And that's what I got with Marcus.

My fairy tale wasn't over. It was just beginning.

Preston and Amanda from *Just for Now*

AMANDA

When I was sixteen years old, I was positive that I would never love anyone as much as I loved Preston Drake. Sure, he was my brother's best friend and only saw me as a kid, but I loved him. Every daydream I had was of Preston. Even though he was a major player and he flirted with all females, I loved him. Not once did I think I could love a man as much as I loved Preston Drake.

And I was right. Even at sixteen I was so very right.

In three days I was supposed to be marrying the man I had loved for the past seven years.

Tears burned my eyes as I ran my fingers over the white satin of the dress I'd had made specially for me. For our special day. The day I had dreamed of long before Preston Drake loved me.

"Amanda?" Willow asked as the door to my bedroom opened. "Are you okay?"

I started to nod, then said, "No."

Her hand rested on my shoulder. "What you saw . . . I think that text message was something that he needs to have a chance to explain. Once Marcus finds him, if he lives through that, then you should talk to him, sweetie. Don't call it all off just yet. Give him a chance, if he isn't in the hospital, to explain himself."

I didn't want Marcus to hurt him. Even after seeing that text on Preston's phone. He'd left his cell in the car when I had dropped him off this afternoon after we'd had his final fitting for his tux.

> Greg: Same place. Ready to be fucked just as hard as you did it last time. My pussy is all wet.

I had sat in my car, staring at the text message from Greg, who I knew he worked with. And was, the last time I checked, a guy. Twice I had almost dialed the number, but I hadn't been able to. Checking his other contacts, I found another Greg but it was a different number. The only explanation was that he was using Greg's name to save some . . . some . . . slut's phone number. I felt ill again.

"I just can't believe this. I thought . . . I mean, he acts like he loves me. He is always with me. He never once gave me any hint. . . ." I trailed off, staring at my wedding dress.

"He adores you. That's why this text makes no sense. So just take a deep breath. Let's have a glass of wine. You can come back to my place if you don't want to stay here."

I had stayed in the apartment I lived in with Preston, waiting on him to come home. He had to work tonight. Marcus had gone after him immediately. Willow had called Dewayne and Rock and warned them to go after Marcus. She was afraid he'd kill Preston.

"I just don't see how there can be an explanation for this," I said, sitting down on the chaise beside me.

"If you called the number, maybe that would answer your question. Maybe Greg was . . . joking. . . ." She trailed off.

That wasn't believable. But neither was the fact that Preston was cheating on me. He loved me.

"I'm calling the number. There has to be an explanation. We need to figure it out before your brother kills your groom," Willow said, taking the phone off the bed, where I had dropped it and left it.

She pressed the number and held it to her ear. I watched her, holding my breath. When her eyes went wide, my stomach dropped and my chest felt like it had exploded.

"Who is this?" she asked, going from surprised to angry. "Jill who? . . . Willow Hardy. Now answer my question." Willow was scowling. "How do you know Preston Drake?" Willow closed her eyes and swore. "She hung up."

I couldn't talk. Or breathe. Or talk. I bent over and grabbed my knees, wanting to wake up from this nightmare. That had to be it—this had to be a nightmare. An awful one.

"Her name is Jill Vick. She was at the club. I heard Jackdown playing in the background."

Jill Vick. It wasn't Greg. It was Jill Vick.

I didn't know a Jill Vick. I didn't know anyone with the last name of Vick.

Oh God, I wanted to scream but I couldn't breathe enough to scream.

"I was trying to stay positive about this, but now I hope Marcus beats his ass," Willow said, throwing the phone back on the bed.

"We're getting married," I said, looking up at Willow. "Saturday. We were going to promise forever to each other. I don't understand."

A sob burst out of me, and I curled up on the chaise lounge and let the pain in my chest free. I had to do something before I completely broke in two.

"I'm sorry, sweetie. I'm so sorry." Willow sat beside me, trying to soothe me, but it didn't help. Nothing would ever help. I couldn't get through this. I would be broken for life.

PRESTON

After the crew Dewayne had working on the condo going up on the east beach left, I went through and made sure things were unplugged and expensive shit was locked up. It was Dewayne's night off from doing this.

When he brought me on a couple of months ago, I had agreed to take over some of his responsibilities so he could get home to his family. Soon I would be taking off for a week for my honeymoon, so I owed him extra time this week. He didn't demand it, but I felt like it was the right thing to do. He'd hired me as soon as he could give me a job that paid what my bouncer job had paid.

I hated working nights, and he knew it. This had fixed my problem. I had a fiancée at home I wanted to be snuggled up to naked in my bed. And fucking. Lots and lots of fucking. Grinning, I picked up the trash that had been left behind, then headed down to the Dumpster. These guys were pigs. They left empty Coke bottles and chip bags all over the place. What was the big deal with cleaning that shit up?

Headlights lit up the empty parking lot, followed by a second set of headlights and then a third. What the hell? Was there a parking lot party about to go down that I had to put a stop to? I just wanted to get home to Manda.

Stupid teenagers.

Closing the lid of the Dumpster, I turned and started

walking toward the headlights when a car door slammed and I heard Marcus yell my name. Confused, I stopped in my tracks.

"You motherfucker, I'm going to KILL YOU," Marcus roared, and I realized something was seriously wrong. Marcus was my best friend and would be my brother-in-law in a couple of days. Was this a joke?

"Preston, back the hell up! Marcus, stop and ask him first before you commit a murder." Rock's voice came out of the darkness.

"He's right, Marcus. Let him talk first. If he's fucking around, we'll all beat him to hell," Dewayne called out.

I heard a scuffle and Marcus yelling as Rock demanded he calm down.

Moving out of the headlights that were blinding me, I walked toward them. Once I had the lights out of my eyes, I could see my three best friends in what looked like an argument. Marcus was swinging his arms and yelling about killing me, and Rock and Dewayne were holding him back.

"Can I ask why the hell you want to kill me?" I asked, trying to figure out what had brought this level of anger out in normally levelheaded Marcus.

"Are you fucking around on Amanda?" Dewayne asked with a snarl.

What the fuck? "No! Fuck NO! Why would you even think that? Is that why he's lost his mind? He thinks I fucked around on Manda? My Manda, who I adore more than my own life? Are you shitting me?"

"I told you he didn't do it. There's an explanation, Marcus. Calm down, dammit, and let him talk," Rock said, jerking Marcus's arms back as Marcus glared at me. Some of his rage had cooled as he studied me.

"Let me go. I'll let him talk first. But he better have fucking proof! Do you understand me? FUCKING PROOF!"

Dewayne eased up on him. But Rock didn't let go.

"Promise you'll let him talk. Amanda is gonna want him alive if he didn't do anything wrong," Rock said.

"I swear. Let go," Marcus snapped, jerking free of Rock's loosened hold on him.

Then he started toward me, and Rock was back on him.

"I just want to ask him!" Marcus roared.

"Then do it with several feet between you," Rock replied calmly.

"Fine," he yelled, jerking free again, his eyes so full of pain and fury that it wasn't even Marcus. I'd never seen him like this. Not even the time he had found out I was seeing Amanda.

"You left your phone in Amanda's car today. You got a text from Greg," Marcus said in disgust. "But Greg doesn't have a pussy that you can get wet. So Amanda was confused about that and found out that the Greg you used to work with is in your phone but with another number."

"Wait . . . what?" He was talking about wet pussies and Greg from work. None of this made sense.

"Do you have a woman's number that you're disguising as Greg's in your phone because you're fucking her behind Amanda's back?" Dewayne asked.

"HELL NO!" I yelled, furious that they would even think this.

"I knew he wasn't cheating on her," Dewayne said, throwing up his hands like he was always right. This time he was. Very fucking right.

"You've got some serious explaining to do, then, because I just got a text from Willow. She called that number on your phone, and a girl named Jill Vick answered. She was at Live Bay. Willow could hear Jackdown playing in the background. When she asked her how she knew Preston Drake, the girl hung up on her," Marcus said, not sounding as angry, but more like he needed proof.

"Does Manda think I've cheated on her?" I asked, looking at the three of them.

"Of course she does! She's a fucking mess!" Marcus replied, raising his voice again like he was about to go off. This all made sense now. Amanda . . . I had to get to her. Holy fuck. She'd be crushed.

"I gotta go talk to Manda. Now," I said, stalking past them.

"NO! You're going to Live Bay with us first. We're finding

this Jill Vick and figuring out why the hell her name is in your phone under 'Greg,'" Marcus said, reaching out and grabbing my arm.

I loved the guy, but he was not going to make me let Amanda think for one more goddamn minute that I had cheated on her. Fuck that! "I. AM. GOING. TO. AMANDA."

"Okay, look. I'll go to Live Bay with you," Dewayne told Marcus. "I know you're angry because Amanda is so torn up, but he needs to get to her to fix this. She needs him to fix this. We will go figure out who the hell Jill Vick is."

I pulled free of Marcus and ran to my Jeep. When I jerked open my door, I remembered where I had heard that name before. "Jill Vick is that brunette at Live Bay with the big fake tits and the pink tips in her hair. She's been coming on to me for months. I just ignore her and she goes away."

"I know her! You asked for another server last week because of her," Dewayne said, snapping his fingers.

I nodded. "Yeah. That's how I know her name. Rick told it to me when I went and asked him to keep her away from my table for the rest of my life."

AMANDA

"Hey," Willow said, standing up when her phone rang and putting it to her ear. "He didn't. I knew he didn't. . . . Stop it, Marcus. . . . You're too emotional about this. Calm down.

Do Dewayne and Rock believe him?" She was pacing back and forth, and I was hanging on her every word. "See! They believe him. . . . I'm only staying until she tells me to leave. I won't stay here until I hear from you if she wants me to go." Willow looked at me and rolled her eyes. "Go figure this out and leave us alone. She's going to be fine. He's telling the truth. You know in your gut he is. . . . Love you, too," she said, then hung up.

"Preston is on his way here. Marcus said he's desperate to get to you. He swears he's never touched anyone. And Jill Vick is the waitress at Live Bay with the pink tips in her hair, who Preston asked Rick to move from his table last week. Apparently, she was flirting with him."

I remembered her. She had really big boobs. I was jealous, and Preston got pissed when she wouldn't take a hint. I didn't know he'd had Rick move her, though. "She kept showing Preston her cleavage, or trying to. He wouldn't look at her, and he kept pulling me closer to him until he was behind me, wrapping his arms around me. But I have big-boob envy, and hers made me feel self-conscious."

Willow sat down beside me and patted my knee. "I think we have a case of someone setting Preston up. He's on his way right now. When he gets here, do you want me to stay or go?"

I didn't want to talk about all this in front of my sister-in-law. "You can go," I told her. "Thank you for coming, though."

She nodded. "It ain't over yet. If Marcus doesn't get some proof, he's going for Preston's throat. Dewayne and Rock are still with Marcus, though, so they should keep your fiancé alive and your brother out of prison."

If she wasn't being serious, I would have laughed.

The door to our apartment flew open. "Manda!" Preston called out.

"He's here," Willow said, then stood up. "I'll let y'all talk."

Willow was walking to the bedroom door when Preston called my name again, sounding panicked.

"She's in here," Willow replied, and just as she walked out, Preston came barreling in, looking like a man on a mission.

"Swear to God I have no idea how that number got in my phone, and I'd never, ever fucking ever touch anyone but you," Preston swore, wrapping his arms around me and pulling me up. "I don't fucking know that bitch. I just know that's what Rick called her when I asked him to keep her the hell away from me. She got to my phone somehow. I'll figure it out, but I need you to believe me. Never, baby. God, I would never do that to you."

The desperation in his voice as he held me so tightly that it was hard to breathe was all I needed. He was telling me the truth. This was the man I knew. The one who loved me. The one I trusted with my life. My happiness.

He was mine.

"I believe you," I said, reaching up to touch his long blond locks. "But I can't breathe."

His arms loosened a little, and he continued to stand there breathing hard. "Swear to God," he said again.

"I know," I assured him.

He was rocking me now as we stood there. I could feel his heart slamming against his chest. This had scared him. All my pain was now replaced with sympathy for him.

"Did Marcus touch you?" I asked, trying to pull back to look more closely at his face, but he wouldn't give an inch. He buried his face in my neck.

"No. But only because Dewayne and Rock held him back while he yelled."

"I'm sorry," I said as I tried to calm him.

"Don't apologize for this, Manda. This shit was because of me. Not you." He finally eased back enough to kiss me softly. "Just you, pretty girl," he said against my mouth.

"I know," I assured him.

"Gonna marry you, pretty girl."

I smiled at that reminder. "Yeah."

"I need you now, pretty girl," he said as he trailed kisses down my neck and started making quick work of my clothes. "Hate that you've been crying. I don't want you to cry. I hate it. I want you smiling," he said against my collarbone. "Only crying you need to do ever is my name when you come."

"Mmmmm," I agreed as his attention moved to my breasts, which he was very happy with. He didn't seem to mind their small size. He made me feel perfect and beautiful.

He was my one.

PRESTON

My phone had been swiped from the table last week, when I was dancing with Amanda while Rock went to get a beer. The waitress Rick had sent me was a friend of Jill's, so she did the dirty work. Jill's plan was to send naughty texts until either Amanda saw it or I called the number, and if I called, she was going to try to talk me into meeting up with her.

The other waitress had sung like a bird when Rick called all the waitresses into the office and asked about it. Jill was fired and so was the waitress who had helped her.

Marcus no longer wanted to kill me, and we were now back to being happy about becoming family. Not that we weren't family before. Dewayne, Rock, and Marcus had been my family since second grade.

I hadn't been allowed to see Manda all day. All damn day. Willow said it was bad luck. I tried telling her that nothing about Manda was bad luck. Willow had laughed at me and gone back to guarding Manda.

The wedding pictures that could be taken without me seeing my bride had been taken, and we had one hour before the wedding started.

I wanted to see my pretty girl. I didn't like waking up to find a note on the pillow explaining that Willow had come and taken her away in the middle of the night. I wasn't liking my future sister-in-law very much right now.

"Where are you going?" Dewayne asked with a smirk when I turned down the hall of the chapel toward the bridal room.

"Exactly where you think I'm going," I told him.

"Just got an hour. Can't wait until then?" he asked, amused.

"You're next. When you're wanting to see Sienna and they won't let you, you're gonna need help. You cover for me, and I'll pay you back."

Dewayne nodded, then chuckled. "Yeah, I got this. Go see your girl."

That was an easy sale.

I ducked behind the corner when the door to Manda's room opened. Willow said she needed to go check on Eli and she'd be back soon to help her. Smiling, I waited until Willow was out of sight and I made a run for it.

The knob turned and I slid inside the room, closing the door and locking it behind me.

Amanda sat with her back to me, wearing a white lacy bra

and matching panties, and—God help me—she had on a frilly garter belt and thigh highs. Jesus . . .

I must have made a sound because Amanda spun around.

"Preston," she said in a surprised whisper. Then she started giggling. "Willow will be furious."

I could give a rat's ass what Willow was gonna be. "Stand up," I said as I took the three long strides that got me to my bride.

She stood up, and the shiny white heels I'd missed with all those other things—now I saw them.

"How the fuck am I gonna get through the ceremony knowing you look like that underneath?"

She shrugged playfully. "Maybe that's why you weren't supposed to see me."

That was bullshit. I didn't like that rule at all.

"Manda, you're wearing a thong," I said as her ass cheeks flashed me.

She nodded.

"Sit on that table," I said, stalking her as she backed up and sat down on the table behind her.

"Now, pretty girl, spread those legs for me," I demanded, and she did exactly as I told her.

"Put those heels up on the table, but keep those thighs open wide."

My bride did just like she was told. Grinning, I went down on my knees, watching her face while I did it. She had known while I was telling her what to do exactly what I was planning on doing to her. She wanted it.

I had a naughty bride. "When my pretty girl walks down that aisle toward me wearing white, her thighs will be wet from my mouth," I said, then pulled the thong aside and began tasting the sweetest candy in the world.

"Preston," she moaned, reaching for my head. Her hands grabbed fistfuls of my hair. I glanced up at her—her knees up high, legs wide open, arms reaching down to hold my head between her thighs—and it was the most fucking erotic thing any groom had ever seen on his wedding day.

"Sweet pussy," I said with a smile, and she watched me with her mouth open. Those lips of hers had been perfectly painted the pink I'd helped her decide on. I wasn't going to mess that up until I got to kiss her in front of everyone.

There was a knock at the door, and her eyes went wide as her attention shifted from me to the door.

"It's locked," I assured her.

"But—"

I didn't give her a chance to stop me. I played dirty and began sucking on her clit like a lollipop.

Her eyes rolled back in her head, and she kept her hands on my head to hold me there.

"Yes, yes, yes, there, just . . . like . . . that," she panted, then squealed as she tried to keep from being loud.

I lapped at her until she laughed and pushed me back.

Grinning up at her, I wiped my mouth on my sleeve and stood up.

"Don't clean that up. I want to say my vows knowing how wet you are. That little slip of satin you're calling panties is drenched. I like it."

Amanda was gasping for breath.

"Oh, for GOD'S SAKE! Preston, you have the rest of your lives for that!" Willow called through the door.

Amanda started giggling again.

"I get to taste you all night," I said, licking my lips. "Before the reception I'm gonna need to fuck my wife."

She puckered her lips like she was thinking, then sighed. "I guess I can manage letting my sexy husband have his way with me before we go dance and celebrate."

"That's good to hear," I said, then pressed a simple kiss to her nose so as not to mess up her makeup. "I'll let you get dressed. See you in a few. I'll be the handsome guy at the end of the aisle. Come get me."

AMANDA

Preston blew me a kiss, then opened the door and walked out.

"I can't believe you," Willow said to him as she walked past him into the room.

Preston shrugged, and Willow burst out laughing.

When she closed him out of the room, she turned to look at me. "I guess if a bride is going to have wild, hot sex with her groom minutes before the wedding, it would be Preston Drake's bride," she said, then shook her head and laughed again.

"I'd say I'm sorry I let him stay, but . . . I'd be lying."

"I know you would. I walked up on the end of that and heard enough to know I didn't want to stand too close to the door. I backed up and kept everyone else away. You can thank me later for saving your mother the horror of hearing you get off."

My face flushed and Willow laughed. "Girl, it is too late for blushing now." She turned and got my dress, which I had taken off after pictures so I could use the restroom and touch up my makeup. "Time to get this back on you. It's almost time for you to marry Sea Breeze's very own reformed playboy."

Oh, he was still a playboy. He was just my playboy.

I lifted my arms and let Willow drop the dress over my body.

"Sadie, Eva, Trisha, and Jess are all ready to go line up. I made sure before I left them to come back and check on you.

"Thank you." I wasn't sure how I would have done all this without Willow. My mother had her hands full with my little sister, Larissa. The idea of that just made me happy.

Willow had stepped up and been the best matron of honor on the planet. My maid of honor was Sadie, but Willow had left Sadie to take care of the bridesmaids while she took care of me.

"You're welcome. I loved being a part of this," she said, smiling at me in the mirror. "Let's go do this thing."

Larissa met me in a dress full of white tulle as I opened the door. "You look like a princess," I told her as she spun around for me.

"Daisy May has a dress just like mine. Just like you said." She beamed at me.

"I'm sure you both will be the prettiest princesses these people have ever seen."

Larissa held up her basket. "It's empty. Daisy May is keeping my petals until it's time. I kept spilling 'em by accident. She didn't want me to lose them, so she said she'd keep 'em for me."

"Come with me. I'll get you and Daisy May ready to walk down the aisle, and you can toss those petals all you want then. Just wait until it's time," Willow said, grinning at me as she moved Larissa back to the lineup.

The bridesmaids had already started to head inside as the music played. Sadie smiled at me. "You look beautiful."

"Thank you."

Her eyes flashed with humor and she leaned close to me. "Is it true you had a little pre-wedding activity?"

I blushed again. Apparently, they all knew what had happened.

"Figured it was. You are marrying Preston Drake, after all," she said, then turned to walk through the doors.

"Girls, you two go once you see me get to the front," Willow told them, and they both nodded.

"I got this," Daisy May informed her.

I bit back a laugh. She really did know what she was doing. She'd done this a few times already.

Daisy May nudged Larissa. "Your turn. I'll be behind you."

Larissa shot me a toothless grin and headed down the aisle too fast, and she tossed all her flowers out before she got halfway there. But she was happy and adorable.

My dad walked up beside me and held out his arm.

"He makes you happy, right?" he said, staring down at me.

"Yes, Daddy. More than anything in the world."

He nodded. "Then it's time I gave you away."

I patted his arm and held on as we walked toward the man of my dreams waiting on me.

Jason and Jess from *Misbehaving*

JESS

I stood in the mirror and looked at my stomach. It was at that point where I looked fat but not yet pregnant. I was not liking this phase of pregnancy. My boobs were bigger, and Jason loved that. Until today I hadn't minded. I loved knowing I was carrying Jason Stone's baby.

He had classes all day, and I wanted to surprise him at lunch. But when I texted him, he said he had to go to the library and get some research pulled from some blah, blah, blah stuff I didn't understand.

By the time he had responded to my text, I was already on the Harvard campus and had to turn back home. Girls my age in tight tops and cute little skirts were all over the place. They were all smart and brilliant like Jason.

They looked like everything I wasn't, and I hated them. I hated that he was there every day with girls like this. I was at home, pregnant, taking online college courses because my nausea had kept me from actually attending college in person.

While I'm at home, he's here living this life of a college guy, seeing everything I took away from him. Tears welled up in my eyes as I stared at my own image in the mirror in front of me. I was ruining his life. I was nothing like what he deserved. I had my body and looks before, but now I was losing that. And what did I have to even compete with those girls?

I had nothing. I was exactly what his mother said: a weight around his neck.

"Jess, baby, are you crying?"

I jerked my head up to see Jason coming in the bedroom door, moving directly toward me with a purposeful stride. Seeing him dressed in his white oxford shirt and slacks, looking like one of those elite people I will never be, sent my tears into a full-blown sob.

I hadn't made friends here because no one liked me. I wasn't like them. I was different. Jason had even distanced himself from his friends at school, and I knew why. They didn't like me. I wasn't classy and rich.

Jason's arms wrapped around me and pulled me against his chest. "What's wrong, sweetheart?" His voice was so gentle and patient. Which only made me cry harder.

"You're scaring me, Jess," he said in a concerned tone as he ran his hand over my head and then cupped my face. "Tell me what's wrong. I hate it when you cry."

I tried to control my sobbing and wiped at my tear-streaked face, now worried because I was going to be all red and blotchy. Not exactly something a man wants to come home to.

"Did someone say something to you? I swear to God, if they did I'll kill someone. . . ."

He had been forced to defend me a lot in this world. Now that we didn't do much with the crowd he used to spend time with, it happened less. I shook my head so he would calm down. I sniffed, swallowing the newest onslaught of tears that were threatening to break free.

"I'm a . . . weight . . . around your neck," I choked out, my words followed by a sob.

"Has my mother been here?" he asked angrily.

I shook my head. "No, it's just . . . just the tr-truth," I hiccupped. "I don't fit into your wo-orld. I just hinder your life," I finished, then buried my face in his neck.

His arms tightened around me. "You put color in my life, Jess. You make me laugh and you give me a reason to smile even when things are shit. You're my world. I don't know where you're getting this bullshit. Baby, you never have been and will never be a weight around my neck. Ever."

I kissed his neck and sniffled. His words always helped steady me. The past month, my emotions had been a roller coaster. My usually tough exterior had crashed and burned somewhere around twelve weeks of pregnancy. And everything hurt my feelings.

Jason ran his hands over my widening hips and cupped my butt. "No panties. Fucking hot," he said, smiling. "I missed you today. I hate being away from you. Wish I could put you in my pocket and take you to all my classes with me."

Smiling through my tears, I kissed him under his chin. "I'm too fat to fit in your pocket."

His hands squeezed my bottom. "Nothing about you is fat. You're all curvy and soft and carrying my baby. Most perfect woman on earth."

He finished that sweet little statement, then covered my mouth with his. Hungry for him, I groaned and opened for him. The gentle thrust of his tongue as it swirled around mine before moving out and back in made me think of where else I'd like him to thrust into my body. I wiggled against him, feeling his erection pressing against my stomach.

"I forgot to mention: always so hot and horny, too," Jason said with a growl, reaching for my nightgown and taking it off me with one hand. I was completely naked underneath.

"What do you need, baby? What will make you feel good? It's time I take care of my girl, and I'm all yours."

When a man like Jason Stone offers to take care of you, it's hard to put thoughts together.

Anything he did would make me happy. But I knew exactly what to do to make him crazy. He had always loved my butt, but now that it was fuller he was positively obsessed with it. I turned around and put my palms on the dresser, sticking my bottom out to him and spreading my legs. "I need to be fucked," I said sweetly, glancing back over my shoulder at him and batting my eyelashes teasingly.

His eyes were hot and glued to my ass. He lifted his gaze from what I was asking for to look at me. I made the pouty lips that drove him nuts. "Hurry, I'm all achy."

"Holy fuck, Jess," he groaned, jerking his shirt off without even unbuttoning it, then ripping his pants off faster. "I love this ass. And the naughty girl it's attached to. She fucking owns me."

He grabbed my butt cheeks with his hands and squeezed, then slapped my ass, watching it jiggle. With another growl he soothed the skin pink with his hands, and then bent down to kiss each spot he'd slapped.

I jiggled my bottom myself this time. "It's tingling. Please," I begged, and bit my lip. His eye swung back to my face, and he bent over me and kissed my lips, then pulled the one I had been biting into his mouth and sucked.

"You want me to fuck you? That's what will make my girl happy?" he asked me in a husky voice that made me shiver.

"Mmm-hmmm," I replied, and pressed back against him.

His hands grabbed my hips and he entered me, sliding

inside me slow. The muscles in his neck stood out as he threw his head back and closed his eyes. He was beautiful. And when he did that, he was so fucking hot.

"Best pussy in the world," he panted, and then his eyes opened and found me looking back at him. "My pussy. My tight, hot little pussy," he said as he rocked back and forth into me.

"Yes," I agreed, letting my head fall forward. Each time he was fully inside me, he hit the spot that made me cry out. "All yours."

"Fuck yeah, it is," he agreed. "Love you, Jess. Love you so much. But I also love this pussy."

Smiling, I looked up and found him watching me in the mirror. His eyes were smoldering with need and lust. I loved knowing I made him this out of control. I liked testing my good boy. Making him act like the bad boy he only was when he was in bed with me. "Harder," I said, then licked my bottom lip. His eyes flashed and his grip on my hips tightened.

"Jess," he panted as our gazes stayed locked. He wanted me to say more.

"Today I needed you so bad I had to play with my pussy. I wanted your big, hard cock so bad," I said, pouting. "I got so wet."

He shuddered. Hearing me talk dirty to him was going to send him blowing before he was ready. But he wanted it anyway.

"You touched my pussy. . . . If I'd known you needed me,

baby, I'd have skipped the class to come home and fuck my girl."

"I wanted your dick down my throat," I told him, watching his face morph as he fought off his release. His hand slipped down until he was rubbing my clit in rhythm to his thrust. "Making me gag on it while you pull my hair," I said through my panting.

"JESS, fuck, baby." His voice was strangled as he pounded into me harder.

My orgasm slammed over me, and I grabbed the dresser before I screamed his name and pushed back against him.

"Fuuuuuck!! GAAAHH, FUCK YES, Jess," Jason cried out as he jerked behind me, filling me with his release.

I fell forward and rested my head on my arms. He was still buried deep inside me. I could feel his cock jerking with each shot of come.

He began caressing my back, then moved around to rub my breasts, then my stomach. "You are incredible. I swear to God, I don't know how I manage to leave this bedroom." He chuckled, then slowly pulled out of me. "Stay," he said in a whisper. "Let me see my come run out of you and down your legs."

I trembled and stayed still. Jason could be extremely naughty when he wanted to be. Tonight he was definitely being a bad boy.

"There it is. Right down those creamy, smooth thighs. Damn, that's pretty," he breathed, dropping to his haunches and putting a hand on each of my butt cheeks and spreading them so he could see better.

"You going to let me move anytime soon?" I asked.

He ran his finger over the folds now coated with his release. "This makes me want to fuck you again. Damn, Jess, I will never get enough of you."

"Then let me move and we'll go take a very long shower," I suggested.

Jason stood up. "Deal."

JASON

Jess stood in the kitchen with a frown on her face as she stared at the recipe in front of her. Lately she had started cooking meals every night. I tried to tell her she didn't have to, but she really wanted to. So I was letting her. Times like this, when she looked adorable while trying to figure something out, made it worth it. However, sometimes actually swallowing the food she made was difficult.

I walked up behind her and grabbed her expanding waist. "Need help?" I asked, and she yelped.

"You scared me. I didn't hear you come in," she said, dropping the recipe and turning around to kiss me.

"Probably the fact that you have the radio so loud the neighbors can hear it," I replied.

She laughed, then grabbed the remote to the stereo system

and cut it off. "Sorry. It helps me think. What are you doing here? I didn't think you would get home until eight. I was just now starting on dinner."

I leaned back on the counter and brought her with me to stand between my legs. "I decided the study session could suck it. I wanted to take my girl out tonight. I missed you."

She gave me that sexy smile I had been in love with from the first moment she flashed it at me. "I thought I gave you some extra loving this morning to keep you happy through the day."

The blowjob I had woken up to had been fantastic. "Baby, all that did was have me thinking about this sweet mouth all day," I told her, leaning in to kiss her.

She wrapped her arms around my neck and sank into the kiss too. If I let this go on too long, we would end up stripping naked in the damn kitchen. Lately we were doing it all over the house.

I broke the kiss. "What do you say? You want to go out with me and get some dinner? You can order dessert, and then we can come back and you can give me my dessert."

Her eyes flashed. She knew what I wanted for dessert. "Okay. Yes. This recipe is too complicated, anyway."

I took a nibble of her neck, then stepped away. "Let's go."

She smirked at me. "You know I'm not dressed to go any-where. I need at least thirty minutes."

"Jess, seriously, baby, you can't be any more beautiful. If you pretty this up any more than it already is, I'm going to end up in a fight tonight because some stupid fucker is looking at my woman."

She laughed and slapped my arm. "You're so full of crap. I'll be quick."

I watched as she hurried to the bedroom.

It took her thirty-six minutes, but seeing her all fixed up and feeling good about herself was well worth it. She was glowing, and I loved that. Jess woke up beautiful. She didn't have to do anything to make herself breathtaking. But it made her feel good about herself. That was what mattered.

The past couple of months she was acting different. I knew she was supposed to be emotional, but she seemed like she was trying to hold on to me. Like she had to work extra hard or something. Like with cooking me meals. That was the beginning of it. Now we were having sex like rabbits.

As much as I loved the fact that she would drop to her knees and start sucking my cock at any moment, it bothered me that she was doing it. Before, our sex life had been good. No, it had been incredible. But lately she was desperate about it. Like she was trying to fulfill every fantasy I'd ever had.

When I tried to talk to her about it, she either distracted me with sex or she started talking about something else entirely.

And although I had a cleaner come in and clean the place three times a week, Jess was also cleaning. Something was wrong with her. I just needed to figure out what.

I thought about calling her mom, but I didn't know if she'd have any insight on this. She wasn't living here with us, and she didn't see what Jess was doing. Plus, telling her mom that she was suddenly sucking my dick all the time didn't seem appropriate either.

I had to figure this out on my own.

I wanted Jess happy. Not trying to make me happy. She made me happy by breathing. I didn't need her to become Martha Stewart with a naughty side. I liked Jess just as she was.

The waiter at the Italian place I knew Jess loved seated us at a table. She had tried to tell me she wanted to go eat Thai food. That was a lie. I was the one who loved Thai food. Once again she was trying to give me what she thought I wanted. This was getting out of hand.

Her eyes lit up as she took the menu and started reading it. That was what made me happy. Seeing my pregnant fiancée drooling over food. She was craving things. I knew she was, but she wouldn't tell me. I would come home and she would have gone and bought strange items she never used to eat.

"I want you to order three things. Eat what you want and we'll take home the leftovers for you to enjoy for the rest of the week, in case you crave it and I'm not there."

Jess glanced up at me from her menu. "How did you know I was trying to decide between three things?"

I smirked. "Because you're mine and I know you. The ricotta and Grana Padano gnocchi, pesto lasagna, and cannelloni are always hard for you to choose between. Just get all three."

Jess pressed her lips together and closed her menu. "Fine, then. Read my mind. I guess I'm predictable."

Laughing, I shook my head. "Jess, you are anything but predictable. And I love that about you."

She tilted her head as she looked at me. "Really?" Like she didn't believe that I loved that.

Jess didn't normally need reassurance like this. Another new thing that bothered me.

"Jess," I said, leaning on the table and closer to her. "I adore everything about you. You shouldn't question that by now."

She beamed at me and looked like she let out a sigh of relief.

"Jason, what's up? Hardly see you off campus," Jamieson Kennedy said as he stopped beside our table. He glanced at Jess, and I could see the glint of appreciation in his eyes. It was something I was learning to deal with. Jess was beautiful, and men would always notice.

"I've got better things to do when class is over," I told him with a smirk, then winked at Jess.

"Jason, hello. We missed you at study group last night," Vivian Northrop said as she walked up beside Jamieson.

They were on-again off-again and had been for years. That social circle, they seemed to inbreed and keep dating just each other. It was weird and boring. Vivian, however, liked to remind me we had once slept together. Not something I ever thought about until I worried that she was going to bring it up. Especially in front of Jess.

"Vivian. You both have met Jess," I said, nodding toward Jess as she suddenly looked like she would rather be anywhere else.

"Oh, I didn't realize you were still together. I thought . . ." Vivian was elbowed by Jamieson and they both put on those fake smiles I hated.

"You thought what?" I asked her, annoyed now. Because I made it very clear I was with Jess and brought her up regularly.

She waved it off like it was nothing. "I just haven't seen you around outside of classes, and I assumed you were in a serious relationship."

Scowling, I reminded myself that she was just a bitch. "I am in a serious relationship. I'm engaged," I told her, and reached for Jess's hand and covered it with mine. "To Jess."

Vivian acted shocked as she looked at Jess, then turned her head. "Oh, well, I'm sure your mother is thrilled," she said. "I'll see you later, Jason." Then she walked off.

Jamieson shrugged. "That's just Viv. You know how she is," he said, making an excuse for her.

"Yeah, I know," I replied.

When he walked off, I looked over at Jess, who was staring down at her lap. I squeezed her hand. "Hey, don't get upset over that. Vivian is a grade-A bitch. She's uptight and likes to say things that make her feel better about herself."

Jess only nodded. Then I saw her take a deep breath as she lifted her head to look at me. "It's okay. I'm used to this by now." The small smile she was forcing didn't fool me.

"Is that what is bothering you? The elitist assholes around here? Because none of them matter. Nothing they do or say matters."

She sighed and glanced away, looking out over the dining room. "I know. It's okay."

No, it wasn't okay. "Jess," I started, but then the server walked up.

I let Jess place her order. She only ordered the lasagna. So I ordered what I wanted, and her other two choices boxed up to go. I wasn't letting Vivian freaking Northrop ruin Jess's dinner.

JESS

When lunchtime came the next day, I was really thankful that Jason had ordered my other two favorite dishes the night before. I put a little of both on a plate and heated them up. I had a hard time going to sleep last night. Once I had finally fallen asleep I slept so hard that I hadn't woken up when Jason left this morning. He had gotten up and made his own coffee, and left without even a kiss from me.

It had ruined my morning. I worried over not being what he needed. What I thought would make him happy. Last night he'd been determined to go eat at my favorite restaurant and, in the end, I had wished so hard we were eating Thai. Running into those uppity people who saw me as less than them had taken away my appetite. I hadn't wanted to eat.

Under Jason's watchful and concerned eyes, I had forced it down. Or at least half of it. I couldn't do more than that.

At some point Jason would realize what he's done. I was just sitting here, waiting on him to figure it out. He is brilliant and going to do big things. What could I do? Make clothes? Who wants me to make them clothes? No one. That's who.

I sank down on the sofa with my plate of food and rubbed my stomach. We were going to be parents while Jason still went to his Ivy League college. Soon there would be diapers and sleepless nights and hardly any time for sex. How soon would it be before some girl in one of his classes took away all his stress and met his needs?

My appetite vanished again. I set my plate down and stood back up. I shouldn't have been eating all those carbs. I was going to get fat. I needed to go for a walk instead. I had to have my perfect body so that when our baby was sleeping, I could keep Jason interested in me.

Would we be married then? Jason hadn't talked about setting a date. When he proposed to me, I hadn't been pregnant. Now that I was, he didn't seem really excited about making a wedding happen. Which was not helping me feel safe in this relationship. I wanted to go see my momma. Talk to her about all this. She'd make me feel better. Being around people who didn't look down their noses at me would be a nice change.

My cell phone rang just as I was lacing up my tennis shoes. It was Jason. I pressed it to my ear. "Hey, you," I said, trying to sound happy.

"Hey, baby. You slept good. I liked seeing you all curled up in bed like an angel this morning." His voice made me smile.

"I'm sorry I didn't wake up to tell you bye."

"Don't be. I liked leaving you tucked in and resting. I was just heading to lunch, and I know you have Italian food in the fridge, but I thought you might want to come to the campus and eat with me."

I looked down at my leggings and off-the-shoulder shirt I was wearing. No makeup and my hair was in a ponytail. "Right now?" I asked, hoping he'd say, *No, in half an hour*.

"Yeah, sorry it's late notice, but a meeting with a professor was canceled and I realized I'd have time to eat today."

I wanted to see him. And I didn't want to turn him down. "I don't look great. I was about to go walking. I'm in my workout clothes."

Jason chuckled. "Noted. But, baby, you look gorgeous no matter what you're wearing. Come eat with me. Please."

The Vivians of Harvard were going to love this. I was going to give them something to make fun of for weeks. Maybe months. "Okay, I'll head that way now."

"I'll wait for you in the courtyard outside the main cafeteria."

Great.

The whole way there I prepared myself for all the preppy, skinny girls who'd look at me like I was a bug that needed to be squashed.

But seeing Jason's smiling face when I rounded the corner to the courtyard made it all not matter. He beamed at me and started walking toward me with purpose. When we reached each other, he grabbed my face and kissed me hard. It was a claiming kind of kiss he liked to do in public. It made me feel special and loved.

When he pulled back, I heard a catcall and a whistle. Someone else told us to get a room. Jason was oblivious to all of them. "Hey, baby," he whispered, then pressed one more kiss to my mouth. "Come on. Let's go eat."

His arm slid around my back as we walked to the cafeteria. I felt eyes on me as we stepped inside. But I didn't focus on any of them.

"They have lasagna today, but I don't think it will compare

to last night's. But the chicken parmesan is good. I think you'll like that."

"Sounds good. I trust you," I told him.

He led me over to a table and pulled out a chair for me. "Wait here. I'll go get the food. They don't have your soda, but they have Sprite. You want that?"

I nodded and smiled up at him.

He winked, then headed to get in line.

I was the only pregnant girl here. I didn't have to look around to know. The girls who got into school here didn't get knocked up.

The chair beside me moved, and a guy sat down with his gaze directed at my chest. "This seat taken?" he asked.

"Yes," I replied.

This one actually had a sweater tied around his neck. Seriously?

"I've not seen you around here. What classes are you taking?"

Had I not just told him that seat was taken?

"I don't go here. And that seat is taken."

He grinned and leaned forward. "That explains it. You don't look like the girls here. But I do like the way you fill out a shirt. Who you here with? Boyfriend?"

"Me. Move, Devin," Jason snarled, slamming down the tray in his hands, making me and Devin jump.

Devin stood up. "Damn, Jason, get a grip. I was just making your friend feel welcome. It was obvious she was an outsider."

Jason took a step toward him, and the angry clench in his jaw told me Devin needed to run. "She's my fiancée, dickhead. And the fact that she doesn't fit in here is one of the many reasons I love her."

Devin shrugged. "Got it." He held up his hands in surrender. "Leaving now."

Jason stood there glaring at him until he was happy with how far away Devin had moved. Then he swung his gaze to mine. "I'm going to go get you a drink, but I'm trying to decide if I need to take you with me."

I started to say something when he grinned. "I'm kidding. I'll be right back, and I'm sorry about him. He's a jackass."

JASON

By the time the weekend arrived, I was exhausted. Between keeping up with my studies and assignments and making sure Jess was happy, all I wanted to do was sleep.

When my eyes opened on Saturday morning and I focused on the alarm clock beside the bed, it was after eleven. I hadn't slept that late all semester. I heard the shower going, and the smell of coffee and pancakes filled the apartment. Smelled like Jess had been up for a while.

Tossing the covers back, I stood up and stretched. I was

still naked from the last round of sex we'd had the night before. After getting off for the third time in one night, I don't think I came back from the last one. All I could remember was holding on to Jess as pleasure coursed through me.

I had to have passed out on her after that.

I went to the bathroom, and the glass shower was steamed up but I could still see my gorgeous fiancée rinsing the shampoo from her hair. She had her eyes closed and her head tilted back. Opening the shower door, I stepped inside and she snapped her eyes open.

Her surprised gasp turned into a smile.

"Morning," I said, sliding my hands around her slick body and pulling her to me. "It was cold in bed alone."

She laughed. "Some of us can't sleep all morning. We get hungry," she teased.

"Smelled that. You make me any?"

"Of course."

I moved my hand down to gently touch her between the legs. "Are you sore? Because I am, and I'm thinking if I'm sore, then you gotta be."

Jess opened her legs for me and rocked on my hand. "A little," she whispered. "But if you're sore, I can kiss it and make it better."

I caught her under the arms just as she started to go down on those knees again. "No," I said, stopping her. The frown that puckered her brow made me smile. "Sit," I said, pushing her to the bench behind us. "And open," I commanded. Then I went down on my knees.

"Jason, I'm . . . fine. . . ."

"I'm not. I'm hungry," I replied, opening her legs wide with my hands.

With the first lick, she shuddered. With the second one, her hands made it to my hair. I began teasing her and pleasuring every spot but the one place I knew she needed my tongue.

When she started pulling on my hair and begging, I gave in and flicked her swollen clit with my tongue, then pulled it into my mouth and sucked. It was a good thing I had plenty of hair because she pulled so hard I was sure she tore some out.

"JAAASON!" she cried, trembling as her body convulsed and her thighs held my head in a firm grip while she rode the wave.

When her legs went lax and she fell back against the wall, I pressed a kiss to her stomach, then a couple to the inside of her thighs before standing back up and sitting beside her. "That's my favorite breakfast."

She giggled and laid her hand on my shoulder. "Yeah, well then, I'm really lucky. I was going to kiss yours and make it better, though."

"This morning I needed it to be about you. As much as I love it when you're between my legs, I like being the one to make my girl cry out in pleasure."

She smiled up at me, then kissed my chin. "Thank you."

"You're welcome, but are you thanking me for the awesome way I eat breakfast or for wanting to?"

"Both and neither. For loving me."

I reached over and pulled Jess into my lap. Then I cupped her face in my hands. "Don't ever, ever, thank me for loving you. You are my every dream, crazy woman."

Jess wrapped her arms around me and sighed happily. Maybe this was it. Maybe whatever she was dealing with was gone now. God, I hoped so.

JESS

The next week was easier. I wasn't filled with the fear of losing Jason as much. We had spent the weekend watching movies, curled up on the sofa together and eating Chinese takeout and pizza. Having a lazy weekend had helped my emotions.

Even though this week Jason had stayed out late twice with study groups, I had managed not to panic or get needy. He seemed happier too. He wasn't always asking me what was wrong.

Tonight, however, we were going to an event. His friend Finn's birthday was tonight, and Finn loved to have parties. He threw the most parties of any human I knew. Because he had more money than God, it was an *event* instead of just a party. Finn and Hensley were Jason's only two friends I liked. They were nice to me, and I felt comfortable around them.

I chose a dress I had recently made, and went without panties or a bra. The dress hid my baby bump but accentuated my boobs so that a bra was impossible. The pretty blue was a color I had recently developed a thing for. And the fabric had a creamy, soft feel to it. My hair was down, and I had on the heels Jason had bought me a couple of months ago when I had been drooling over them.

The look on Jason's face when I had walked out of the bedroom had given me the extra self-esteem I had needed to face this crowd. He had followed it with a "Goddamn, you're hot."

We pulled up to the country club that I had only been to once and had never wanted to return to. It had been a family meal that ended badly. Sadie had basically told off Jason and Jax's mother.

Before I walked in, I needed to know who would be there. Or if one person would be there. "Will Johanna be here?" I asked.

Jason nodded, then slid his hand around my waist. "And she'll feel very inadequate when she gets a look at my beautiful fiancée. Don't worry about her."

I tried to believe that, but I knew just how attractive Johanna was. I also knew she had slept with my man. That drove me nuts. I hated her bad.

The doors opened for us, and we were greeted by two men in tuxedos. Then we headed to the ballroom. When we walked in, the place was already packed. Dancing was happening, and everywhere there were groups of fabulously dressed people with fancy drinks in their hands.

"JESS!" Finn yelled as he saw us walk in. Jason chuckled beside me.

"I think he's already drunk," he said as we approached the birthday boy.

"I think you're right."

"You came! Dance with me, Jess. Let her, man. It's my birthday," Finn said, reaching out to touch me.

Jason pulled me back fast and shook his head. "Happy birthday, Finn. But my woman is off-limits. Find another."

Finn stuck out his bottom lip and stomped his foot. Yep, he was definitely drunk. "But I wanna touch her."

Jason tucked me closer to his side. "You touch her and when you wake up sober your nose will be broken. Got it?"

Finn burst out laughing, and then slapped Jason on the back. "You are so whipped."

Before he could say anything else, someone came up to talk to him and he forgot about us. Jason pulled me away from Finn and we walked over to the bar.

"If he wasn't drunk and one of my best friends . . . ," Jason muttered. "I need a drink. You want a club soda? Splash of cranberry juice?"

I nodded and Jason turned to order himself a whiskey straight and me a club soda. I saw a girl I had met when we went to a party in New York City. Our night had ended badly and I'd gone home alone.

"Hello, Jason. Haven't seen you much this semester," the girl said, flashing her smile at Jason and completely ignoring me, even though we had met before.

"Hey, Vanessa," he replied as he handed me my club soda, tinged pink from the cranberry juice.

"You and Jo haven't been doing anything together lately," Vanessa said, finally giving me a quick glance before looking back at Jason.

"No. Since I'm engaged and expecting a baby, I don't spend any time with other women. I got the one I want," Jason replied, then took my hand. "Enjoy the party, Vanessa," he said without looking at her as he led me away.

"I remember her from New York," I told him.

"Sorry. She's a vulture," he said.

I nodded, and then Jason stopped to speak to some people who didn't seem very interested in me. As they discussed a class they were taking, I looked around the room.

When a feminine voice joined in, I turned my focus back to the group talking.

"You can borrow my notes. I need them too, but if you want to stay after class you can get a copy of mine. I'll only ask that you take me for coffee in return," she said, flipping her red hair over her shoulder.

"You've got all the notes?" Jason asked, instead of telling her he wouldn't be taking her to coffee.

"Yes. Every last one. I'm detailed," she replied. Why did she sound like she meant that another way entirely? I was not a fan.

"That would be great, Phoebe. Thanks."

Wait, what?

"No problem," she said, and then they all started talking about stuff I knew nothing about again.

The feeling of not fitting into this world started to sink in again. I fought it off, but each time Phoebe said something and Jason laughed, I cringed. She was tall and slender. Too slender. And she was in three of his classes. They were majoring in the same thing.

"Jess," Hensley said, walking up to us with a glass in his hand and smiling. I liked Hensley. He was okay.

"Hey, Hensley," I replied.

"Dance with me, Jess," he said, waggling his eyebrows at Jason.

"No, Hensley. Go away," Jason said, sounding amused.

"I'll dance with you, Hensley," Phoebe said, pushing through the group to walk entirely too close to Jason before sliding an arm around Hensley and whispering something in his ear while she looked at Jason.

Hensley's eyebrows shot up. "Dirty, Phoebe. I like it," he

said, and pulled her out to dance with him. I was glad to see her go, but when she smirked at me over Hensley's shoulder, I knew I hadn't imagined things.

JASON

Jess's hand grabbed my arm. "Take me to the restroom," she said, close to my ear.

I put our glasses down and took her to the toilets closest to us.

"Looks like that one is empty," I told her. There weren't separate women's and men's. There were just six private bathrooms. Three on each side of the hall outside the ballroom.

She opened the door, then turned back to me and grabbed my hand to pull me inside. "You need me?" I asked, confused.

Jess closed the door and locked it, then turned around and grabbed my face and attacked me. I let her plump mouth have its way as I enjoyed the ride. I wasn't sure what this was about, but lately I had learned not to question it.

"I'm not wearing panties," she said against my lips. "Fuck me." Her hands moved to tug her dress up and reveal her round little ass in the mirror behind her.

Fuck.

I unsnapped my slacks and got my dick free while I took over the kiss.

"I want your titties free so I can see them bounce while I fuck you," I told her, reaching for the zipper of her dress. I had already been able to tell she wasn't wearing a bra. It was driving me—and every male here—crazy. I'd had to keep myself from covering her up with my jacket.

She stepped out of the dress as it fell to the ground, and I broke our kiss so I could pick it up and hang it on the purse hook behind the door.

My beautiful Jess stood in front of me, wearing those hot silver heels I had bought her when she'd all but cuddled with them a few months back after seeing them in a store window.

I was letting my eyes slowly take in this view just when Jess lifted her leg and propped it on the closed toilet seat. "I need you in me, Jason."

Damn.

I grabbed her hip, jerked her forward, and then slid inside her already wet cunt. "Shiiiit," I growled, burying my head in her neck and moving in and out of her as she met me with each thrust. "This what you wanted, baby?" I asked as I licked at her neck.

"God, yes," she moaned, and put her hands on the sink to brace herself. I moved back enough so I could see her heavy breasts bouncing.

"You want me to pull out so you aren't leaking come all night?" I asked her as the walls began to squeeze my cock in a way that would send me shooting off in a moment.

"Inside me," she panted.

We weren't gonna be able to stay here long if she was walking around without panties and with come between her legs. I'd walk around with a semi, unable not to think about it.

Jess moved her leg up and wrapped it around my hip. "Yes, yes, oh God, yes, that's . . . I'm gonna . . . AAAHHHH!" She threw her head back and her body jerked under my hands.

Between the sight of her coming and the knowledge that someone was bound to hear us in here, I followed right after her, crying out as I filled my girl. Holding her to me.

It wasn't until after I slowly came off my high that I realized how strange this was. Why had Jess dragged me away from the party to do this? I knew pregnant women were horny, but this seemed different. She was wild and clinging to me while she fucked. Like she had to hold on to me.

"You're gonna regret not making me pull out," I said, kissing the side of her face.

"I never regret that," she replied.

I wanted to believe that she was as satisfied as I was and that this hadn't been some way to reassure herself that I was hers. She didn't have to use sex to hold on to me.

"Jess," I said, brushing hair off her forehead, "as much as I love the fact that you just brought me in the bathroom at a party to fuck my brains out, I'm worried you did it for the wrong reasons."

She stiffened under me. "I just wanted you."

This wasn't the place to talk about this, but we were going to talk about it soon.

I cleaned her up and dressed her. Then I straightened myself up while she got her hair and makeup touched up. When I finally opened the door and Jess walked out, Phoebe stood there, staring at us with wide eyes.

I was worried Jess would be embarrassed, so I started to make up an excuse. But Jess turned back to me and kissed me, pressing into me. Then she smiled with a pleased grin and turned back around and strutted past Phoebe, looking like one very cocky female. I glanced back at Phoebe, who wasn't smiling. And then it dawned on me: Phoebe's suggestion that I buy her a coffee in exchange for borrowing her notes had upset Jess.

I had never intended to take Phoebe to get coffee. I was just gonna buy her one and take it to class as a thank-you. But Jess didn't see it that way. She was marking her man.

I laughed and shook my head. Then I went after my outrageous female. Never a dull moment with Jess. God, I loved that woman.

JESS

The rest of the night Jason kept his hand on me at all times. He didn't talk to other girls, and he kept asking me about my wet thighs. By the time we left, I was ready to get him back home and have a longer and louder session in bed.

Back at the house, I slipped off my shoes and put them in the closet. When I turned around, Jason was leaning against the door frame of the bedroom with a grin on his lips. "So, you showed Phoebe who owned me tonight. I'm not complaining, but next time you don't have to resort to those kinds of measures. You can just tell me it makes you uncomfortable. Phoebe is a flirt, and I've ignored it for so long I don't even notice it. But I get why you did it."

Walking out of the bathroom to find Phoebe standing there looking at us was even better than I had hoped. I had needed to remind Jason how I could make him feel. And I had needed to remind myself that he wanted me. That I was the one who turned him on.

"I didn't know she'd hear us," I said honestly.

He chuckled. "I'm sure you didn't, but I'm betting that the fact that she was the one who caught us made your night."

I nodded. No point in lying.

Jason burst out laughing and covered the space between us in two long strides. "You are so crazy. She doesn't compete with you, Jess. No one does. For me: You. Are. It."

"They intimidate me. All of them. They're like you. I'm not." That was as honest as I had been with him.

Jason nodded. "Yeah, they all have the same career goals I have. Some even more than I do. Most more than I do. We all grew up similarly. But not one of them has ever made me feel like I couldn't breathe without them. Not one of them is you, Jess.

And they never will be. They don't know how to make their own clothes. They don't know how much fun an entire day of lying on a sofa watching all the Rocky movies can be, or how to get out of bed looking like a fucking goddess. Only you, Jess. Get that through your head, baby. But if you want to pull me into restrooms and fuck me in order to remind me how much I want your sexy little body, then please do. Because that was hot. Seriously hot."

His words brought tears to my eyes, and a laugh bubbled out of me. Was I losing it with this pregnancy thing?

Jason held me and we stood there while I composed myself.

"I love this closet," he said. "Smells like you. When you aren't here and I'm missing you, I come stand in here. The other morning when you were sleeping, I came in here before I left and just took a deep breath."

I tilted my head back and looked up at Jason. "Really?" I asked, amazed.

He grinned. "Yeah. I'm as insane about you as you are about me. You just keep forgetting that. I feel like I'm failing you somehow. I don't want you to doubt how obsessed I am with you."

"Next time remind me that you smell my closet when you miss me. I think that'll help," I suggested.

"I'll do that."

Over the next month I managed to get my emotions in order. I was still jumping Jason regularly, but he didn't seem to mind how much I wanted sex. Jason said that news of our little escapade in the restroom during Finn's party had gotten around, and now he was the envied one among his friends. He seemed to think it was funny, and I was glad my moment of jealousy hadn't caused issues.

Today was Friday, which was my favorite day of the week. It meant I would have Jason for two whole days. Even when he studied he was here, so I wasn't missing him. I worked on some new maternity outfits for myself while he read.

I was getting cleaned up after finishing my daily courses online. I wanted my business degree. I had finally decided I wanted to design my own clothing, not work for someone else. Maybe I would make a kids' boutique line. I wasn't sure yet. But I knew that to run a business, I needed a degree.

The door opened and Jason walked in, carrying two large paper bags and wearing a smile on his face. "I'm home."

Laughing, I hurried over to him and kissed his face. "I see that."

He kissed me back, then pulled away. "Don't start that now. I'll have you naked and up against a wall before we know it. And before we play, we have work to do," he said, then held up the bags he was carrying.

"Work?" I asked, confused.

"Yep. Work. The fun kind," he assured me, and walked over to the coffee table and put the bags down.

I followed him as he began to pull out . . . pamphlets?

"What is that?"

Jason held up a handful and handed them to me. "They are destinations. Wedding destinations. We need to decide so I can use my brother's fame and power to get the date and location you want."

I reached for the pamphlets he was handing me, but my mind was not processing this fast enough.

"I've been busy with school," Jason continued. "You've been busy with school and fucking my brains out. And while I've enjoyed that part very much, I need a date set. I'm ready to make you Jess Stone. I am done being patient and giving you time. You're deciding this weekend."

"Anywhere," I said honestly. I would not cry because he had two bags full of locations for weddings. I would not cry because this was so incredibly sweet.

He glanced back at me as he pulled out his own handful to go through. "I want to marry you. I'll marry you anywhere you want. Hell, Jess, I'll go to Vegas and let Elvis do it. But you deserve the dream wedding. The one you've thought about since you were a little girl, and by God, I'm giving that to you. Having a brother the world worships is handy for some things. This is one of them. Now, come sit with me and let's figure this out."

He sat down and held his arm out for me to join him.

I sniffled and smiled. "Okay."

I sat close to him and put my pile in his lap. "Let's look at each one together until I see one I like."

"Nope. You gotta love it. I won't stop until this is everything you ever wanted."

I laid my head on his chest. "You're everything I ever wanted."

He kissed my head. "Good. So do you want Elvis to do this, then?"

Laughing, I shook my head.

"Didn't think so. Let's start with the East Coast locations. We can move west from there."

JASON

The sun had decided to shine today. It was early spring in south Alabama, and the breeze could be chilly if the sun wasn't out. But today it had shown up. The colorful peonies (yes, I know what those are now) decorated the ends of the rows of white chairs and were woven into the wooden arbor I stood under right beside my brother.

"When we used to play out here in the summers, you ever imagine this?" I asked, grinning, already knowing the answer.

"Hell no," he said with a chuckle.

I nodded to the glass balls with candles lit in them hanging from the trees. "I hope we don't set the place on fire."

Jax grinned. "I think we're safe."

Glancing around, I saw several pairs of eyes watching us with big, cheesy grins. Trisha Taylor, Amanda Drake, and Willow Hardy all held bouquets of peonies and wore dresses similar in style but not identical. And each one was a different color, matching one of the peonies all over this place.

"Y'all are supposed to be quiet at this point," Marcus said from the other side of Jax, a smirk on his face.

Daisy May Taylor and Larissa Hardy came walking down the aisle, tossing petals to the ground as they smiled at the friends and family watching them.

"This is it," Jax whispered when the music, which had been chosen after lots of debate and changing of minds, started up.

My chest tightened and then my heart started pounding as I waited for Jess to turn that corner of trees. White satin appeared first, and then came my girl. Her eyes found me immediately, and all the things that were ever wrong with the world were right now. I had never thought I would settle down. Then a wild, gorgeous blonde with a baseball bat waved down my car and climbed inside. My world had never been the same since.

I heard Jax's sharp intake of breath, and I knew the cause. But right now all I saw was Jess. I couldn't look at anything or anyone else.

She'd spent the past month making her dress. She had worked late into the nights and put so much love into it. It was perfect. She was perfect. When she reached me, I stepped down, took her hand, and pulled her to my side. My brother stepped down and took Sadie's hand, and they stood to the left of us.

When they were planning this, Jess and Sadie both considered letting their mothers walk them down the aisle. They'd both been raised by just their moms. But in the end they had decided to walk down side by side to meet us.

"You're breathtaking," I whispered as I stared down at Jess in awe.

"Thank you," she said, smiling so brightly it put the sun to shame. "I love you."

"I love you more," I said as I tucked her hand in my arm and held her beside me.

I glanced over at my brother, who held his bride on his arm, looking as completely consumed as I felt. Sharing this day with each other wasn't our idea. The girls had come up with the idea of a dual wedding at Jax's Sea Breeze home. They had wanted to get married where we all had good memories. Near the family and friends who had watched us fall in love. Who had been there through the ups and downs.

And it was perfect.

"We are gathered here today," the minister began, and Jess squeezed my arm.

This was it.

It seemed, in my attempt to give Jess her fairy tale, she'd

given me mine. And I hadn't even known I'd had one. Until now. This was it.

The vows were said, and although my brother was famous for his lyrics, my vows were exactly how I felt. I didn't try to make them as pretty as Jax's would be. But mine were ours. Mine and Jess's. Our story. Our beginning and our forever.

"You both may now kiss your brides."

My favorite part of the ceremony. I cupped Jess's face in my hands and stared down at the beautiful woman who was now my wife. "Hello, Mrs. Stone," I whispered before taking her mouth and kissing her.

The cheers faded away as I held my wife in my arms.

My wife.

Damn, I was a lucky son of a bitch.

Krit and Blythe from *Bad for You*

BLYTHE

So many numbers . . . So many people . . . Oh my God.

I sat at my desk, staring at the screen of my MacBook. I hadn't been able to do much else for the past hour. There were just too many freaking numbers. I hadn't expected this. Never in a million years had I expected this.

But it was there. Was it wrong?

Gripping the edge of my desk, I blinked several times and took a deep breath. When the numbers remained the same, I pinched myself. Ouch. Yeah, I was awake. This wasn't a dream.

I heard my phone ringing, but I couldn't answer it. My eyes were completely glued to those numbers. Talking right now wouldn't be possible. I was speechless.

I wasn't sure how long I'd been sitting there when the door

of our apartment flew open and Krit stalked in, frantically call-ing my name.

Hearing his voice snapped me out of my state of shock, and I lifted my gaze to see my beautiful boyfriend with his pale blond hair and striking blue eyes looking at me like he was terrified.

"You're okay," he gasped. "Fuck . . . Goddamn, love, you scared the shit out of me. I've been calling for the past hour. I even had Green come up and knock on your door."

I hadn't heard Green knocking, but, then again, I'd only noticed my phone ringing once. "Come here. Come see," I managed to say.

"What is it?"

He came behind me, his hands resting on my shoulders as he pressed a kiss to my head. "Wait . . . are those your book sales?" he asked, awe in his voice.

"Yeah . . ." I nodded, then let out a laugh. "I'm just . . . Can you believe this?" I asked, turning to gaze up at him.

Krit's smile was so full of pride my heart felt full. "Hell yeah, I believe it. Those stupid shits who sent you rejection letters didn't know what they were doing. This proves it. You're bril-liant, baby. I never doubted that."

I had spent seven months trying to get a literary agent for my finished novel. It hadn't happened for me. After ten rejections, I did some research online and found out about self-publishing.

It took three more months of getting an editor and having the manuscript cleaned up, finding a cover artist to do my cover, and building an online presence. Two weeks ago I had clicked publish on the three top ebook retailers.

I hadn't even let Krit tell our friends. Knowing my words were out there for people to read was terrifying. Within days bloggers had started reviewing it. I wouldn't look at the sales numbers all week because I was afraid to.

"Can you believe that in two weeks' time eight thousand people have bought my book? They've read it!" I was amazed.

"Babe, it's about us. That's some good shit," he teased.

I shook my head and stood up, putting my hands on my hips. "Krit, that's . . . that's twenty-four thousand dollars in just two weeks." Even saying it out loud sounded insane. Crazy! People did not make that kind of money in two weeks. Especially not college students.

"What?" Krit asked slowly.

I hadn't discussed pricing with him, or how much profit I received per book. This was where he got the shock. "Twenty-four thousand. I make three dollars a book," I explained.

Krit's eyes went wide, and then something happened. The excitement and pride that had been there faded. Something else took its place before he turned his head away from me. "That's amazing, love. Really amazing. I knew you'd do it. You deserve it," he said, finally glancing back at me. "I gotta get back to class.

I'll see you tonight," he said, then kissed me hard on the mouth before walking out of the apartment we shared.

What the heck had just happened?

KRIT

Going back to class was pointless. My head was fucked up. Everything was fucked up. This was just the beginning for her. Two weeks and she'd made what it took me about six months to make. Holy shit.

I needed to talk to my sister. No, not her. She's a woman. I needed to talk to Rock. He'd understand before Trisha would. The diamond ring I'd been making payments on for the past six months didn't seem so damn impressive anymore. Eight thousand dollars had kicked my ass, but I was making the final payment on it this Friday.

Planning how to propose to Blythe had been an even longer ordeal. I had changed my mind ten times already. I was sure I had decided what I wanted to do now, but after this . . . could I?

FUCKED! This was so fucked.

Twenty-four thousand goddamn dollars. Motherfucker, that was insane. And it was going to get worse. She was going to be making millions at this rate. She was almost finished writing her second novel. So then she'd have two books out there making this kind of money.

I pulled my bike over and called Rock.

"What's up?" he said by way of greeting.

"Where are you? I need to talk."

"I'm over at the condos Dewayne has going up. I was going with him and Preston to get some lunch. Want to come with us?"

Telling Rock this was one thing. He was family. This wasn't shit you shared with other people. "No, just need to talk to you. When will you be done with lunch?"

"Wait a sec," Rock said. "D, I gotta go meet up with Krit. I'll catch up with y'all later." Then he said to me, "I'm headed to my house. Meet me there in five."

I slipped my phone into my pocket and turned my Harley back to the road before heading to my sister's house.

By the time I arrived, Rock's truck was parked outside and he was leaning against it with his arms crossed over his chest, watching me. I didn't normally come to him with stuff. He usually gave me advice I didn't want. The truth was, Rock might be just a couple of years older than me, but he had become a safe place for me when I was a scared kid. When he had walked into our lives, I was fourteen and trying to keep my sister alive. Then Rock Taylor had stepped in and saved us both.

He was my family.

I parked my bike by his truck, then walked over to him.

"Sounds serious," he said, studying me closely.

"It is. I think. Fuck, I don't know." This was so damn confusing.

"Let's hear it."

I had come here to tell him my problem and get advice. Backing out now was a pussy move. With a frustrated sigh, I looked at the man I considered a brother. "I can't propose to Blythe. Not anymore. It won't look right," I blurted out. That hadn't been exactly the way I wanted to say it, but that was what came out.

My biggest fear. The one thing that was haunting me and driving me mad.

Rock frowned. "You mean after spending all that money on a ring and working shifts for Dewayne to make extra cash, you aren't gonna propose? What the fuck happened?"

"She . . . she published her book. She didn't want me to tell anyone. She did it two weeks ago," I explained.

Rock grinned. "That's awesome. Why didn't she want you telling people?"

"Because she was nervous. Scared. Hell, I don't know. I just didn't say anything. But it's doing better than she expected. Much better. Like five figures better in two damn weeks."

Rock let out a loud laugh. "No fucking way! That's great, man. What's the problem? I bet she's thrilled."

He wasn't getting it. Frustrated, I shoved my hand through my hair and groaned. "Yeah, it's great. She is thrilled, and I'm happy for her. Don't get me wrong. I'm so damn proud of her. But . . . but now that she's making this kind of money, I can't go and propose. That's like me saying that now that she's big money, I want to get hitched."

Rock frowned. "That's not the truth. You've been working your ass off to get her a ring that was bigger than anything
Blythe expects."

"Bad timing," I snapped.

Rock finally got it. "Shit."

"What do I do?" I asked him.

Rock sighed and shrugged. "Dude, I don't know. I've never
had to worry about Trisha thinking I wanted her for her money.
Maybe this isn't a permanent thing and it won't be this much
money in the future. When she's making less money, would you
feel better proposing then?"

"I hate waiting. I want my ring on her finger. It's just the
idea of her thinking I could want her for anything less than
just *her* kills me. I worry that doubt would be in the back of her
mind. I want to ask her to marry me, but when I do it, I want
her to understand that she is my fucking universe. Being with
her in a cardboard box would be fine as long as she's curled up
next to me. I just need her to be happy. Now all this fucking
money . . ." I wanted to scream in frustration.

"Wait. Give it a week or so. Maybe a month. If you're
worried about the money. In all honesty, I don't think Blythe
will think you are proposing because she's had success with
this book. When she sees that diamond you got her, she's
gonna know you've been working for this for a while."

"Or she's gonna think I got it on credit, planning to pay it off once I'm married to a wealthy woman," I grumbled.

Damn money. It had to make everything complicated. I just never thought it would make *my* life complicated.

My girl had written a novel—gone after her dream and achieved it. Instead of celebrating, I was bitching about it. How screwed up was that?

She deserved this. I needed to get over myself. The time would be right eventually. I just needed to wait for it.

BLYTHE

Krit's strange reaction and quick departure today had bothered me so much I couldn't focus. I closed my computer and cleaned the apartment, then went to get groceries to try to keep my mind off his odd behavior.

Around four Krit came walking in with his usual charming smile and pulled me into his arms to kiss me senseless. He managed to erase all my concerns with that one possessive lip-lock. We cleaned each other in the shower—several times—before getting ready for Jackdown's gig tonight at Live Bay.

"Don't forget you have to sing tonight," Green called out as he walked in the back entrance, leaving me and Krit out here alone. It was a ritual now. Sometimes they all left us alone so we could make out. And other times we just kind of . . . did it. Depended on what Krit needed.

"Fuck off," Krit yelled back at him, annoyed.

I grabbed his face and moved his attention to me. "Be a good boy."

Krit gave me his wicked smile. "That's no fun, love," he said, slipping a hand between my legs. "Good boys don't do this."

His finger thrust up into me with ease. I was always wet when Krit was around me. His face and the way his mouth moved when he talked, not to mention his piercing, just . . . made me aroused most of the time.

"They don't?" I panted, trying to play along as he found the spot inside me that always sent me spiraling into oblivion.

"Uh-uh. They don't have a clue," he whispered against my ear, then bit my lobe before licking my neck.

I held on to his shoulders while he brought me to my climax.

When I came down, he pulled his finger out and moved it to his mouth to suck on it.

Giggling, I shook my head. "You are a very bad boy. I'm very lucky you're *my* bad boy."

He moved closer to me and cocked his head to the side as a crooked grin appeared on his face. "You like this bad boy, love?" he asked, running his damp finger, which I could smell myself on, down the side of my face.

"He's okay," I teased, knowing that what he really wanted was for me to tell him I loved him.

He pouted, and those full lips of his made my heart skip.

"That ain't nice. I'm obsessed with your sweet cunt, and God knows I love you. I better be more than okay."

I reached up and rubbed my thumb over his pouty lips. "You know that I love you. I screamed how much I loved you earlier in the shower. So loudly our neighbors banged on the wall to shut me up."

The wicked laugh that vibrated his chest was delicious. "When my head is between your legs, tongue-fucking you, it doesn't count. Of course you love me then."

I was getting better about not blushing when Krit talked dirty, but sometimes I still did. Like when he talked about how much I loved for him to kiss me there.

"I love you, Krit Corbin. So very much," I assured him.

He closed his eyes, pulled my thumb into his mouth, and bit it gently. "That's it. What I fucking need to hear," he said, then opened his eyes and slipped his arm around my waist. "Let's go do this."

We walked into the back entrance, and Green shook his head at us like we were naughty children. It wasn't like Green didn't mess around with girls backstage. Just last week I'd walked in on him nailing a girl against the wall in the green-room. I saw a flash of his butt and her breasts before I slammed the door in horror.

Krit had been more than pissed that I had seen Green's ass, and he had lost it on everyone, yelling about not fucking backstage. They pointed out that we messed around backstage, so he amended it to "lock the fucking door."

I had stopped thinking that Krit would want me out in the audience with everyone eventually. He never wanted me anywhere but back here so he could get to me and see me. Because if he saw a guy in the audience get close to me, he'd lose it and jump off the stage and end up in jail.

So to help my man and his temper, I stayed back here with him. He sang and looked at me most of the time, but no one seemed to notice or care. Girls still threw their panties and bras at him. They screamed that they wanted to have his babies and needed fucking. I could hear it all up here, but I no longer cringed.

He didn't care what they said. Not once had he seemed tempted by them.

When I first met Krit, he had shared the apartment above mine with Green. Now I shared that apartment with him, and Green lived in my old apartment underneath. The band had become my family. So had Trisha, Rock, and their kids. I hadn't had a real family before, so having people in my life who loved me was the most wonderful thing in the world.

I took my special corner and sat down on the seat Krit always had for me. He winked at me as he tugged off his shirt, showing his pierced nipples and tattooed chest. His sexy ripples of muscle made me squirm in my seat. Soon he would be all sweaty onstage, and his hair would be even messier than it already was.

It was no wonder I let him take me out back or to the green-room during intermission and have his way with me. Just listening to him was already a turn-on as it was, but seeing his sweaty, naked chest and the way he moved onstage made me a puddle. I was always ready to get my hands on his slick body.

"Are you Krit's girlfriend?"

I glanced over to see a blonde who reminded me of the angel on the top of the Christmas tree every year at the church. Her hair was long and golden and curled at the ends. She didn't have on makeup, which was odd for groupies. They were normally all lacquered up. Granted, this girl didn't need makeup. She had the kind of features that were timeless. I started imagining her as a heroine in my novel.

"Blythe, right?" she said, snapping me out of my thoughts.

"Uh, yeah." I nodded, confused as to how she had gotten back here.

She grinned at me. It was a real smile. Genuine. "I'm Trinity, Matty's cousin. I'm visiting him because my mom wants me to move close to Matty and go to South Alabama for college. I don't think he's real thrilled about it, though," she finished, biting her lip nervously. "But he said that you'd be back here and that you were nice."

Matty was the drummer for Jackdown. He also looked nothing like this girl, who was younger than me by a year or two maybe. Her accent was different. It had a twang to it that I didn't recognize.

"Where do you live?" I asked as she pulled up a chair beside me.

"A little town in Texas you've never heard of." She grinned again. Two dimples appeared. She reminded me of a doll. That was it. She had the face, hair, and dimples of a doll. "It's called Berryville. If I leave, the population will go from 999 to 998. I don't know how they'll make it." There was teasing in her tone. I liked her.

"Wow. Yeah, you might want to rethink that," I replied.

She giggled, then pulled her legs up in the seat. "So, Matty says you live with Krit and are very important. I'm not to do or say anything that would offend you. I will admit I'm a little nervous about that. Krit seems scary."

I glanced out to see Krit frowning as he looked over at us. He'd be over here in a minute. This was going to bug him.

"He's scowling at me. Should I move?" she asked in a quiet voice.

I shook my head. "No. You're fine. I swear. Krit is just intense. When he finds out you're Matty's cousin and not some groupie back here trying to upset me, he'll chill out.

About that time Matty walked up to Krit, grabbed his shoulder, and said something in his ear. Krit nodded, then looked at me for reassurance.

I gave him a thumbs-up.

He relaxed and went back to warming up and checking the sound.

"Does that mean I get to stay?" she asked.

Laughing, I nodded.

KRIT

The girl beside Blythe looked young and innocent. Matty said it was his cousin visiting from Texas. He swore she was nothing like him and that she and Blythe would get along great.

So far Blythe had been fine. Though the girl had kept talking to her and kept Blythe's attention off me. I didn't like that. I wanted all her attention. Yes, it was selfish, but fuck that.

During our first break I was at Blythe's side before she could stand up. "Come here, love," I said, pulling her up and into my arms. I was sweating, but she never recoiled or acted like it bothered her. She came to me willingly. I loved that.

"Krit, this is Trinity. Trinity, this is Krit," Blythe said, introducing us.

"Nice to meet you, Trinity. But I've got to take my girl away for a bit, yeah?" I hooked my arm around her neck and led her backstage, away from Trinity and her chatty mouth.

"What was that about?" Blythe asked, staring up at me.

I didn't meet her gaze. I was hiding my selfish behavior the best I could. She was damn near perfect and she loved me, this fucked-up asshole. I had to hide my worst traits the best I could.

"Krit Corbin, are you jealous of . . . a girl?" Blythe's amusement was obvious.

I didn't respond.

"Ohmygod, you are. Krit, seriously? I don't swing that way at all. Granted, she's a very beautiful girl, but I'm in love with you."

I bent my head and kissed her temple. "Yeah, you are."

She giggled and laid her head on my sweaty chest. "What am I going to do with you? You're just getting worse."

"Keep me. That's what you're going to do with me."

She slid a hand up my chest and left it over my heart. "Yes, I am in fact going to keep you."

That made me feel better.

"I wasn't jealous of her. I just didn't like that she was talking so damn much. I like seeing your eyes on me."

Blythe nodded. "Got it. And I know, but I was trying not to be rude."

Figures. Blythe didn't want to be mean to anyone. She was sweet and kind and mine.

"We can go out and see Trisha. I saw her walk in with Amanda a few minutes ago. Or we can go to the greenroom and fuck."

She laughed out loud, and my chest squeezed at the sound. "I don't know, Krit. . . . What do you want to do?"

I turned her toward the greenroom. "With you, love, that answer will always be fuck. I'm obsessed with your cunt, remember?"

She shivered in my arms, and I opened the greenroom and

barked at the stage guys to get out before closing the door and locking it behind them.

"Pull that skirt up," I growled as I stalked her until she was pressed up against the wall.

Of course that's exactly what she did.

BLYTHE

"Do you know Green very well?" Trinity asked me.

I kept my eyes on Krit so he'd be happy. He was like a spoiled little boy. It cracked me up. "Yes, I know him pretty well. He's Krit's best friend."

Trinity didn't say anything for a few minutes, and I was tempted to glance at her. She had asked a random question and then ended the conversation.

"He's very talented. I wasn't really expecting that, given what I had seen of him so far. I mean, I didn't mean to say he was dumb or anything. . . . It's just that I noticed him . . . or, well, I had to notice him because he came over to Matty's with some girls, and he wasn't sober, I don't think. Matty sent me to my room and argued with Green, and finally the girls left. I came out of the room thinking Green was gone too, but he wasn't. He was there, drinking a beer. He apologized for the almost naked girls he had brought with him, then went on to call me a cock blocker. Matty slapped him on the back of the head, and, well, I was nervous so I went back to my room again. So . . . he seemed not so smart, or maybe he seemed not so dedicated to serious things like being a musician. But he's really good and he's very nice tonight. He hasn't spoken to me, but I've seen him with everyone else. He appears a lot smarter . . . than I originally thought. That didn't sound right either. What I meant to say is that he's really pretty and I'm glad he's got brains in his head. It's a shame when boys are pretty like him and dumb. I'll shut up now."

That was a mouthful. Trinity had managed to get my complete attention with her long ramblings about Green. The two things she said that stood out most were that Green had been ignoring her all night and that she thought he was pretty. That was very interesting. Green was a nice guy, and if he'd met Trinity before, even drunk, I can't imagine he'd ignore her. He never did that.

I studied her for a moment, and the pink in her cheeks told me she was embarrassed about her outburst of information. Did Trinity have a crush on Green? Surely not. He was not only too old for her, but she was Matty's cousin. This would end very badly. Unless, of course, Green's ignoring her meant he was fighting off any attraction to her. It was possible for Green to fall for a girl and change his ways. He was an easier bet than Krit before I came along.

"Green is in law school. He's actually brilliant, and, yes, he's very talented. But you'll learn, if you're around these guys very much, that musicians are an odd sort. They live life their own way. As for ignoring you, I wouldn't read anything into it. He's just focused because they're onstage. He has his game face on, where he flirts with the fans and brings in the crowd. It's what they do."

Trinity looked very thoughtful for a moment, then nodded. "Okay. Yeah. That makes sense. Thanks, Blythe."

I nodded in return and looked back at Krit, who was waiting on me to look at him. I grinned and blew him a kiss. He caught it and pressed it to his lips, then winked at me. I could just imagine the females swooning in the audience right now. I was one very lucky girl.

KRIT

Two weeks later Blythe had sold a monthly total of twenty thousand books.

I had a paid-for diamond hidden under the bed.

All plans to propose were on hold.

FUCK!

BLYTHE

I typed the last word of my second novel and dropped my hands into my lap. The sense of accomplishment and satisfaction that came with knowing I had written two complete novels was extraordinary.

There were still the edits and the rewrites I would need

to do, but the story was complete. Within a month I could upload it and click publish again. The power that came with that surprised me. I hadn't expected this feeling of triumph. Several times over the past month I had thought about calling Mr. Williams. Also known as the man who helped give me life.

I wasn't sure what I would say, though. He did raise me, in the loosest sense of the word. Mrs. Williams, his wife, and not my mother had done most of it. The discipline and emotional abuse—Mr. Williams had just stood back and let it happen. He had only intervened when he thought he needed to.

Since I didn't know he was my father until last year, there was no connection or love there. I didn't find myself wanting to bond with him. To me, he seemed like a hollow old man who relied on the pulpit he stood on every Sunday and told people what Jesus wanted them to do. I had stopped listening to that a long time ago.

In my opinion, Jesus didn't want parents to abandon their kids and let them grow up in a home without love or affection. So he'd failed miserably there. I wasn't of a mind to forgive that.

Calling him and telling him about my book seemed pointless. And he wouldn't approve of it if he read it. There were parts that I had changed and made very fictional, but they were still based on the life he let me grow up in. If anyone would catch on to that, he would.

I put Mr. Williams out of my mind. One day maybe I'd call him—or maybe I wouldn't. He had made no effort to contact me. And I had a family now, and friends. I had the love he'd denied me.

Standing up, I stretched my back from sitting all day long at my desk and went to make a glass of sweet tea. Before I could get to the kitchen, there was a knock on the door. I opened it to reveal Green looking like he hadn't slept in days.

"Green . . . are you okay?" I asked, worried he might be sick. He looked ill.

"No. God, no," he said, running his hand through his hair, then cursing a streak. "I fucked up, Blythe, and I know Krit's not here, but I need advice. From a girl. Or anyone at the moment who I can trust and who isn't an idiot. Then I may need you to lock me in a room and protect me."

This did not sound good. "Come in. I was just going to get some tea. Would you like some?" I asked him.

He shook his head. "No, but lock that door. Bolt it too. Just in case."

"You're starting to frighten me, Green."

He walked over, dropped onto the sofa, and buried his head in his hands. "He won't murder you. Just me. He's gonna kill me, and I fucking deserve it. But she's just so . . . and her hair . . . and she smells . . . FUCK! What did I do? I swear to God I'm never drinking again."

I sat down on the chair across from him. "Slow down. Let's start with who is going to kill you."

Green pulled his hair as he kept his head down. "Matty."

Oh no. "Green . . . what did you do? Did you, uh . . . touch Trinity?" The fact that he was ignoring Trinity at the gigs for a week and a half, and then two nights ago he kept looking at her, then jerking his gaze away had caught my attention. But I decided it was harmless.

"She was a . . . virgin," he choked out.

Was? Oh no. Ohno ohno ohno . . . "Green, please tell me she was willing . . ."

He dropped his head farther into his lap and groaned. "God, yes she was willing. I'm not a fucking rapist. But she was so fucking willing about everything I did that I missed the signs. Until I was inside her, being squeezed to death by her tight pussy."

"TMI, GREEN!" I stopped him.

He lifted his head and frowned. "Yeah. Sorry, it was. But I didn't know, Blythe. I seriously didn't know. I was drinking, and Matty was passed out. She woke up and all that hair of hers was messy and she wasn't wearing a bra. Then she smiled at me with this cute little sexy look, and she has fucking dimples so damn deep, GOD! I'm just a man, Blythe. I'm just a motherfucking man who fucked his friend's virgin cousin."

He was really in trouble. Matty was going to kill him, or he was going to go to jail. "How old is she? Did you get her age first?" I asked, ready to go hide him if I had to.

"She'll be nineteen next month. She's legal. I already asked Matty her age back before things went weird with us. That's her fault too, because she has that hair and she smells good and she smiles at me and watches me. When I catch her staring at me, she doesn't look away, she just gives me them dimples. Did I mention her hair?"

I bit back a smile. "Yeah, you mentioned her hair a few times."

Green shot up and went back to pulling his own hair with both hands. "I AM SO FUCKED!"

"Where is she now? I mean, did you take her virginity and run over here, or did you take care of her and clean her up and talk about it?"

Green dropped his hands to his sides and let his head fall back while he stared at the ceiling as if it had answers for him. "We . . . you know . . . both, uh . . . finished. And then I did clean her up. She was all dimpled smiles, and I was so pissed. But them dimples were fucking my head up. She said things like it was wonderful and like she'd always dreamed. Then she asked if she could tell Matty we were a couple." He looked right at me with his eyes wide. "A couple, Blythe! She thought because we fucked we were a couple."

Uh-oh. This did not sound good. What had he done?

He sank down onto the coffee table this time and rested his

elbows on his knees as he hung his head in what could only be described as shame. "I told her she should have told me that she was a virgin. That I'd never have slept with her. I blamed it on drinking too much whiskey, and then I told her I had too much going on in my life to be in any relationship. That I fucked girls, I didn't date them. . . . Then I left."

Oh, Green. How could you?

"When did you leave her?"

"I came straight here. I needed a safe place to hide for when she tells Matty."

He was right. And Krit needed to get home. I wasn't sure how to keep them from destroying the place without Krit here to control them.

Poor Trinity.

KRIT

I flung the door to the apartment open and stalked inside, ready to bash heads. I found Green pacing in front of the window and Blythe sitting in the recliner with her legs pulled up under her, watching him with a concerned frown.

She'd texted me that Green had slept with Trinity and Matty was going to kill him. *Please come home. Green is here.*

I told Dewayne I had to go and got the hell out of there. He asked if it was an emergency and if I needed backup. I had told him I wasn't sure—I'd let him know if I did, though.

"You look like shit," I told Green as I walked over to Blythe.

"I didn't know she was a virgin. She was flirting and all fucking over me. And she has this hair." He stopped and cursed.

"He has a big thing for her hair. He will mention it a lot," Blythe whispered up at me.

I slid my hand under my girl's hair and cupped it around her neck. "Is she even old enough?" I asked in disgust.

Green glared at me. "Yes! She is as old as Blythe was when you hooked up."

"I was in love with Blythe," I fired back.

"Not at first! You were obsessed with her. She was just one of your crazy addictions. The love came later."

He was right, but it pissed me off to hear him blow off my feelings for her. "Watch it. Right now I'm the only thing standing between you and Matty."

Green sighed and looked remorseful. "Yeah, I know. I'm just a mess. I can't believe I did that. It's that damn hair . . . and the dimples."

Apparently, Blythe was right. He really liked the girl's hair.

"Did she get mad at you and say she was telling Matty? I mean, is he even gonna find out?"

Blythe tilted her head back. "She thought that made them a couple. He said he fucked, he didn't date. Then he left her."

Ouch. He was so getting his face bashed in.

"You can't stay here in our apartment. I'll make sure you get down to your apartment alive and get bolted in, though. Then we just wait. The girl may not plan on telling him. You don't know her well enough to know if she will. Stay alive until our gig tomorrow night."

Green looked longingly at the door that used to be his bedroom. "I'll stay in that room. I won't come out and bother y'all."

I shook my head and went to the door, and I opened it for him so he could leave. "Not staying here. Give it up. Let's go," I said, pointing for him to exit.

Green glanced out the window again. He was looking for Matty to show up.

"While the coast is clear, you need to make a run for it," I reminded him.

"Fine," he snapped, and finally got the hell out of my apartment.

BLYTHE

Before I moved in with Krit, I never made my bed. It was my one act of rebellion after being forced to make my bed growing up in a strict household. If I messed up while making the bed, I got lashed with a belt. So making a bed isn't something I care for.

However, Krit likes a made bed. For a long time he would make it up in the afternoons when he got home. He never complained or brought it up. He just did it. He liked it nice and straight.

After watching him do this for a while, I decided I could do that every morning. He wasn't picky about how tightly the sheet was tucked in or if the blanket was exactly straight. He just liked it to be neat.

The first time I did it, the grin on his face when he walked into the bedroom made it worth it. Now I do it just to see that smile. He likes that I do that for him. Because he knows it was something I hated before.

This morning I didn't have classes. Instead, I settled in to do some deep cleaning. I was still waiting for Green to call for help. So far Matty hadn't shown up or even mentioned anything. I didn't think Trinity planned on telling him.

Getting on my knees, I pulled out the panties and socks that had made their way under the bed. Most of the time we throw clothes while attacking each other, so things go missing and end up all over the place. My favorite bra was lost for a month because it was behind the dresser.

I figured I would look for all our missing articles of clothing, then dust and vacuum. Several boxes stayed under the bed. They were Krit's, and I never asked him about them. It was mostly CDs, from what I could tell, and keepsake items. I reached under to straighten them and check for anything that might have gotten stuffed between them and the wall.

My fingers brushed against a small velvet box. Confused, I wrapped my hand around it and pulled it out slowly. I knew what came in small velvet boxes, but Krit hadn't mentioned marriage to me. Even though it was all I could think about at the past few weddings we had attended. I loved Krit, and I wanted forever with him, but he didn't seem to be ready for that step. I was content getting to live together.

The small box was black. I held it in my hand while lying on my stomach beside the bed. I was almost afraid to open it. What if there was something in here I didn't need to see? What if this was a ring from his past? Had he given Jess a ring?

No. I wouldn't be jealous of this. I would not jump to conclusions. But there was dust on the box. Not a lot, but still, there was some.

Things could get dusty under a bed fast. After that little pep talk I opened the box.

Nestled in the satin was a huge diamond ring. Of all the things I expected to see, this was not what I had imagined. This ring was expensive. And very real. The inside of the box had the jeweler's name pressed in black ink into the white satin.

Checking over my shoulder to make sure Krit hadn't come home, I decided I was going to try it on. I pulled myself up to a sitting position on the floor and gently picked up the ring like it might break. Then I delicately slid it on my ring finger. It was a perfect fit. I tilted my hand from side to side to see the lights glimmer off the stone. Why did he have this? Was he saving it for me?

If he was, you would think he might have mentioned marriage, or hinted at it. But over the past month he hadn't said anything. In fact, when I had asked him what he thought I should do about the money coming in and where I should deposit it, he suggested I go speak with the bank manager and get some insight on it.

He didn't offer to go with me. He didn't even bring it up again.

That didn't sound like a man who was about to propose marriage.

I reached for the box again and studied the dust on it. He hadn't just gone out and bought it and stuck it under here recently. The more I looked at it, I realized it had been under here a while. It was wishful thinking for me to pretend he had it under here for me. This couldn't have been meant for me. It came off with the same ease it had gone on, and then I placed it back into the box just as I had found it. With a sad sigh I lay back down on my stomach and put the box back in its hiding spot.

I wasn't in the mood to clean anymore.

KRIT

Something was wrong with Blythe. I had asked her if she was feeling okay, and she had forced a smile, then reassured me she was fine. When she wasn't better the next day and continued to seem moody, I had asked her if someone had upset her, and she had said she was fine. A week later, when she was still acting strange and even more withdrawn, I asked her if I had done something to upset her. There was a pause before she said no . . . she was fine.

She wasn't fucking fine.

I just didn't know what was wrong. But I was deciding it was my fault. For the first time in our relationship, Blythe was actually pouting. The only time I felt like we were good was when we were fucking. So lately I'd been doing that even more to reassure myself she loved me and I wasn't about to lose her.

I heard the yelling before I even got to the steps. It was Matty. . . . Shit. When he didn't mention it all week, I figured the girl wasn't going to tell him about Green. Sounded like she changed her mind.

I took the stairs two at a time. When I got to the first landing, where Green's apartment was, the door was open and Matty was yelling something about Blythe needing to get out of his way.

Motherfucker!

I stormed into the room to see Blythe standing between Green and a very angry Matty. She had her hands in the air like she was shielding Green. "Do NOT fucking go a step closer to her," I roared, shoving Matty onto the sofa and wrapping Blythe up in my arms while I glared daggers at my best friend, who had just let my woman be his shield.

"He FUCKED MY COUSIN! I'm GONNA KILL HIM!" Matty screamed, and I felt him move beside me.

I pushed Blythe behind me, then turned to block Matty. "You aren't going to touch him with Blythe in this room. She could get hurt. And before you go committing a felony, let him talk."

"Please!" a feminine voice begged, then started crying again. I jerked my head around to see Matty's cousin and the cause of all this drama watching this unfold, her face red and splotchy. She sure as hell wasn't saving Green with her body. She was letting Blythe do that.

"She's my cousin," Matty yelled. "I would have thought as my friend he would respect that!"

I agreed. But Green had never fucked up like this before. The amount of time he spent going on about the girl's hair and dimples made me think he was more attached to her than he wanted to admit.

"You had to tell him?" I snarled at the whimpering blonde. I didn't get what he saw in that.

She shook her head frantically.

"Don't yell at her! She was here with me, and he followed her." Green finally entered the conversation.

I turned my attention to Blythe. "I need you to go stand at the door away from danger. Can you please do that for me?"

She bit her bottom lip and looked like she had to seriously weigh the options here. Dammit, did she really think she was going to save Green?

"Love, if someone were to accidently touch you, I would lose my mind. This would go down very badly, and they both know it. Both of them need you to get out of harm's way."

Blythe finally nodded and glanced back at Green before going over to stand by the door.

I looked at Green this time. "Why was she coming over here? I thought this was a one-time thing and was over."

Green paled some, then looked like he was angry. "I . . . I called her that day after, you know . . . to see if she was okay. We talked, and then she came over. She's been over a lot this week."

Fuck me.

"I'm going to motherfucking kill you!" Matty shoved past me now that Blythe wasn't in the way, and I had to grab both his arms and jerk him back before he pummeled Green.

"Let them explain first, dammit," I ordered. Then I glanced over at the girl. "Do you like Green? Did you flirt with him and come over here of your own free will?"

She nodded, then wailed. "Yes! I tried to tell Matty that. I tried to tell him I loved Green. But he won't listen to me."

Yeah, well, Green didn't love her, so I was now understanding why Matty wanted to kill him. The chick was seriously naive.

"Green?" I asked, looking back at him. "Did you know she loved you?"

He ran his hands through his hair. Then shook his head. "Not until she yelled it at Matty."

"Did you tell her or make her think at any time that you loved her?"

He shook his head. "No. I just . . . I like her." He glanced at her. "A lot. I like being with her, and I like talking to her."

"And you like fucking her!" Matty roared, trying to break free from my hold.

Green glared at him. "Don't say that. It upsets her. Can't you just shut up and stop doing this in front of her? She's crying and you don't even care. She's scared and upset. Let Blythe take her and calm her down. Then we can get on with this."

Well, that was interesting.

"He more than likes her, dude. Are you listening to this?" I whispered in Matty's ear as I held him back.

"She's too young for him. He'll hurt her. Hell, she already thinks she loves him. How's she gonna handle it when she sees him fucking a groupie?"

Green stalked toward us. "SHUT. THE. FUCK. UP." His face was bright red, and the vein on his forehead was standing out.

"Back up, Green, or I'm letting him loose," I warned.

"Noooo, please!" the girl cried out.

Green glanced over at her and his expression softened. Damn. I almost laughed.

"It's okay, Trinity. It's okay. Just please stop crying." His voice was softer when he spoke to her.

Matty's tension eased some. He heard it too.

Green looked back at Matty. "She's . . . different. For me. I'm trying to figure this out, but I don't want to be with anyone else. It's an exclusive thing, and I respect her. I want to protect her, and I don't ever want to hurt her. I did that once, and I swear to God I won't do it again. Just give us a minute, okay? She needs to calm down."

"He can't fall in love in a fucking week. Give him time," I said, and Matty sighed heavily. Then he nodded.

"Fine. She wants you. You're gonna be good to her. What the hell am I gonna do about it? Her momma should've never sent her for me to watch over. My friends are all fucking dicks. Fucking horny dicks."

I let go of Matty, and thankfully he didn't lunge at Green. He turned to look at Trinity. "He's a good guy. For the most part. But he's not perfect, and as much as he doesn't want to, he *will* fuck up."

Green snarled, and I put up a hand to shut him down.

Matty shook his head, then headed for the door. He stopped when he got there. Looking back at me, he said, "I would have never touched him with Blythe so close. I'm not stupid." Then he turned to Green. "If you do anything other than respect and cherish her, I'll find you where Krit isn't around to save your ass."

We all stood in silence for a moment until we were sure

Matty was gone. Then Green turned to the girl and she ran to him.

I was done with this drama. Blythe walked back into the room and I went straight to her. "Don't you ever scare me like that again."

She gave me a small smile. "I knew he wouldn't touch me. I was the safest thing for Green."

"You don't have to save Green's ass from being an idiot."

She smirked. "You did."

BLYTHE

He knew something was wrong with me. I was trying so hard not to let the fact that he had a ring hidden under the bed with dust on it get to me. But all I could think was that he'd bought it for Jess. As much as I liked Jess, I was so freaking jealous. We had been together a lot longer than he was with Jess. He had been ready to propose to her after only a couple months. We had been together close to a year, and he wasn't even mentioning it.

Today I had given in and cried about it. Every day that passed and he didn't say anything about marrying me, I became more convinced that it wasn't my ring. It was for someone else. Who was now married to another man.

GOD! I hated feeling like this. I loved Krit. Even if he never wanted to marry me, I would stay as long as he wanted me. I was that pathetic. Seeing him smile made my day brighter. When he kissed me, I would forget momentarily that he didn't love me as much as he had loved Jess.

Then the awful fear that he was still in love with her would sink in, and I would be all kinds of screwed up for the rest of the day. Looking at my book sales no longer made me happy. My heart was breaking more and more every day.

I curled up on the sofa with a cup of coffee and covered myself with a blanket. Krit was still asleep, but dreams of him proposing to Jess, which was ridiculous, had woken me up. I needed to get away from him and get my head together.

He would wake up and be upset that I wasn't there beside him. I felt guilty for not being there. His favorite part of waking up was sex. But images of him putting that ring on Jess's hand did not put me in the mood for sex. I wanted distance.

Pulling the cover up, I snuggled up against the morning chill and sipped my coffee. There was no reason for me to be acting like this. I had a wonderful life. Krit did love me. I was sure of that. I had finished two novels, and it looked like maybe I was going to make a career out of this author business. These were dreams I'd had for so long: being loved and writing.

This stupid ring was ruining all of that. I was letting one pretty rock upset me, take away my joy. Maybe if I just told him I'd found it. Explained to him that I'm being a baby about it but that knowing he had been going to ask another woman to marry him bothered me. He would understand why I had been so moody, and then I could let it go.

His feet hit the floor in the bedroom. I could hear him stretch, and I knew exactly what that looked like. All those pretty muscles on display. I loved that view. And because of a stupid ring I was in here missing it.

I think I hated that ring.

When his gaze hit me, I lifted my head from my cup of coffee and looked at him. The frown on his face wrinkled his brow. "Why are you in here?" he asked with his husky sleepy voice.

I had lied to him all week and told him I was fine. It wasn't fair to either of us. The ring was ruining things.

"I found the ring," I blurted out, wishing I had thought that one out better.

His frown deepened, like he wasn't sure what I was talking about. The moment understanding hit him, I saw it transform his face.

"I was cleaning. I wasn't snooping. I just . . . We tend to lose my panties and bras and nighties when you throw them. And your socks. I was checking behind furniture and under the bed. . . ."

Krit let out a frustrated growl and ran his hand through his messy bed head. "When did you find it? Is that what's been wrong with you all week?"

He wasn't denying that it was meant for Jess. He wasn't

telling me it was mine. He was upset. The look on his face was one of concern and maybe fear. Not good.

"Yes. It's been a week. But"—I held up a hand—"it's okay. I think I just needed to tell you. I'm dealing with it. Sure, that's not easy to swallow, but I will. That was before my time."

The confusion on his face was followed by, "What do you mean, before your time?"

I didn't want to talk about this, but it was good for us. We could discuss it and I could put it behind me. "I'm assuming it was for . . . Jess. She was before, uh . . . me."

Krit's nose scrunched up in a look that said he thought I'd lost my mind. Had there been another girl? One he hadn't told me about? One he had loved more than Jess? I was going to be sick.

He stared at me for a few more moments before walking over to sit down on the coffee table so he was facing me. "Love, I never bought Jess a ring. Hell, I didn't even consider it. Why would you think that?"

So there had been someone else. Someone so important he hadn't even told me about her. This was worse somehow.

"Who, then? I thought she was the only serious relationship you'd had."

Krit let out a small laugh like he was surprised by my question. "The only woman I've ever considered forever with is you."

But the ring . . . Oh. Oh my.

"Yeah. You. Just you," he repeated. Then he moved to sit beside me on the sofa. "Why would you assume that it was for anyone else?"

"Because it had dust on it. And you never mentioned getting married. Not even jokingly."

He groaned and laid his head back on the sofa. "I have so fucked this up."

I waited for him to say more. His neck muscles and shirtless body were distracting me a little.

"I've worked for Dewayne to make extra money so I could pay for that ring. It took several months, but I did it. I loved every damn minute of it too. I wanted you to have the best. I wanted the ring on your finger to tell the world you were mine and I cherished you. But . . . but then your book . . ." He paused and clenched his hands in his lap. "It did fantastic. It was fucking amazing, and I was so damn proud of you. I still am. You blow my mind. But I just . . . I couldn't ask you to marry me now. Because I didn't . . . I never wanted you to think . . ." He stopped again and looked at me.

The frustration and fear in his eyes tugged at my heart. I got it now. I understood his worries. Crazy man.

I leaned up and set my coffee cup on the table, then turned my body to face his. Reaching for his face, I held it in my hands and looked into his eyes. "Yes. Yes. A million times yes." Tears stung my eyes as I said the words, but I kept going.

"You are the only man I will ever love. You are the only man I want to spend forever with. You were the first person to love me, and I found that, with your love, I didn't need anything more. You filled every void in my life. My heart was complete with you. So whatever silly idea you have in your head about the money I've made off this book or the books I write in the future, forget them. I don't think you want me for my money." I laughed as I said it.

Krit closed his eyes for a second and let out a breath. When he opened them, he frowned again. "Shit. I fucked this up. I was going to propose to you onstage. I was going to have the crowd hold up lights, and Rick was going to make the place go dark otherwise. Then I was going to get on my knee and tell them all how much I love you while I asked you to be my wife. This," he said, waving at us sitting on the sofa together, "was not the plan."

I laughed again, then leaned in and kissed his lips. "As sweet at that sounds, this is better."

"How is this better?" he asked with a pout.

I pushed the blanket down, reached for the T-shirt of his I was wearing, and removed it. "Because," I said, crawling over into his lap completely naked, "we can do this."

Krit's big hands grabbed my waist, and he muttered a curse before crushing his mouth to mine. I sank down and moaned as his rigid arousal pressed against me. Krit lifted his hips to grind against the anxious tingle already starting up inside me.

Threading my hands into his hair, I writhed in his arms as my breasts brushed against his chest. The pulse between my legs grew more intense with each stroke of Krit's tongue.

"Fuck, love. You're soaking my boxers. So damn hot," he murmured against my lips.

He kissed me like I was some rare savory treat, and I wondered if any woman had ever felt this perfect euphoria or if being owned by Krit Corbin was the only way to experience this.

"Wait. Stop," Krit said as he broke the kiss.

I didn't want to wait. I nuzzled his neck and kept his hard length cradled tightly against my needy heat.

"Shit, love. I'm gonna . . . just give me a minute. I need—" He stopped when I began rocking on his lap. "Fuck. Yeah."

I was suddenly being thrown through the air. Krit pressed me back onto the sofa as his gaze scorched my body while he yanked off his boxers with one hand.

I lifted my leg and threw it over the back of the sofa, opening for him. It only made the flames in his eyes burn brighter. Knowing I had made him turn into this made me quiver with anticipation. I knew how he would make me feel. The blissful wonder he would take me to was addictive. Krit Corbin had managed to make me an addict too. I was as addicted to this man as he was to me.

Instead of grabbing me and plunging into me, he eased over

me, his eyes still locked on mine. Then slowly he began to press until he entered me with a gentle stroke. Gasping, I reached over my head and grabbed the armrest.

His eyes dropped for a minute to my chest. The tip of his tongue came out and licked his lips. "Exquisite tits, love. *My* fucking stunning tits."

I gasped and heaved a sigh, needing oxygen and knowing it would make them bounce and give his lusty gaze a tease.

Lowering his head, he pulled a nipple into his mouth while he slowly began to slide back out of me. Then, just as he got everything but the tip out, he plunged back inside with a groan that curled my toes. "Love this. Can't live without it," he panted, then moved to give my other breast the same attention.

With each luscious rock of his hips, he whispered in my ear how much he loved me. "You're my girl. I love you. So damn beautiful."

When he began telling me how precious I was to him, I crashed into the stars, and it felt like I was flying.

KRIT

When we're old and we have to tell the story to our kids and grandkids about how I asked Blythe to marry me, I'll have to come up with a PG version to share with them. But damn, the X-rated version was so much better.

Blythe's dark hair was curled around her shoulders and splayed across my chest as she slept in my arms. After I had loved my girl thoroughly on the sofa, I'd picked her up and brought her in here to do it again. We constantly had hot, wild sex where she clawed me and I talked dirty to her. But it wasn't often I took my time and let her know just how she had changed my life. How loving her was the best damn thing that had ever happened to me.

I decided I liked it. A fucking lot.

She was exhausted now and curled up in my arms. This was a perfection I never wanted to lose. I'd fight my entire life to keep it. Reaching for her left hand, I took the ring in my hand and slipped it onto the delicate finger that I'd sucked on earlier.

Blythe's eyes fluttered and finally opened. She wasn't looking at me but at her hand, now displaying the ring I had picked out just for her. Only her.

Grinning, I watched as she held her hand up and tilted her hand, watching the diamond sparkle against the sunlight streaming in through the windows.

She bit her bottom lip, and a smile tugged on her lips when she finally turned her eyes to me. "Yes, yes, yes," she said, then giggled.

"You already told me yes, love," I said as I bent my head to kiss her lips.

"I like saying it," she replied.

I paused. "Really? 'Cause I can think of a lot of things I'd like you to say yes to. Might start testing that theory real soon."

"Yes," she repeated.

My life was going to be fucking amazing.

Dewayne and Sienna from *Hold On Tight*

DEWAYNE

A sound no man wants to wake up to jerked me out of my sleep. As I rubbed my eyes, trying to wake up, the sickening hurl came again. Throwing back the covers, I jumped up and ran to the bathroom to find Sienna holding her hair back as she hugged the toilet.

I moved fast, grabbing a cloth and wetting it while reaching to take Sienna's hair for her so she could hold the toilet with both hands. I gave the cloth a one-handed squeeze.

"Why didn't you wake me?" I asked, frustrated that she'd been in here throwing up all alone.

"Don't. You don't want to see this," she said with a groan.

"You're right I don't want to see you sick, but I sure as fuck ain't gonna let you be sick alone."

Sienna chuckled. "We don't know what it will be. We don't get to pick that. If we did, I'd pick a little boy just like you because I love you so much. But whatever we get, we will love it."

Micah thought about that for a minute, and then he frowned. "Will this baby call you Dad?" he asked me, this time looking thoughtful.

I needed Sienna to bail me out here. I wasn't sure answering yes to this was what he needed right now. Or if we were supposed to ease him into the fact.

"Yes, the baby will call him Dad."

Micah didn't look at his mother when she answered. He kept looking at me. Then he puffed up his chest like he was pulling courage from deep inside. "Can . . . can I call you Dad too?"

I wasn't a crying man. Tears didn't come easy for me. But in that moment the room went blurry and I had to blink to clear my vision. Tears pooled at the corners of my eyes and I sniffed. "Yeah, bud. You can call me Dad too," I managed to choke out.

Sienna glanced back at me, and I knew the surprise on her face wasn't because I had told Micah yes. It was because a tear was rolling down my face.

SIENNA

My emotions were already raw. The hormones in my body had hit pregnancy insaneness. So seeing my bigger-than-life man cry over the fact that his nephew had just asked to call him Dad was too much.

I burst into tears and covered my mouth on a sob. I felt Micah's little hand on my back instantly. "I'm sorry, Mommy. I didn't mean to upset you. I don't have to call him Dad."

I shook my head and gasped for a breath. "No. Yes. I mean, I want you to call him Dad if that's what you want. I'm just happy. These are happy tears. I'll do a lot of this while the baby is in my stomach. I did it with you, too."

Dewayne's big form closed in on us, and he bent down and pulled both me and Micah into his arms.

"We have our work cut out for us, bud. She's gonna be a handful," Dewayne teased, and Micah giggled.

Dewayne held us like that for several minutes. It was perfect.

Micah was late for school and I was late for work. But Micah and Dewayne had decided that they needed to fix me breakfast, and then they decided they needed to pack my lunch. It was cute. But if they tried to smother me like this for nine months, I would have to put a stop to it. My eating toast and drinking orange juice was not the most important thing in the world.

I didn't want to tell Hillary or the others at the salon yet. I was just now getting used to the idea that Dewayne and Micah knew. Ever since the sticks had shown me those two lines, I hadn't been able to accept it. My last experience with pregnancy had been bad. Really bad.

My boyfriend was dead, and my parents had shipped me off from my home to live with my aunt, who had treated me like a mere acquaintance. I had made it through morning sickness all on my own. No one had held my hair back and washed my face. No one had made me breakfast and packed my lunch. Those weren't things I had even thought about. Until now.

Micah had been mine. I had suffered through the bad times to be gifted with a beautiful baby boy who made fighting worth it. We had made it together.

Seeing Dewayne and him working together and talking about the baby and taking care of me this morning touched something in me I couldn't explain. I knew we were a family now, that our two had become three. And I loved having Dewayne in our little world. He made it complete.

The idea of having Dewayne's baby and knowing I wouldn't be alone, that he would be there through everything, almost scared me. Or it did scare me. Because it made me want that so much that I was afraid of losing it.

DEWAYNE

I held Micah's hand in mine as we walked across the street to see my parents. After picking him up from school today, I had taken him to one of the shops in town that had baby stuff. I had given him the mission to find something for the baby that we could give to his grandparents. He was supposed to hold on to the gift that was tucked in the brown bag until his mother got there.

It was Tuesday night dinner with my parents. Momma lived for Tuesdays, and for Sundays, when we came over to eat lunch. Micah made it over there for cookies almost every afternoon, but she liked having all of us together.

When she saw the ring on Sienna's hand the first time, she burst into tears and clapped, then went to hugging the breath out of Sienna. I could only imagine what her reaction to this would be. Sure, we weren't married yet, but I was dealing with that tomorrow. I wanted to enjoy this news first before pushing up the date of the wedding. I wasn't waiting another two months. I wanted Sienna to be my wife now.

"When will Momma be here?" Micah asked as we walked up the steps to the house.

"In about"—I paused as Sienna's car pulled into the driveway—"now," I finished.

Micah made a whooping noise and let go of my hand to run over to her. "Guess what we got!"

Sienna smiled at him as she stepped out of the car. Her hair was pulled up in a knot at her neck, and the deep scoop of her top gave me a sweet little flash as she bent down to hug Micah.

"I know what you got. Dewayne texted me a picture of it.

Very good choice," she said, kissing his face, then lacing her fingers through his before standing back up to look at me.

Her smile turned soft and sexy. That was the smile that was mine alone. No one else got that smile. And they never fucking would.

"You ready for this?" she asked me as they walked over to join me.

I chuckled. "Yeah. They're gonna be thrilled."

She stood on her tiptoes and pressed a quick kiss to my cheek. "Need to kiss both my fellas when I get home."

Micah groaned and then pulled on her arm. "Let's go!"

Momma had already seen us coming. The door swung open, and she came out onto the porch, beaming at us as she waved us inside. "Come on in here, y'all."

Micah let go of Sienna's hand and took off up the stairs and straight into the house.

"He's so anxious to tell them," Sienna whispered beside me.

"You should have seen him deciding what to buy," I told her.

She laughed softly, then laid her head on my shoulder. "Thank you. I want him to feel involved. Like this is his baby too."

"It is," I assured her.

"Stop. You're gonna make me cry again," she said, slapping my chest, then kissing my cheek again.

"Stop kissing and get in this house," Momma said as we

in her arms. "Thank you. Thank you. I couldn't ask for a better mother for my grandkids."

When she was done with Sienna, she grabbed me around the waist and held on tight. "My boy's gonna have a baby," she sobbed into my chest.

Dad walked up and hugged Sienna. "If this ain't a surprise." He chuckled, trying to hide the fact that he had gotten a little emotional.

"Dad, can we go eat now? I'm hungry," Micah asked.

Both my parents froze from hearing Micah call me Dad for the first time. Honestly, it was a little intense for me, too. He was my brother's son. But in my heart he was mine. "Yeah, kiddo, we can go eat now," I replied.

Then my mother promptly burst into a new round of happy tears.

SIENNA

When I jumped up from bed and ran to the bathroom two days later, Dewayne was right behind me. He had my hair pulled back and was wetting a washcloth by the time I hit my knees in front of the toilet. Yesterday I had made it through the morning until the bacon Micah had requested for breakfast wafted past my nose and had me running for the toilet. But today I woke up this way.

"I love you," Dewayne said so sincerely as he held my hair

back while I dry heaved. If I wasn't puking my guts out, I would laugh. This isn't where most women expect to hear their men tell them they love them.

Once I was finished, Dewayne flushed the toilet and started cleaning my face for me. I was getting spoiled by this. He helped me up and began fixing my toothbrush for me.

"I can do it," I told him.

"I know" was his response as he continued to put the paste on my brush, then handed it to me.

I laughed as he filled the glass with water for me to rinse and waited patiently like I was a child for me to finish.

When I was done and had dried my mouth, he took my arms and turned me around to face him. "Marry me," he said simply.

"You already asked me that. I said yes."

He gave me a crooked smile. "I mean today. Now. Tomorrow. Just soon."

Today? Had he lost his mind? I couldn't get the wedding together for today or tomorrow.

"Just because I'm pregnant doesn't mean we have to hurry up and get married. Two months isn't that long to wait."

He shook his head as if that was the incorrect answer. "I want a wedding band on your finger. I want your last name to be mine. I want to be able to say 'Have you met my wife, Sienna?'" he said, looking exasperated.

"So I'm to be your trophy wife?" I teased because of his last comment.

He smirked. "Come on, babe. Marry me. Let's not wait."

When the most beautiful, perfect man in the world, who you loved more than life, asked you to hurry up and marry him, it was hard to say no. Especially when he was only wearing a pair of sweatpants.

"Two weeks," I said, trying to sound firm.

He groaned. "Two weeks? That's forever."

Laughing because he sounded just like Micah right then, I slipped my arms around his waist. "Next week is a big week because we go to the doctor. I need time to adjust to the pregnancy and plan at the same time. I don't want anything extreme, but even a little wedding takes some time."

He sighed, then finally nodded. "Fine. Two weeks. But two weeks from today, you will be Mrs. Sienna Falco."

"Agreed."

One week and six days later . . .

I watched as Dewayne walked Micah over to his parents'. The little blue rolling suitcase that Mama T had given him was trailing behind them. He was staying with them for the next week. Tomorrow afternoon Dewayne and I would pledge forever together at a small, simple beach wedding. Then, for our honeymoon, we were going somewhere—but I didn't know where because Dewayne wouldn't tell me.

If Micah didn't love Tabby and Dave so much, I wouldn't have been able to leave him that long. But he'd be so taken care of and spoiled while we were away, I knew everything would be fine. Tonight Dewayne wanted it to be just us. If he didn't get to see me tomorrow until the wedding, then he wanted to spend the night before with me. Alone.

Smiling to myself, I went to the bedroom and slipped out of the clothes I had worn to work today and turned on the faucet to fill up the bath. I needed to be clean. I felt yucky from working all day. Before Dewayne ran his wonderful mouth over me everywhere, I needed a bath.

Once the water was warm enough, I slipped inside and sank down. With a sigh I closed my eyes and laid my head back. Soaking in the tub was one of my favorite things to do.

The front door opened and closed. He was back. I would need to make this bath quick because, even with Micah there, he had been frisky this evening. His hands had kept slipping under my shirt while I cooked dinner.

I felt his presence the moment he filled up the doorway. Opening my eyes, I turned my head to look over at him. "I needed to get clean," I told him.

He smirked. "I'll take you clean or dirty, babe. In fact, I like you dirty."

Laughing, I reached up with my toes and turned off the

water. Dewayne walked over to the tub and picked up the wash-cloth lying beside me, then picked up my body wash. "But bathing you has its advantages too," he said as he dipped the cloth into the water and ran it up my thigh while his eyes roamed over my body. "I'm looking forward to seeing that flat stomach get nice and round," he said as he brushed the cloth over it.

Enjoying his touch, I closed my eyes and let him play all he wanted. His breath was on my face just before his lips touched mine. He licked my bottom lip, then nibbled on it before trailing kisses across my jawbone and down my neck. "Smell good when you're dirty," he whispered. "But I'll make you smell better."

Shivering, I waited for the cloth to touch my body again. But what I felt instead was better. Dewayne had soaped up both his hands and used them to wash my body thoroughly.

This man wrecked me with things like this. He never made me question if he loved me. He never made me wonder if this was forever. With every look and every touch, Dewayne Falco proved to me that I was it for him. That our story was going to be full of happiness and love. Our house would be full of laughter as we raised our children together. Then one day, when we were old and gray, we would sit on the front porch swing, holding hands and talking about all the memories we had made.

Cage and Eva from *While It Lasts* and *Sometimes It Lasts*

CAGE

Today was my baby girl's third birthday. I blinked and she had gone from being a tiny little bundle in pink to wearing tutus and tiaras—literally, and daily. Like all the time. Even when she went to preschool. They had just learned to accept the fact that Bliss was wearing what she wanted.

For a while she had looked a lot like me, but that was fading. Every day she grew to look more and more like her mother. Which only stressed me out. I couldn't imagine dealing with this when she became a teenager. I now understood why Eva's dad had wanted her to have nothing to do with me. I'd have locked Bliss up in her room and thrown away the key if someone like me had shown up sniffing around her.

Chuckling, I reached over and tucked my beautiful wife closer to my chest. She wasn't awake yet. I was trying my damndest to let her sleep late since she had a birthday party to pull off today. I had tried to tell her we didn't have to invite every friend we had and feed them all. But she had told me I was wrong.

I accepted her correction. Besides, it was my baby girl's birthday, and she loved having everyone here giving her attention. She was three going on thirty. She talked like she was grown, and poor Eli Hardy was one of her loyal subjects. She bossed that boy around, and he just took it. His dad would chuckle and say Eli knew a pretty girl when he saw one.

That was funny now, but that shit wouldn't be funny in ten years. Eli Hardy was Low's boy, and I loved him. But he'd better never look at Bliss as anything more than a friend. My little girl was too good for any male out there.

"Mmmm . . . you feel good," Eva mumbled in her sleepy voice as she stretched out, throwing a leg over me.

"Hell yeah, I do," I agreed with her, and she let out a soft giggle.

When she was done stretching and making me horny as fuck, she tilted her head back to look up at me. She didn't say anything at first. Then she gave me a teary smile. "Our little girl is three. How did that happen? She was just born."

I imagined one day we'd be saying this when she graduates from high school, and then when we send her off to college. Then the day she gets married . . . Wait, no. That shit ain't happening. No getting married. Until she was, like, maybe forty, or I was dead.

"She's excited about it. Didn't think she'd ever go to sleep last night," I said, thinking about her telling me who was coming and what games they were going to play.

"She likes to be the center of attention," Eva said, then smirked at me. "A lot like her daddy."

I bent my head and took a nip of Eva's earlobe. "I have no idea what you're referring to."

She giggled and squirmed, pressing her breasts to my chest. All the thoughts of today left me, and I was very focused on my naked wife. Pulling her on top of me, I claimed her mouth with mine.

"Cage, we can't," she said, wiggling on top of me. "We will wake up Bliss."

"We can be quick and quiet. Try not to scream my name," I said, picking her up and sliding inside her easily. "Fuuuuck yeah, that's the way to wake up," I whispered in her ear as she made her sweet, sexy noises and then pressed her face into my chest to smother her sounds.

"You're soaking wet. Someone else woke up horny too," I teased.

She lifted her head and glared at me, then moaned. "Stop talking. I'm trying to be quiet."

I reached back and tugged on her hair, then licked a trail up her neck.

"Cage," she whimpered, then bit down on her bottom lip again.

"Ride me hard, baby. Make it fast," I told her as I lifted my hips and pushed deeper inside.

Pleasure lit her eyes, and I covered her mouth with my free hand. Her teeth bit down on my palm. "Fuck yeah, bite me," I encouraged.

She started rocking back and forth while moaning into my hand. "I said ride me, not play with me."

Her eyes flashed. She lifted her hips, and the slaps of our bodies hitting each other filled the room. Over and over again, until she cried out into my hand and I followed right behind her.

EVA

Being married to Cage York was never dull. This morning was just one example. I smiled as I flipped the chocolate chip pancakes Bliss had requested this morning. The fireworks Cage always managed to set off in my body still left tingles between my legs an hour later. He was just really good at that. And he was mine.

"Can I put on my new sparkly tutu now, Mommy?" Bliss asked from her chair at the table.

"No, sweetie, you could get syrup or chocolate on it. Wait until after you eat breakfast to get dressed for the party," I told her.

She sighed dramatically. Bliss did everything very dramatically. Even sleep. She was impossible to sleep with. The moving and talking that went on was cute but kept us up most of the night.

"Can I wear my boots with my new tutu so I can go help Daddy feed the cows?" she asked.

As much as Cage would get a kick out of her strutting out there in her sparkly tutu and the work boots he had bought her for when she helped him feed the cows and spread the hay, I couldn't let her do that. She'd be so upset if it got dirty before her party. Those were tears I didn't want to happen on her big day.

I scooped her pancakes onto the pink ballerina plate she loved and walked over to set it down in front of her. "You could get the tutu dirty out there too. Maybe you could wear the tutu you wore to help Daddy outside yesterday."

She scrunched up her little nose. "Um, no. That one needs to be washed."

Yes, it did, and whichever one she wore outside to help Cage today would need to be washed too. "Well then, wear your blue one. It's clean."

Bliss picked up her fork and took a bite of her pancakes. "Okay. That works."

The things that kid said sometimes. With a smile I went back to the stove to clean up the mess I'd made from Bliss's special birthday breakfast. It was what she ordered every

Saturday morning, but it was what she wanted, so I made them. I had apple cobbler to make and pasta salad to fix before lunchtime. I had made everything else last night. Including the cake. Cage was grilling ribs for the party because they were Bliss's favorite food.

"Mmmmm, these are good, Mommy. Best pancakes in the whole universe," Bliss said as she ate.

She used to say the world until she recently learned that the universe was bigger.

"That's because I made them for my most favorite girl in the universe," I told her, then focused on cutting up the veggies for the pasta salad.

CAGE

Standing over by the grill with a beer in my hand, I took in the scene in my backyard. My best friend, Willow Hardy, was once again pregnant. She was sitting in the swing under the tree with her feet propped up on her husband's legs. Willow and Marcus's son, Eli, was with Bliss, sliding down the large inflatable water slide we had rented for the event.

Across from them sat Preston and Amanda Drake. Preston was leaning up against the tree, with Amanda sitting between his legs. They laughed at something Marcus said. They didn't have kids yet, but knowing Preston, one would be along soon enough.

Dewayne and Sienna Falco were recently married as well, with a baby on the way. Their son, Micah, was over by the cows, feeding them some of the old bread we had left out for them, with Daisy May Taylor.

Rock and Trisha Taylor's boys were throwing the football with their dad and uncle Krit. I had never imagined Krit Corbin would get married, but damned if he wasn't engaged, with his wedding date set for next month. His fiancée had him so wrapped around her little finger it was comical. It was fun to watch. I understood completely. He thought it was bad now, but just wait until he had a daughter. I sure hoped he had one. All reformed players needed a little girl of their own.

"Those smell good."

I turned my attention to the newest arrivals. Jason and Jess Stone were in town for the week, visiting her mother. Jess was another one who had surprised me. Jess had been trouble back in the day. The girl had caused all kinds of shit. But then Jason Stone had rolled into town, and it had all changed. Jess's diamond ring and wedding band flickered in the sun as she rested her hand on her pregnant belly. She was due any day now. At least, it sure looked like it.

"Sadie and Jax sent a gift too. They wanted to be here, but Sadie's on bed rest still," Jess said as she held up two presents wrapped in shiny pink paper.

"Glad y'all made it. Eva is over there, setting up the table with Larissa and Trisha's help. Beers are in the cooler, and sodas are in the big ice bucket over under the tree."

"Thanks. Need any help here?" Jason asked.

"Nah, I got it. Go get yourself a beer and relax. Soon enough you'll have a kid to chase around."

Jason grinned and turned to look at Jess. I had never pictured Jess with a preppy Harvard boy. But those two worked.

Bliss saw them arrive and jumped down from the slide in her new tutu swimsuit and ran for Jess. It was Bliss's big day, and she was going to soak it all up.

"Hey, beautiful," Jess said as Bliss got to her. "I love that swimsuit. I need one."

Bliss did a twirl for her and then curtsied. "Thank you. It's a birthday present from Amanda," she said.

Jess nodded as if that made complete sense. "Amanda would find the perfect gift."

"You can put my presents over on that table," Bliss informed her. "And if you want some snacks, we have dips and chips and Goldfish."

My little hostess. She was her momma's child. Most of the time.

Eva glanced up at Jess and Jason and waved. They headed over toward the crowd.

"Daddy," Bliss called out. She had stopped running back to her friends and was looking at me.

"Yes, sweetheart?"

"I love you bunches and bunches. Thank you for making me ribs." Then she turned and ran back to the slide.

For that kind of thank-you, I'd make her anything she wanted.

Her mother called her a charmer and said she got that from me. Grinning, I figured maybe she did. It had taken some pretty damn intense charm to land Eva. I watched her as she talked to Jess. The way her dark hair blew in the breeze and her pretty blue eyes sparkled—God, that woman was beautiful. She'd taken my breath away the first time I saw her.

Glancing over to the front porch, I remembered the day she had walked out onto it, looking down her nose at me. Those shorts on, showing off all those legs. Her sassy mouth had been a fucking turn-on. My summer job working on her father's farm had looked a hell of a lot brighter after getting a look at her.

Once I had thought I couldn't be loved. Eva had proved to me I was, in fact, worthy of love. And anyone worthy of Eva's love is fucking amazing. So therefore, I'm pretty damn special.

Eva's eyes met mine across the yard, and she gave me that smile that was just mine. This was our life. We'd made this. Our friends were all here, and soon every last one would be married. Kids would be born, and our families were growing. Hard to believe four years ago every one of us but Rock was living the bachelor life. Looking for something but not knowing what we needed.

Just like magic, each one of us had had that someone special walk into our lives and love us enough to fight for us. Life is funny that way. Fate happens, and it's better than what you had imagined in the first place.

Eva was so much better than anything I ever could have thought up for myself. She was more. So much more.

"Daddy, watch!" Bliss yelled, and I turned my attention to my little girl as she held on to Eli's hand and they slid down the slide, laughing together, until they hit the water pooled at the bottom.

When they stood up, everyone clapped. Bliss, of course, did another curtsy. Because my baby girl was a princess, and she fucking knew it.

She was Cage York's daughter.

BLISS YORK

As much as I loved the big, crazy family I was a part of, when we all got together at Dewayne and Sienna's beach house, things could be overwhelming. There was so much talking and kids were everywhere. It was like this bunch couldn't stop reproducing. Jeez. At some point they need to stop *doing it*.

I wasn't one of the oldest of the kids. Jimmy, Brent, and Daisy May Taylor were all in college now, and they didn't hang around with the "kids." They got to hang out with the adults. Micah Falco and Larissa Hardy were both driving now, and they were in their own little teenage world. So that left me and Eli to make sure Eli's sisters, Crimson and Cleo, didn't kill each other. There were only two years between them, and at ten and eight they seemed ready to start a war every time they were left alone together. It made me thankful I didn't have a sister. But I had brothers. Three of them. Cruz, Cord, and Clay were all under ten. It was a miracle they hadn't burned something down yet. Mother would just laugh at them and look at my daddy like these crazy males were wonderful. Only my daddy was wonderful. My brothers were out of control.

Then there was Hadley Stone. She was ten, and I'll admit she did act older than most kids her age, but she was like a celebrity because her dad was famous. She couldn't go out and play with the rest of the kids without a freaking bodyguard. It was weird. She had one sibling, Evangeline, who was only three.

You would think all those kids would be enough to drive a person batty. But noooo, there were more of them. Micah wasn't the only Falco kid. His younger brother, Jude Falco, was ten, and his sister, Mila, was five. Then there were the Drake boys. God help us all, they were quite possibly worse than my brothers. I'd feel sorry for this town when the York and Drake boys all had cars. Hendrix, River, and Keegan Drake were all the exact ages of my brothers. They were the terrible six. Or at least, that was how Eli and I referred to them.

The last group was ten-year-old James Stone. He was Jason and Jess Stone's son. They also had a daughter, who was eight, and, well . . . they were going to have their hands full with her.

That was all I was saying. Juliette Stone was a rounder. She kept the terrible six on their toes, and that's saying something.

Saffron and Holland Corbin were the last two kids in this craziness of reproduction. They were identical twins, but they were complete opposites. Saffron did everything she could to get attention, while Holland was normally in a corner with a book. For ten-year-olds, I liked them well enough. I used to say their parents were the only sane ones in the lot. They had twins and stopped. But today the big news was that Krit and Blythe were expecting a baby by Christmas.

Now that I knew what sex was, I was horrified every time another one of the adults told us they were pregnant. Did they just, like, have sex a lot, or was this an accident? Did they plan it? Ugh! I didn't want to think about it. I was just glad my parents seemed to be done with their four. After having three boys in a row, I think my mom was too nervous to try again. She wasn't getting another one like me. I'd told her that, and she had laughed at me. Then she'd said I was more like my father than I thought I was. I didn't mind being like my dad. I looked just like my mom, or so my uncle Jeremy says every time he sees me: "Spitting image of you, I swear, Eva."

That makes me smile because my mother is beautiful.

"Hey," a deep voice says, and I jerk my gaze off the waves crashing on the shore and look up into the sun. There is definitely a male there, but I don't recognize him. Shading my eyes,

I see he is not only a guy, but he is rather remarkably gorgeous. He looks a little older than me. Maybe fifteen or sixteen.

"Uh, hey," I reply, not sure what to do about this. I know everyone in Sea Breeze around my age. I feel like I'm related to most of them.

The guy sat down beside me, but instead of doing it in an awkward way like most people, he made it look cool. He was also wearing jeans on the beach. Granted, it was fall and the breeze was cool, but still. I didn't look long at his black combat boots, which were super awesome.

"You live around here?" he asked, leaning back on one arm and turning toward me. He appeared so casual and sure of himself. He had to be a lot older than me. Eli could never pull that off and appear that badass.

"Yeah, my whole life. Well, not all of it. I lived the first years on a farm about thirty miles from here. But Dad got the baseball coaching job at the college, and we moved here to be closer. Plus, most of my family is here." I was just sharing my life with this guy. He had asked if I lived here, not for my life story. My face felt hot, and I looked away from him, praying he'd just leave. But he didn't laugh at my silliness.

"I'm visiting. My grandpop lives here now. Moved here about six years ago and opened up a restaurant."

I turned back to look at him, and the color of his silver eyes was rattling. A girl could only handle so much. Eyes like that needed a warning with them: *Be careful of insanely hot eyes.*

A smirk tugged up the corner of his lips, and I realized those lips were just as impressive as his eyes. "Reason why you're out here mumbling to yourself?" he asked.

Once again my face flamed red and I looked away from him. This time he did chuckle. I wanted to bury my head in the sand and wait for him to leave the crazy girl on the beach alone.

"Hey, I'm sorry. I didn't mean to laugh. You're just really cute. With the blushing stuff."

Oh God, he called me cute. This gorgeous boy who was way too old for me thought I was cute. Breathe, Bliss. Breathe. You will pass out if you don't breathe.

"You got a name?" he asked me.

I straightened my shoulders and tried not to look like the idiot I had been acting like so far. "Bliss York," I informed him like I was filling out some form. All businesslike.

His smirk turned into a grin. The way his eyes sparkled that silver color when he was amused made that breathing thing I was trying to do hard.

"How old are you?" he asked, studying me closely.

He probably thought I was one of the silly ten-year-olds. I was positive even Holland could have handled this better than me, and she rarely talked to anyone.

"Thirteen," I said, waiting for him not to believe me.

He nodded as if that was what he had thought.

"How old are you?" I asked.

"Fourteen," he replied.

My mouth fell open. This guy with all his coolness was just fourteen?

He acted so much older. Eli was thirteen, like me, and he was so not this mature. He was also easier to be around because, although Eli had really nice blond hair and pretty green eyes, he was just Eli.

"You look surprised," he said with a smile. "Do I not look fourteen to you?"

I swallowed and tried to breathe again. When this guy's eyes were on you, then you forgot how to talk or do pretty much anything. "I, uh, yes, I mean no, I mean . . . You just look older than that. And you act older. I didn't think . . . I thought . . . Never mind." I stopped my ramblings and once again thought of burying my head in the sand.

I really needed to give myself a break. There were not any guys around here who looked like him. Any girl faced with this kind of . . . of . . . perfection would also freak out. His dark hair was cut short, but there was a messy thing he had going with the top that seemed to be a little longer.

He laughed again and I dropped my eyes to the sand.

"Ah, come on, Bliss York. Look at me again. I didn't mean to laugh, but you make me. I can't help it."

"Well, you make me nervous," I blurted out.

"I do? Why?"

I was not telling this beautiful boy that he was beautiful. So I just shrugged.

"Bliss!" Eli's voice called out, and I turned to look toward the Falcos' to see Eli waving at me to come back. I stood up quickly and glanced back at the guy, who also stood up, but he did it smoothly, without the clumsiness of my attempt to scramble up. The last thing I needed was Eli telling my dad I was talking to a boy.

Daddy would lose his mind.

"That your boyfriend?" the guy asked, and I laughed this time.

"Eli? Uh, no. He's like my brother. . . . No, my brothers drive me nuts. He's more like my cousin. Or best friend. Our parents are close."

The guy's mouth curled into a pleased smile that made my knees weak. I had to walk back to the Falcos' and Eli. I didn't know how I was going to do that if Mr. Gorgeous kept smiling at me.

"I gotta go," I told him.

"If you're sure," he replied.

I was positive. This guy was the epitome of cool, but he had not met Cage York yet. And he didn't want to. "I, uh, yeah. My parents are probably looking for me."

He smirked. "Okay. Maybe I'll see you again, Bliss York."

It hit me then that I had no idea what his name was. He'd had me in such a scrambled mess with that face of his that I'd never asked.

"Yeah, maybe. You never told me your name."

That sexy grin was back, and he glanced out at the waves, then back at me. He tilted his head in that way guys in the movies do and you swoon. He had it nailed, and I was so about to seriously swoon.

"Nate Finlay."

ABBI GLINES is a #1 *New York Times, USA Today,* and *Wall Street Journal* bestselling author of the Rosemary Beach, Sea Breeze, Vincent Boys, and Existence series. She never cooks, unless baking during the Christmas holiday counts. She believes in ghosts and has a habit of asking people if their house is haunted before she goes in it. She drinks afternoon tea because she wants to be British but, alas, she was born in Alabama. When asked how many books she has written, she has to stop and count on her fingers. When she's not locked away writing, she is reading, shopping (major shoe and purse addiction), sneaking off to the movies alone, or listening to the drama in her teenagers' lives while making mental notes on the good stuff to use later. Don't judge.

Abbi maintains a Twitter addiction at @AbbiGlines and can also be found at Facebook.com/AbbiGlinesAuthor and AbbiGlines.com.